D1562742

THE

HUNT

TWISTED KINGDOMS BOOK 1

FROST KAY

Copyright

The Hunt: Twisted Kingdoms Book One

Copyright © 2019 Renegade Publishing, LLC

First Edition

All rights reserved. No part of this publication may be reproduced, stored in a retrieval system, or transmitted in any format or by any means, electronic, mechanical, photocopying, recording, or otherwise, without written permission of the author.

This book is a work of fiction. Names, characters, places, and incidents either are the product of the author's imagination or are used fictitiously. Any resemblance to actual events, locales, or persons, living or dead, is purely coincidental.
For information on reproducing sections of this book or sales of this book go to www.frostkay.net

Cover by Story Wrappers

Copy Editing by Madeline Dyer

Proofreading by Kate Anderson

Formatting & Design by Jaye

Also By Frost Kay

THE AERMIAN FEUDS

Rebel's Blade

Crown's Shield

Siren's Lure

Enemy's Queen

King's Warrior

Warlord's Shadow

Spy's Mask

Court's Fool

DOMINION OF ASH

The Stain

The Tainted

The Exiled

The Fallout

MIXOLOGISTS & PIRATES

Amber Vial

Emerald Bane

Scarlet Venom

Cyan Toxin

Onyx Elixir

Indigo Alloy

THE TWISTED KINGDOMS

The Hunt

The Rook

The Heir

The Beast

ALIENS & ALCHEMISTS

Pirates, Princes, and Payback

Alphas, Airships, and Assassins

HEIMSERYA

History of the Kingdoms

Once upon a time... Elves, Shapeshifters, Giants, Dragons, Humans and Merfolk were all at peace—all equals. Their lands and kingdoms were prosperous, and their enemies didn't dare attack for their armies were formidable. Generations passed and the people began to forget what was most important—love, courage, loyalty.

That was their downfall—for in self-indulgent ignorance they allowed darkness to creep into the land like a thief in the night. It started out slowly.

The Merfolk let vanity take root deep in their hearts, the Dragons became greedy from the skies, the Giants grew bloodthirsty, the Humans covetous, the Shapeshifters prideful, and the Elves allowed apathy to squeeze compassion from their hearts.

It was said that the earth rumbled and cracked, shaking the core of the world. When the tremors ceased, the Jagged Bone Mountain range surrounded the Elvish kingdom, cutting the elves off from every other living creature.

The Dragons abandoned their own kingdom and made their home in the Jagged Bones, threatening all who approached their lairs—making it impossible to pass through the mountains—though the Giants tried. As if the mountains of the Jagged Bones craved blood and hatred, many lives were claimed in the senseless violence there.

Upon witnessing such death, the Merfolk retreated to their watery homes, content to bask in the beauty of the sea and their own splendor, only occasionally consorting with pirates when it amused them.

Years passed and the myths faded from the world's mind.

The Elvish kingdom became the Wilds, the Giants sequestered themselves in their own kingdom of Kopal. The Fire Isle Kingdoms were forged by mercenaries—the offspring of pirates, Sirens, and Merfolk.

For a time, the Shapeshifters of Talaga held an uneasy peace with the Humans of Heimserya. The two kingdoms needed each other to survive, that all changed with the birth of a new plant and a royal son.

An extraordinary flower—the Mimikia—was discovered in Talaga. When distilled, it was a powerful drug capable of healing any wound. It was practically magical. The applications were limitless and its worth immeasurable. In their pride, the Shapeshifters boasted of their discovery, of their brilliance.

Word reached the Humans of this new source of wealth. They coveted this new miracle plant and the temptation proved to be too much for the newly crowned king who sought to enrich his kingdom. With his greed dawned a new era of bloodshed, prejudice, addiction, and depravity.

Welcome to the Twisted Kingdoms.

Prologue

The world wasn't always a place of war, depravity, and death.

Her mum used to tell her stories of a time when Shapeshifters, Elves, Giants, Merfolk, Dragons, and Humans shared love and unity. A time when kings were honorable, their men chivalrous and valiant.

A time of peace.

Those were times of fairytales.

In the icy land of Heimserya, fairytales didn't exist.

Not anymore.

Chapter One

Tempest

The pungent scent of herbs perfumed the air as she pulled a plant from the ground just like Mama. Delight filled five-year-old Tempest as a ladybug crawled across her dirty knuckles, a bright splash of red against her own pale skin.

Her nose wrinkled as a horrid odor blew through the glen, polluting her playground. Tempest tipped her head back and scanned the meadow as the scent grew stronger. *What was that?* It didn't belong in the forest. Her brows drew down as she spotted wisps of smoke swirling on the wind.

A sheen of sweat broke out on her body, and she pushed her hood from her tiny face, frowning. It was so hot today. Her mum said it was going to be chilly.

A worm wiggled in the dirt, pulling her attention from the smoke. Temp pushed some dirt over the top of him.

"Goodnight little worm," she whispered as she pulled another herb from the ground.

She paused as another wave of heat rolled over her. Tempest straightened and pulled at the neck of her frock, hating the heavy, itchy fabric. Something just wasn't right. It was warmer than normal. Too hot for spring.

Unnatural.

She froze as a scream pierced the air. The herbs tumbled from her fingers as she recognized the voice.

Mum.

Tempest abandoned her collection of plants and bolted back toward the cottage, her little heart hammering in her chest. Why was her mama screaming like that? Was it a spider? A monster?

Her feet pounded against the loam-covered ground, the heat increasing with every step. Tempest slowed and her mouth gaped as she spotted the biggest fire she'd ever seen. Gargantuan licks of flame teased the tops of the trees that stood like giant sentinels around her home. Terror filled her body down to her very soul. Something was horrifically, painfully wrong.

She picked up her speed and sprinted toward the hissing, fiery beast. A rock jabbed into her slippered foot, but she scarcely felt the pain. All she could think about was getting home and finding her mum. Mama would know what to do. She could tame the fire.

Her breaths came in pants as she broke through the ring of trees surrounding their home. Tempest stared at the towers of fire that greeted her, five times taller than her little form. Fire demons had almost engulfed everything. Her house was being devoured before her very eyes.

"Mama?" she whispered.

Her mother was nowhere to be seen.

A soul-piercing scream caused Tempest to jump and the hair along her arms to raise. Was her mama in there? Her eyes searched the flames desperately, seeking the owner of the screams. She took one step forward and held up her arm to block the heat from her face. The blaze caused tears to leak from her eyes.

"Mama," she tried to call out, but she choked on black, poisonous smoke. She coughed and tried again. "Mama, where are you?!"

She screamed as the windows exploded, raining fragments of glass. Tempest winced as she accidentally stepped on one, the heat of the glass burning through her slipper. She blinked at the thousands of scattered shards on the ground, looking like the first frost of fall.

It was wrong. It was spring not fall. Even though none of it made sense, it was almost magical how the glass glittered on the ground, reflecting the writhing flames and clear blue sky high above.

A hysterical giggle started in her belly, and she took another step toward the house. The flames danced like fiery demons above her home. Why were they there? She and Mama were good people. They'd never done anything bad. Her mum always helped those in need. In fact, the week prior Tempest had found a stranger in the meadow near her home. She'd dropped her flowers when he'd stumbled out of the darkest part of the woods, covered in blood.

So much blood.

Perhaps another little girl would have cried at the sight of him—but not Tempest. She had asked him if she could help and he'd promptly passed out. Her mama had always said it was their responsibility to help if they had the power to. When Tempest had screamed for help, her mum came running to her side, and between the two of them, they'd hauled the man back to their cottage to tend to his wounds. He had strange, animalistic ears poking out through his hair. They were different from hers, but she didn't care. Temp had only wanted to touch them because they looked *so* soft.

Her mum had called him a shifter.

Tempest didn't have much experience with shifters. Their cottage was far from any nearby villages, so they didn't have many visitors. Much to her disappointment, the man certainly hadn't been talkative, since he'd slept on Mama's cot most of the time.

The shifter. Maybe he could help. "Shifter! Help!"

He didn't come.

A wave of heat slammed into Tempest, instantly drying her tears and leaving her cheeks dry and itchy. Unbearable warmth pressed down on her, causing her to sob. The fire raged and a sense of helplessness settled over her. She needed help.

"Help!" she wailed again. The shifter had to help her.

A flash of movement through one of the broken windows caught her attention. She wiped her stinging eyes with her sleeve and squinted. There he was: the shifter. He leapt through the window and scrambled across the glass-covered ground, coughing.

Tempest glanced back to the window, waiting expectantly for her mum to follow. Nothing. Smoke billowed from the jagged-toothed window, but her mum still didn't appear. She turned her attention back to the man. He lifted his head, and his eyes met hers. They stared at each other as the world burned down around their ears.

"Where's Mama?" Tempest croaked.

It was as if her speech had broken the spell. As soon as the words had passed her lips, he fled through the forest.

"Where are you going?" she screamed. "My mama is in there. Help me!" Why hadn't he helped Mama? Surely, he heard her screams? "Come back!"

A chill ran down her spine and she stilled, tears dripping down her dry face. How could he leave Mama? What was she supposed to do? Mama was screaming for help...

Tempest twisted back around to face her burning home. Something wasn't right. It was quiet. Too quiet. Aside from the roaring of the fire, she couldn't hear a thing. No screaming or shouting. No cries for help.

Nothing.

"Mama!" Tempest yelled. "Answer me, Mama!"

Again. Nothing.

Terror for her mum pushed past Tempest's fear of the

fire, and she found herself reaching for the front door's handle, despite the danger raging around her, determined to find her mum. As much as she was afraid, she knew she couldn't leave her mum alone. They were a team. Always together.

The metal was blindingly hot; she flinched away, whimpering, before wrapping her hand in her thick winter cloak and forcing herself to touch it again. With a desperate push, the door wrenched open, rewarding Tempest with a solid blast of boiling air and thick, acrid smoke. Her lungs screamed. She closed her watering eyes as she took a few unsteady steps into the cottage, the heated floorboards scalding the soles of her feet through her shoes.

Every instinct in Tempest's small, fragile body begged her to run away. She would die in here if she stayed, but she couldn't leave Mama. Tempest forced her streaming eyes open and took trembling step after step into her rapidly deteriorating home.

The cottage groaned as if it was in pain and she shrieked when a beam crashed from the ceiling, blocking her path. Tempest darted to the left and scurried toward her mother's bedroom.

A figure slumped in the doorway, blackened by soot, and dangerously close to being burned by the cruel touch of a flame.

"Mum—Mama!" Tempest sobbed, closing the distance between her and her mum without thinking about the encroaching fire. "Mama, wake up." She struggled to turn her unconscious mum onto her back, willing for her to be awake. She shook her mum's arm. "Please get up."

But she didn't. Tempest laid her chapped cheek against her mum's chest. It was too still. Understanding dawned and she pulled back, shaking. Her mum wasn't breathing.

"Please wake up," Tempest begged. "Please. Please. Pl—*ah!*"

She flinched away when a searing pain crawled through the bottom of her feet and up her legs. The flames surrounding them burnt away her leather slippers, reaching her skin even as she watched it happen, helpless.

Tempest's gaze swung from her mother to the front door and back again. She wasn't strong enough to get the two of them out of the cottage—her mum was just too big, and she was *so* tired. Sobs racked her chest and she hugged her mama, barely able to stand the heat any longer.

Her mum's voice floated into her mind: *If I'm not here, you must take care of yourself, Tempest. If there is danger, flee. I will come for you.*

"I love you, Mama," she wept.

She kissed her mum's cheek, and, with one final tear-filled glance, Tempest stumbled toward the entrance of the cottage. She blinked at her mum's bow laying abandoned on the floor somehow untouched by the flames. Kneeling, her little fingers curled around the heated wood of the bow and she dragged it out of the only home she'd known.

Numbness seeped into her bones. Tempest didn't feel

FROST KAY

the glass cut her feet, nor the burns on her hands and legs as she wandered to the edge of the trees that bordered their land, dragging her mum's bow. She turned and stared blankly as everything she loved was consumed by the fiery beast. The cottage released one last protesting groan right before the entire building collapsed. The earth rumbled beneath her abused feet as if acknowledging the end of a life.

Her breath came in wheezing pants and Tempest's legs crumpled. Time ceased to matter as she watched the flames rapidly consume what was left of her home and flicker out of existence. It was all gone. She tipped her chin up when her belly growled, realizing the sun had moved across the sky.

Slowly, she stood on shaking legs and began walking into the forest. The sun said its final farewell and the stars came out to play, but she kept walking. Her mama said the forest wasn't safe at night, and even though her feet ached, her throat parched and scratchy, and her brain numb, she knew her mama was right. Tempest huddled deeper into the remains of her tattered cloak as the blanket of a bitterly cold night set in.

Tempest tripped when she stumbled across a cottage. One second she was in the woods, and the next surrounded by homes. Her eyes rounded as she counted the cottages. Two, three, four. No, five, then ten. It was the largest number of houses she'd ever seen before.

A village. She'd always dreamed of visiting the village, but now it seemed to lack the excitement. All she wanted

9

was her mum or… her papa.

"Papa," Tempest whispered, the word a puffy little cloud upon the air.

He'd not visited her in a long time, but her mama said that he loved her even if he couldn't come. Her face screwed up as she tried to remember what else her mama had said about Papa. He lived in a city. She eyed the houses around her. Maybe he lived here.

"Hello, there!" a stranger called. He lifted a lantern high in the air.

His smile fell when he shuffled closer, his eyes widening behind his spectacles. Tempest held her hands up and stared at her pale arms streaked with soot. Her clothing was blackened and burned. So dirty.

"Can I get some help over here? Quick!" he yelled, closing the gap between himself and Tempest as he spoke.

Her mouth watered and her belly growled. He smelled of bread. "Papa?" Tempest said again. "Where is my papa?" Someone had to know where he was.

The man who smelled of bread knelt in front of her and smiled kindly, his eyes reminding her of a snowy owl. He stroked her matted hair.

"Who is your papa, child? What happened to you? Where did you—"

He paused, bringing a lock of her hair closer to the lantern light. He fingered a patch of her ash-covered, periwinkle blue hair. The man gulped, then glanced behind him as several other villagers reached the two of them.

"The Hounds," he said. "Get the Hounds. Now."

Hounds? She'd always like puppies. She gaped as more and more people joined them, forming a loose circle. There were so many people. Too many voices. Too many faces. So many colors. Tempest trembled and her skin crawled as too many pairs of eyes watched her. Why was everyone staring at her?

Her stomach cramped as she inhaled, the scent of burnt flesh clinging to her. It was too much. Tempest bent over and vomited all over the nice man's shoes. A large hand settled on her back and rubbed in circles.

"It's all right, dear. Everything will be all right," the bread man crooned.

She began to cry in earnest. He was lying. Nothing would be okay. Her mama was gone. And where was her papa?

"Somebody clean her up, for Dotae's sake!" somebody insisted.

"But she—"

Thundering hooves against stone rang sharply behind her. Tempest lifted her head weakly. She watched as the crowd parted and a regal man swung down from the biggest horse she'd ever seen. He looked like something out of a fairytale.

And he had hair like hers.

Blue hair.

Special hair.

"She's a child," the blue-haired man announced. His voice was low and booming. He pushed past the crowd with his grey horse in tow and knelt next to her. "Just a scared, hungry child, nothing more. What is your name, lass?" he asked softly.

Tempest blinked wide eyed at the man before her. His hair was so blue it was almost black in the moonlight, as were his eyes. Though his face was impassive, there was something innately kind about him. She clung to his arm as if her life depended on it—because it did.

"T-Tempest," she stuttered.

"Hello Tempest, I'm Dima," the man replied.

"Are you my papa?" she asked, trembling. He had hair like hers. He had to be.

"No, lass," he said gently and gestured behind him at several men on horseback who had completely parted the crowd. Each and every one of them had variable shades of blue hair, like Tempest's. "I'm one of the King's Hounds, as are these men." He slowly tugged on one of her dirty blue locks. "We're your family. Aren't you lucky we were staying here this evening?" He held his hand out to her. "Let's get you cleaned up. You must be thirsty. And starving, no doubt. Baker, bring along some bread, if you will?"

She eyed him and the scary-looking men behind him. They didn't seem to be bad and she was so tired and hungry. Tempest took his hand and flung herself into his arms. Wasting no time, he picked Tempest up as if she weighed nothing at all and tucked her against his chest.

Then the man who had first spied Tempest nodded sagely. "My wife just made a fresh pot of soup. I'll bring some of that, too."

She yawned and blinked slowly, the world blurring into utter darkness.

Chapter Two

Tempest

13 Years Later

In the blink of an eye everything was gone—the fire, the forest, the screaming, the village—but the smell of smoke lingered upon the air, as if it had somehow managed to travel through Tempest's dream into the realm of consciousness. It always started the same. The acrid, foul, suffocating scent of smoke choking her.

Her eyes snapped open and she swung up into a sitting position on her bed, rubbing away the sheen of sweat that had covered her forehead. But the smoke wasn't a remnant of her memory—it was a signal that breakfast was being prepared in the barracks' kitchen. Her stomach rumbled, but she didn't think she could eat a bite.

Even now, after dreaming about it for what felt like the millionth time, Tempest still couldn't shake the horror of watching her mum die. It never got easier. She glanced around the long rectangular room, eyeing the peacefully sleeping Hounds in the barracks.

Lucky bastards.

Every Hound had his own share of horrors that kept him up at night, but she was the only one who screamed in her sleep, and on occasion wandered from room to room in a panic, scratching at the walls trying to escape a nightmare that only existed in her mind.

Despite being wide awake, she lay back down and closed her eyes. Her heart began to slow as the effects of the dream wore off, and Tempest forced herself to relax. She couldn't change the past, but she could control her future.

Today was the most important day of her life.

She clenched and unclenched her hands in an attempt to calm the nerves that vibrated like a strummed violin in her chest. There wasn't anything more she could do. Tempest had trained all her life for this and she wouldn't let a little thing like a nightmare pull her focus from what was most important.

Today her future began.

Today, Tempest would face the Trial, and with it, her fate as the first female Hound would be decided.

Chapter Three

Tempest

Tempest's stomach was a lurching, sickening mess of nerves, excitement, and hunger. She'd barely eaten the night before in anticipation of today.

Tempest's belly released an irate growl.

She regretted it now; the idea of keeping down any food before her Trial seemed impossible despite the emptiness inside her.

But she had to eat. Tempest needed all the strength she could get, but first thing was first. She needed to prepare. Food could come later.

She sniffed her armpit and her nose wrinkled. Scratch that, she needed to bathe first.

Tempest whistled as she stretched and got out of bed, the cool stones seeping through her thick woolen socks. The sound came out as shaky as she felt at first, but by the time she'd padded over to the wash basin, her voice evened out and her whistle became tuneful. The melody had stuck with her since she was a child. She didn't know the melody's origin—perhaps it had been one of her mum's almost-forgotten lullabies?

What would her mum think of Tempest's decision to join the Hounds? Was she making the right choice? The memory of her mum's cries echoed through her mind, causing Tempest's eyes to sting with the threat of tears. She pushed away the memory and took a fortifying breath.

No one had been there to protect her mother from the miscreant. If there had been a Hound there, surely things would have turned out differently. Tempest liked to think that her mum would be proud to the see woman her daughter had become; eighteen years old, fully grown, strong and healthy, and ready to take on the world as a Hound.

She *hoped* her mother would be proud of her.

In truth, it wasn't just her mum's lullabies Tempest barely remembered, although she could recall her mother's lifeless form inside the burning cottage, Tempest could not recall what her mother's face looked like, nor the touch of her hand, nor the sound of her voice.

Only the sound she'd made as she screamed.

As if on cue, the soul-wrenching scream began again in her mind.

"Just *stop it,* Tempest!" she uttered, disgusted with herself.

She lifted her head and stared at her distorted reflection in the warped mirror that hung above the wash basin. Now was most certainly not the morning to engage in such dark, macabre thoughts. Tempest scrubbed herself extra hard with the rough-woven washcloth, as if its soap-laden scratchy fibers could somehow wipe her mind clean as well as her body. She knew the only thing that could ultimately stop her dwelling on her dream was to focus on the upcoming Trial. Her rebellious stomach lurched again as goosebumps pebbled along her arms from the cool air.

The outcome of today would decide her future.

Tempest ghosted her way back to her cot and paused at the foot of the bed, staring at the garment bag holding her ceremonial garb from the king. She reached out a hand but paused, not wanting to see what he'd chosen.

"Go on now, girlie," Maxim's deep voice rumbled softly from her left.

She glanced at him from the corner of her eye and received a sunny smile that twisted the scar across his lips into a gruesome picture—well gruesome to most, anyway. To Tempest, he was one of the dearest men. He slapped a meaty hand against his thigh, which was the size of a tree trunk. Maxim leaned closer, his bed groaning underneath his huge form.

"Don't be shy now. Open it," he urged.

Tempest steeled her nerves. She was made of sterner stuff than this. It was only an outfit.

From a king who hates you.

She ignored the thought and untied the bag. Her breath seized as she got an eyeful of the garment she was expected to wear.

Dotae, no.

Quickly, she swiped the bundle from her cot and darted behind the screen her uncles had built for her. They didn't care for modesty, but they cared for *her* to be modest. Again, she peeked at the ceremonial garb in the bag. How in the hell did the king expect her to fight in such a thing?

Under ordinary circumstances, Tempest would don a form-fitting, pale grey shirt made of stiff, thick linen, with bony doe-skin breeches and matching over-the-knee leather boots. Then she'd lace on an armored bodice, guards for her lower arms, elbows, and shoulders, and a belt laden with loops of leather to hold various bags and weapons. The sheath for her favorite dagger would be tied around her right thigh. Lastly, she'd braid her hair and equip herself with a sword, a dagger, her mother's beloved bow, and a fresh quiver of arrows.

Simple. Practical.

But today was not a normal day.

No, today Tempest's outfit was far more stately. Decorative. *Fashionable,* as her best friend Juniper, a maid from the castle, had told her. *More womanly.*

Tempest wrinkled her nose at the additions to her armor.

"It can't be that bad, girlie," Maxim called.

"It can," she muttered, frowning at the sad excuse for armor.

Carefully, she lifted the raven-feathered bodice that attached around her neck with a gilded, silver buckle.

Tempest twisted the piece back and forth. Where was the damned back to the thing?

She dropped the article of clothing to the ground and dug out the shoulder guards. Tempest hissed as she got a good look at them. Or rather—a look at it. There was only one, a singular shoulder guard made of overlapping plates of lilac-stained metal on top of silver chainmail, complete with dozens of hanging chains that were present for purely aesthetic reasons.

Bloody useless reasons.

With care, she set the damned thing next to its disgrace of a breast plate. She brushed her finger over one of the fine delicate chains. *Winters bite.* It would be impossible to untangle the chains. If she'd had her way, Tempest would have tossed the shoulder guard across the room.

Finally, she pulled out the last pieces of her ensemble.

"Ridiculous," she snarled quietly.

She pinched the thigh-skimming black leather skirt that had been cut into ribbons and the deep purple half-cape that, she assumed, was to drape over her bare shoulder.

"It can't be that bad," Dima, another one of her uncles, added softly. "Put on the basics and we'll help you with the rest."

"Basics?" she murmured. They hadn't given her the basics. Her gaze moved back to the top. One wrong move, and her tits would be shown to all. Tempest held her hand out over the screen. "I need my half corset."

A beat of silence, and then rustling.

Normally, she wasn't shy. Living with men nearly all her life had taken most of the embarrassment away, but when Maxim's hand reached over the screen holding her dingy corset, heat scorched her cheeks. Tempest snatched the undergarment from his scarred fingers with a quickly muttered thank you.

A shiver ran down her spine as she pulled her sleep-shirt off and unwound the band from her breasts. With deft hands, she snapped the corset in place and stepped outside the screen, presenting the room with her back.

"Could someone lace me?" she asked, her voice just a touch too high.

"I've got you," Maxim muttered, his tone gentle.

Tempest stared blankly at the grey wall as her uncle cinched her corset. Of all the things she imagined for Trial day, this wasn't it.

"Is that too tight?" her uncle asked, knotting the corset strings.

She wiggled and then jumped in place. Her breasts didn't budge, and she could breathe, so that was a plus. "It's fine."

With scalding cheeks, she moved behind the screen and plucked the feathered nightmare from the floor. She clasped the buckle around her neck and waist, securing the raven-feathered bodice. Next, she painstakingly adorned the lilac-stained shoulder guard. Frigid chains slid over the bare skin of her biceps and back. Tempest shuddered and rubbed at her arms, hating the feeling of being so exposed.

Tempest bent to pick up the skirt and shimmied it over her thighs, settling the high leather waist beneath the bodice. She glared at how much of her legs were on display. She looked like a trollop. How was she supposed to fight in such a state?

She clenched her jaw and came to a decision that wouldn't earn her any favors from the king. Tempest would wear his gifts, but she would do it *her* way. The warrior way.

"Could you pass me my leather leggings?"

Someone tossed them over the top of the screen, the leather slapping her in the face.

"Thanks."

Tempest tugged on the familiar pants and sighed as the soft black leather caressed her legs, bringing with it a modicum of calm. She snatched the cape from the floor and kicked the garment bag against the wall. Now all she had to do was leave the sanctuary behind the screen.

Be brave, Temp. It's just fabric.

She blew a periwinkle strand of hair from her face and twisted her lips in distaste. She would also have to wear her hair hanging free. She didn't like that one bit; it would be a disadvantage in combat to have such free-flowing hair

"I should have cut it all off," Tempest muttered before venturing out from behind the screen.

Silence. Pure silence greeted her as she moved to the trunk at the end of her cot. It was difficult to ignore the looks of her uncles and fellow Hounds as they appraised her outfit.

"Is he trying to get you killed?" Maxim burst out first.

Tempest's mouth popped open in shock. That was treason, and she knew she wouldn't be the only one to think so.

Dima's tall, thin form stepped next to Maxim and he slapped the hulking man on the back of the head. "Are you stupid? You'll get her killed with your nonsense."

Maxim scowled and rubbed at the back of his head and gestured toward Temp. "Do you have eyes? She's completely vulnerable."

Dima turned his calculating gaze on her and cocked his head, his deep blue braids slipping over his shoulders. "Is that all you have?"

Tempest swallowed hard, her mouth dry. "Among other things."

She turned back to her trunk and yanked out her metal gauntlets and pulled one over each of her forearms. Next, she tugged on her boots that she'd shined the night prior. Her stomach rolled as she plucked a comb from the chest and yanked it through her hair. Pain pricked her scalp, but she welcomed it. It helped her focus.

With a final tug of the comb through her hair, she threw her mother's bow onto her back and made sure her sword and dagger sheaths were secure. Murmurs followed her as she moved to stand in front of the mirror. Tempest studied her reflection, inspecting her overall outfit with a begrudging sense of admiration. She supposed she *did* look good. Great, even. But playing up to her femininity—

not to mention indulging in the theatrics so beloved by the royal city of Dotae—made Tempest somewhat uncomfortable. She wanted to be judged on her ability to act as a Hound, regardless of gender. Tempest certainly didn't care she was female, and nor did the rest of the Hounds.

My uncles.

She glanced at Maxim and Dima who were whispering heatedly between the two of them. Tempest counted herself lucky to have been raised by them. She crept out of the barracks and strode toward her favorite thinking place.

The training yard was still empty. The sun was hanging low on the horizon, and morning drills did not start until it had fully risen and the Hounds' bellies were full. Tempest nimbly jumped onto the fence, swinging her legs below her after she'd settled into a perfectly balanced sitting position on top of the narrow wood. A faint breeze blew her hair around her face, tangling her loose locks together.

"I really should have cut it," Tempest whispered, echoing her sentiments from before, though Madrid—the intimidating Head Hound—had ordered her not to. For the Trial, at least. It was clear they thought it important to play up the fact Tempest was a young woman, no matter that she'd been training with the Hounds far longer than most of the other trainees her age.

"Will you stop complaining about your hair?"

Tempest stilled for just a moment, then relaxed as the

familiar frame of Dima joined her. He leaned against the fence, frowning as he stared straight into the rising sun. The man was as tall, lithe, and thin as he'd been the day he'd found five-year-old Tempest, and his midnight-blue hair was just as dark as it had always been, but there were a few tell-tale lines of ageing around his eyes. Though Dima was quiet and reserved—he rarely showed his emotions on his face—he always seemed to know when Tempest needed somebody either to talk to or to act as a patient ear for her complaints.

"It's stupid that I cannot tie it back today," Tempest said, but even as she spoke, she realized she sounded like a petulant child. For a moment, it seemed as if Dima might smile at her, though Tempest knew that was all but impossible; the man had smiled at her just three times in her entire life.

Perhaps, if she passed her Trial, he would make it four times.

"Just play up to the crowd for one day. Do what they want, when tomorrow comes you can do whatever you damn well please."

Tempest said nothing. She knew Dima was right, of course, but having *anyone* tell her how to act or look grated on her nerves to no end. "I don't care that I'm the first woman vying for a position in the Hounds. It's all a means to an end. All I care about is—"

"Avenging your mother," Dima cut in, not unkindly. "I know, Tempest, I know. But you're an adult now, and, with that, comes responsibilities—such as doing what the king wants you to do."

"He doesn't even *want* me to be a Hound." Tempest knew she was right; the monarch had made no attempt to hide his dislike of her. Her outfit solidified her suspicions.

"Then prove him wrong—show him that women belong in our ranks. Actions speak louder than words, as well as you know."

Tempest's lips curled into the smallest of smiles. She turned her head to face Dima. "Is that why I still have a bruise on the back of my leg?"

"You didn't heed my advice to guard your back so, yes, I'd say that's why."

"I don't have any openings now, I'm sure of it."

Dima rolled his eyes and swung off the fence. "There's more to life than fighting, you know. You say you're here to avenge your mother. What will you do once you achieve that?"

Tempest didn't reply, and Dima merely sighed.

"You will make a fine Hound—we all know that. Just consider whether it's *actually* what you want to do with your life."

Tempest mulled over his words long after he was gone. In truth, she had no idea what she wanted to do outside of this one, all-consuming goal. She'd never thought she needed another one. *I guess Dima is right,* she finally concluded. *At some point I may want more than revenge. But, for now, it's more than enough.*

"Well somebody looks awfully angry," came an airy, sing-song voice—the kind of voice that belonged to somebody who'd already been up for hours and was wide awake.

Tempest grinned. "Morning, Juniper. Your shift must be over soon—the sun is in the sky!"

"It's over now," her best friend replied, snowy-white hair puffing out around her shoulders as she collapsed against the fence, uncaring of getting dust and dirt upon her dress. Juniper looked at Tempest perched above her, before pulling out a cloth-wrapped package and proffering it to her. "Here. Breakfast. I imagined you wouldn't be able to stomach typical barracks food today so I pilfered you some goods from the palace."

"Dotae be good, I love you," Tempest cried in delight, opening the package to reveal freshly baked, flaky pastries, still warm to the touch. Two of them were savory, two of them sweet; Tempest tore into one filled with cinnamon and vanilla first, her nausea instantly forgotten in the wake of her favorite food being hand-delivered to her.

Juniper giggled at her friend's shameless display of happiness. "Feeling better now? You looked about ready to murder someone, and your Trial doesn't even start for another three hours!"

"Much better, thanks." Tempest's words were muffled and warped around mouthfuls of pastry, but she didn't care. With a supreme effort, she swallowed down the overly large bite she had taken. "I was just thinking about my mum's death."

"Hence the expression. Did you have that dream again?"

Her friend gazed at her with concern.

She nodded.

Juniper knew everything Tempest could remember of her past; she was one of her very few female friends. Though the girl was a shifter—which initially set Tempest's teeth on edge as a child—Juniper was gentle and soft-spoken and never judged Tempest for her crass, uncultured way of living, unlike how the ladies of the court often did. Her shifted form was an owl, hence her working at nights in the palace. The two often spent twilight and sunrise together—the beginning of one of their days, and the end of the other's.

Juniper pointed at a pair of men jumping over the fence opposite them to enter the training yard, preparing to spar. Tempest fought back a grimace as she realized one of them was Levka, but her mood improved when she saw the other man was his father, Maxim. The monster of a man grinned at her and waved a comb in the air.

Tempest winced, knowing he had plans for her unruly hair and snarfed down the last of the pastries. Her boisterous, bawdy uncle had always been the one to braid her hair as a child. One day she'd asked him how he knew so much about women's hair. Her nose wrinkled as she recalled the discussion that had ensured afterward. Maxim had been delighted in giving Tempest an especially colorful explanation of how men and women created children.

If only I could scrub that from my brain.

Her attention moved to his spawn. Too bad his son

hated her.

She'd grown up with Levka and was only a handful of months older than him. It didn't improve things between them that her Trial was before his. He viewed it as a huge insult to his person, least of all because he did not believe women should be Hounds in the first place. Despite the fact that Tempest had spent three or four nights a week eating dinner with Maxim's family and that Maxim himself doted on Tempest, Levka had always refused to warm to her.

And she hated it. Things could have been so different between them if he'd only accepted her. She'd always wanted a sibling.

"You're watching Levka as if you'd like to punch him in the face again, Tempest," Juniper said, as if she were discussing the weather instead of impending violence.

Tempest could only laugh. "More like that's what he thinks of *me,* though by his logic I'm simply too frail to take a punch to the face. I can't wait to pass my Trial and show him I can do this just as well as he can. Better, even."

"Oh, come now, you can't be that blind."

She glanced at her friend. "What do you mean?"

"Never mind that Levka definitely knows you're better than him and it drives him *insane,* and that he's jealous his dad loves you so much—"

"I've never done anything to keep Maxim from him. I wanted to be his friend. His anger is not my—"

"I never said it was," Juniper interrupted her, "and that wasn't my point, anyway. Don't you think that he maybe likes you? As in—"

"Oh, please don't finish that thought. For the love of Dotae *do not finish that thought.*" The boy had never looked at her with anything but contempt and disgust.

Juniper stared at her as if she thought Tempest was over-reacting. "It wouldn't be impossible, you know, especially when you're dressed like this." She waved a hand in Tempest's general direction and smiled approvingly. "I love the new look, by the way. Very intimidating."

Tempest snorted. "As intimidating as a woman of the night."

"So dramatic." Juniper rolled her eyes. "You've never had time for boys before, Tempest. You've been so focused on becoming a Hound. But after your Trial—what next? Are you going to continue to be aloof and alone all your life? Because I know for a fact there are more than a few pairs of eyes on you, you hopeless, beautiful fool."

Tempest's cheeks flushed before she could stop herself reacting. She shook her head wildly. "I have no time for such things right now. Maybe not ever. I have more important things in my life than dealing with boys."

Boys lead to babes. Babes led to a life she didn't desire.

"Finding someone who loves and accepts you isn't important?"

"Well, you love me, don't you?" Tempest gestured around the practice yard. "And my uncles love me, and I love them. I don't need anyone else."

She had her family. A family that had welcomed her

with open arms. Many people faced with her situation wouldn't be able to say the same thing. In her own eyes, she was blessed beyond measure.

"Yes, but one day—not too far in the future, I hope—I'll be married, and I'll have children, and then we won't have as much time for each other. And, for all we know, we may live on opposite sides of the kingdom in a few years. Having someone to look forward to seeing when you get home isn't such a bad thing, you know." Juniper's expression relaxed into an almost dream-like state. "And that's not to mention the feeling you get when someone you really like kisses you—how your skin is set on fire when he holds you in his arms, and when—"

"And that's my cue to limber up," Tempest cut in, embarrassed for both herself and for Juniper's lovey-dovey ramblings. She leaped off the fence, stretching both of her arms above her head. "Will you be watching the Trial, Juniper?"

Her friend nodded enthusiastically as she got up from the ground. "Of course! I'm missing my bed and everything for it. You better not fail."

"Such kind words of encouragement."

Juniper touched Tempest's elbow very lightly, causing her to turn and face her. "On a more serious note, Tempest, please be careful. Be safe. Don't do anything rash today."

"Being a Hound doesn't exactly lend itself to those things."

"Tempest—"

"All right, all right," Tempest replied, holding up her hands in resignation. "I won't be stupid. Happy?"

"Reasonably so."

"Go get some rest before the Trial, then. I wouldn't want you falling asleep during it!"

Juniper grinned. "Of course not. See you later, Tempest."

"You, too."

Tempest stretched and performed her morning weapon's drill in relative silence after that, though she knew almost every pair of eyes was on her over the next two hours. But aside from Levka and a couple of his trainee friends, all other members of the barracks were incredibly supportive of Tempest. They wanted her to succeed. It did not matter to most of them that she was a woman, and to those that opposed her on such grounds... well, they could not fault her skill, no matter how hard they tried.

Eventually it was Maxim who put a hand on Tempest's shoulder to stop her practicing. The man looked down at her with an uncharacteristically serious expression on his face. "It's time, Tempest." He scrutinized her hair. "Let's do something about this mane before you head off to the arena to get yourself prepared."

Tempest found that she could no longer form words. Her throat had closed up entirely, like a bee had flown inside her mouth and stung her. So she nodded, avoiding the vicious smile plastered across Levka's face, who was standing slightly behind his father.

Maxim frowned and gently pulled her to the fence. He drew the comb from his pocket and began to work through her twisted hair. "Do you want me to walk over there with you?" he asked softly. "I can if you like. I think Dima and Aleks are already there, otherwise I'd ask them to take you—"

"No, it's fine," Tempest finally managed to utter as she ran her hand along the cape she'd left hanging from the fence. "I can make my way there on my own. I wouldn't be much of a Hound if I couldn't, right?"

"You're more than just a Hound," her uncle said, his deep voice smooth, as his fingers finished a braid on her right side and began working on the left.

"I have to keep my hair down," she whispered.

"Right, it has to be down, but it was never specified *how* it was to be done."

Her lips curled up into a smile. "I love you, Maxim." If there was anyone she could count to be on her side, it was him.

All too soon, he finished her hair and spun her to face him. Her uncle reached over her shoulder and pulled the fine cloak from the fence. He helped her clasp it around her neck and then placed his hands on her shoulders, his hazel eyes serious.

"Take care in the Trial, girlie," he said, his voice gruff.

"I will."

Maxim yanked her into a bear hug, and she inhaled his smoky scent.

"Show those bastards what you're made of." He pulled

back and cupped her pale cheeks. "Show them what the House of Madrid stands for."

She grinned and Maxim mirrored the smile she gave him.

With a salute to the rest of the Hounds currently training in the yard, Tempest turned on the spot—flashy half-cape billowing out behind her as she did so—and headed for the arena, and her impending Trial.

It's now or never, Mum. Now or never.

Chapter Four

Tempest

The roar of the crowd assaulted Tempest's ears as she neared the entrance to the arena. Personally, she didn't see why the Trial had to be public, since it was technically an exam to get a job. But the people of Heimserya flocked to Dotae to watch new Trials, and Tempest's was no exception. Her gaze dropped to her outrageous outfit, and she fingered a silky raven feather. Today, they'd get a show.

Tempest's stomach clenched as she eyed what was perhaps the largest crowd she had ever witnessed for such an event. Nausea rolled through her, making Tempest regret wolfing down the pastries Juniper had brought her.

She stared blankly from her niche, hidden from the swarm of nobility buzzing with excitement and taut with the anticipation of blood. Her lip curled. Violence was a necessity of life, but Tempest didn't take joy in it. The revelers were already well on their way to finishing entire wineskins, and it wasn't even noon yet. They were drunk on spirits and the promise of blood.

Revolting.

A deep gong rung, signaling the Trial was to begin soon.

Tempest stepped out from her hiding spot and moved through the well-dressed crowd, ignoring their gasps and calls, her face a mask of stone. It was only when the commoners spied Tempest in her flashy Trial garb did her apathy melt away. They gasped and cheered, waving wildly from the stands high above. A surge of pride filled Tempest as she gave them a genuine smile. She was one of them, after all. She'd come from nothing. She represented hope. Vengeance for her mother had been her driving motivation for so long, but, in that moment, Tempest enjoyed a flicker of happiness for making the decision to follow the path of a Hound, purely that she represented those who were downtrodden.

She would pass the Trial.

If not for her mother, then for the people who'd supported her. *And* to show that both commoners and women belonged in the ranks of the most elite group of fighters and spies. Everyone deserved a chance to live their dreams.

She scanned the crowd and frowned when she spotted a little boy who looked anything but excited. He was crying in a corner, cradling a hand to his chest. Her eyes narrowed as she noticed a dark red stain on the front of his tunic. She'd bet her mother's bow it was blood. Her scowl deepened as she examined the people around him. Nobody seemed to notice him, or, if they did, they thoroughly ignored him.

Her attention turned back to the arena. The others hadn't arrived for their Trials yet. If she hurried, she could help the poor little one.

Tempest closed the distance between herself and the boy with ground-eating strides. She slowed her pace when he noticed her and cowered farther into the stone wall against his back. Holding out a hand, she smiled softly at him to let the child know she meant him no harm.

"Hello, little one," she said as she bent low beside him. "What's wrong? Did you hurt yourself? Where are your parents?"

He peered at her with wide, tear-filled eyes. His ice-blue irises and snowy hair which were akin to Juniper's.

An owl shifter.

She hid her grimace. Shifters set her teeth on edge, but she wouldn't let that get in the way of helping the youngster. His people may have caused problems in Heimserya, but he was innocent. She would not condemn him for crimes he'd been no part of.

Tempest pointed at his hand that held a jade dagger with an intricate handle, its blade smeared with red. He'd cut his palm open; the wound was bleeding all over the boy's tunic. She studied his ragged clothing. A fine blade. Too fine for a commoner.

Focus on the task at hand. You're not here to interrogate

him.

"Do not be afraid," Tempest soothed, stroking the boy's hair as she did so, the downy strands tickling her palms. "What happened to you? Do you want me to take you to the healer's tent?" Aleks, the resident Hound healer—one of Tempest's favorite uncles out of her multitude of them—would be working in there already, preparing for the Trial. He'd happily help the boy out, if Tempest asked him.

The boy's upper lip trembled. "I didn't mean to cut myself," he whispered, "but I didn't know what to—what to do with it, and—"

Tempest gently took the blade from him, wiping it on the ground to remove the blood before sheathing it beside her other dagger. She smiled. "Luckily I know exactly what to do with a dagger. Let me keep hold of it until we get you to the healer's tent, then you can tell me all about what happened, all right? What's your name?"

"T-Tomas," he said, a shy smile crawling upon his face when Tempest held out a hand to him. He took it, tiny fingers apparently even smaller within Tempest's grasp, and waddled along beside her toward the tent. She ignored the crowd asking after her as she passed; she barely had enough time to sort Tomas out before the Trial started.

"Aleks, I need your—" Tempest began as they pushed through the tent flap, her nose wrinkled in distaste. An odd, sickly-sweet smell filtered through the air. It was cloying in Tempest's nostrils, unfamiliar and thick. It wasn't outright vomit inducing, but it set her teeth on edge.

Aleks really works with the oddest drugs.

"Tempest, what are you doing here? You should be announcing yourself to the king!" Aleks exclaimed, looking up from the notes he was poring over in order to frown at her. But his expression relaxed when he saw Tomas. "I see you found another lost wee one."

Tempest drew shallow breaths through her mouth and tried to ignore the odor. Tomas coughed as she hauled him on top of a cot that was most likely prepared for *her,* should she injure herself today.

"What do you mean *another?*"

He chuckled. "Well, there was that little girl Sasha last week, and the twins the month before that, and—"

"Well it's not like anyone else is helping them out, are they?" Tempest retorted. "Somebody's got to help them." If she hadn't stepped in, she doubted someone would have taken it upon themselves to help the wee one.

"You know, I agree with you, Tempest," Aleks said gently.

"Then have Madrid tell the king to funnel more money into the orphanages."

"Tempest—"

"I know, I know," she interrupted, sighing heavily. "Now is not the time. Well it *will* be the time once I'm made a Hound." She'd lucked out as a child, being born to the Madrid line. If she hadn't, well... life would've turned out very differently for her. The orphanages were a joke. They were workhouses for little ones who had no one to protect them. Even thinking about it made her feel sick.

Her thoughts must have shown on her face because the healer squeezed her hand once, before diverting his attention to Tomas and began to clean his wound. "I do not doubt that. You will do a lot of much-needed good once you're sworn in."

Tempest loved that Aleks had never once doubted her. The number of days and nights she'd spent inside his room as a child, feverish and sick and hallucinating, had brought them close together. Sometimes, Tempest had imagined her own father was sitting beside the healer, watching over her as she fought the latest sickness she'd contracted. Other times, Tempest believed that Aleks himself *was* her father—his hair was an identical shade of periwinkle to hers.

On more than one occasion, Tempest had almost asked him if she was his daughter.

Almost.

But Tempest was scared of the truth—Hounds were not allowed to hide their children in obscure cottages in the middle of a forest, away from Dotae. To do so was treason. If Aleks really was Tempest's father then she had to believe that he'd had good reason to hide her—so she stayed silent, content with the fact that she had amazing uncles to look after her. They'd all had a hand in raising her.

"Right, off with you," he said, waving for Tempest to leave the tent. "I'll look after—"

"Tomas," she supplied, smiling at the boy.

"Tomas." He arched an eyebrow at Temp. "I hope that I don't see you in here again today!"

Tempest laughed. Of course, Aleks wouldn't want her to get injured, though, in all likelihood, she would. No one came out unscathed from their Trial.

"I shall endeavor to be careful," she said, remembering that she had told Juniper the same thing.

Aleks stepped closer and kissed the top of her head. "Fight well."

She nodded and winked at Tomas before she left the tent. Tempest edged around the screaming crowd and jogged down two flights of stairs, her belly a riot of nerves. The chants and stamps upon the wooden floor of the stands vibrated through her feet, and the sounds from the brass trumpets of the royal band rung in her ears. The scent of warm, sweet, and spicy pastries, roasted nuts, and salted meat perfumed the air. Her bare arms prickled as thousands of pairs of eyes roamed over her as she stepped into the arena. It felt as if everybody in the royal city of Dotae was here to see her succeed... or—for some of them, at least—see her fail.

I won't fail.

In the very center of the arena stood a platform upon which Madrid, the head Hound, was standing. Waiting for her. But Tempest knew she had to kneel before the king first, so she turned to face the royal stand at the northernmost point of the arena.

She bowed deeply, her long braids almost touching the

ground. "Your Grace," she called out, as loud as she could make her voice. Tempest was pleased that her voice did not tremble, but her legs felt as though they'd turned to jelly.

King Destin seemed barely interested enough to acknowledge her presence. He side-eyed her from his throne, looking younger than his forty years. He was wrapped in a sumptuous, fur-lined coat of ruby red to keep out the chill of the day. He didn't speak a word, merely waving a hand toward Tempest to indicate that she could begin the Trial.

She huffed, relieved that he didn't say a word about her alterations to the outfit he'd gifted her. Tempest marched toward the raised platform, her stride sure as she locked eyes with Madrid. He was a tall, icy man, who rarely raised his voice or visibly lost his temper. But when he grew completely still... that was when one knew they were in trouble. Tempest respected him greatly, though she was understandably rather intimidated by him. The man was a legend.

"Welcome, Tempest," he said quietly when she stepped onto the platform and bowed slightly. And then, in a much louder, booming voice, he addressed the crowd. "Welcome one and all to the most auspicious of Trials— our first female Hound trainee!"

The crowd thundered their approval as Madrid once more turned to face Tempest.

"Now, the first part of the Trial is to test your observation skills."

A pre-emptive shiver of adrenaline ran right through Tempest as she waited to hear what her first task would be. She eyed the covered table to her right. What horrors were hidden under the decorative cloth?

Madrid held out his arms, pulling her attention back to the Hound master. "Somewhere in the crowd there is a small child with a jade dagger strapped to their…"

She blinked. It couldn't be that easy.

"Do you mean this one?" Tempest asked without thinking, pulling out said dagger from the sheath on her thigh. She dropped to her knee, proffering it to Madrid.

He frowned at the blade in suspicion. "Where did you get that?"

"From a little boy I spotted about ten minutes ago," Tempest explained. "He seemed lost and nervous, and he cut his hand on the dagger. He didn't know what to do, so I helped him and took the dagger off his hands." Her lips pursed. "It seemed odd that a wee one would possess such a fine weapon."

Madrid seemed torn between bemusement and respect. But then he nodded, acknowledging that Tempest had passed the first round.

She hid her displeasure, schooling her face into a blank mask. It was wrong to use children. Tempest hated the fact a confused, scared little boy had been used as part of her Trial, especially because he'd hurt himself. If she came out victorious at the end of the day, Tempest swore that she'd speak to Madrid about it.

"A keen sense of those around you and the ability to

earn a stranger's trust are vital skills for a Hound," Madrid said, addressing the crowd as well as Tempest. "The fact that you passed the first round without even being aware of it is testament to your skills in such areas. However—" His face was grave as he stared at Tempest. "I do not think you will pass the next test so easily."

Oh, Dotae be good, what's next?

Tempest managed to keep her expression neutral, despite her nerves and anger.

Calm down. Anger is a distraction you cannot afford.

The next section would be brutal. She had seen a handful of Hound Trials over the past few years, and not a single champion had passed. Each and every time the tests were different. It was impossible to prepare for one's own Trial simply by watching what champions of bygone days had done.

Tempest rolled her neck and ignored the cool wind whipping her decorative cape and loosely braided hair around her face. She was on her own.

"The next test will examine your knowledge of poisons," the head Hound said, indicating a covered table that stood on the platform alongside them.

Damn.

He yanked the cloth off the table, exposing three bottles of liquid all various shades of blue. Their stoppers were ornate and intricately carved with designs of leaves and flowers.

All around, the volume of the crowd swelled, everyone presumably wondering what on earth was going to happen next.

The vicious grin that crossed Madrid's face was anything but pleasant. "You have five minutes to work out which of these is deadly, which of these will send you to sleep, and which of these does nothing at all. How you determine which is which is entirely up to you."

Double damn.

Tempest gulped. She was good with poisons when not put on the spot. Aleks had drilled her on their identifying properties over and over again, yet she still struggled. She wasn't the best out of the trainees—that was, in truth, Levka—but she was still better than most. But never had she been faced with identifying such things *in front* of a gigantic crowd.

She kept herself from biting her lip, not wanting to give away her fear. Now was not the time to show fear. She needed to show courage.

It would have been easier if she'd fought someone first.

She crossed the platform over to the table to investigate the bottles and her brow furrowed in concentration. Tempest curled her shaking fingers into fists and inhaled deeply five times, completely aware of the crowd's attention as she employed the calming tactic Dima had taught her as a child.

Stop thinking about them. Focus on your task.

Tempest shut out all sounds around her and squinted at the liquids. All three were of a similar viscosity. All three were translucent. She unstopped them and carefully inhaled the way she'd been taught to. Her lips pursed. All three smelled a little bitter.

Wonderful. They were near-identical. *No one said becoming a Hound would be easy.*

"Two minutes down," Madrid said, startling Tempest.

Twisting her hands together, she stared at the bottles as if they might have suddenly changed their appearance.

Think, you fool. Think. There is a clue here. If it isn't the liquid itself, then—

Her gaze narrowed on the bottles. She picked the vials up, one after the other, inspecting their beautifully carved stoppers. She recognized the flowers on two of them, but not the third, but it was all she needed to work out what they were.

She held up the second bottle for the crowd to see. "This is the poison," she announced. "Blue bottle is nightshade. It's full of atropine and solanine. Incredibly poisonous. The third bottle is dyed blue using bluebells, but it is harmless. I do not recognize the first bottle, so it must be the sleeping agent."

"Are you certain?" the Hound master asked.

"I am."

He waved a hand at the third bottle still clutched in her hand. "Test it."

Although Tempest knew she was right, it was harder than she expected to tip the bottle to her lips and drink the liquid. She swallowed the bitter draught and stared impassively at Madrid, not backing down from his challenge.

Madrid's stone expression melted into a grin that was

anything but vicious this time. It was ecstatic and tinged with the smallest touch of pride.

"The first one does not come from a plant," he explained, "so the flowers depicted on the stopper are fictional. Well done, Tempest."

Some of the tension in her shoulders melted away. She'd done it. She'd passed the second test. And she wasn't going to die. A hysterical laugh threatened to burst from her chest, but she swallowed it down.

The crowd rose to their feet and screamed, but Madrid held up a hand to quieten them. In the space of a moment, they were silent. So silent it was eerie.

"Now, you might be thinking you're glad we're onto the fighting round of the trial," he told Tempest. "But something tells me you won't be so happy when you see who your opponent is."

Tempest stilled. Madrid's face was serious once more, and there was something about the way he kept glancing at the king that told her that, perhaps, the head Hound himself was not so happy with who had been chosen as her opponent, either. But King Destin nodded his head and smirked down at Temp, his gaze pointedly staring at her braided hair.

So he *had* noticed her outfit modification. It hadn't been smart to go against his wishes but being dead seemed like a worse alternative. She swallowed hard and studied Madrid, who in turn nodded at a pair of soldiers guarding a set of heavy wooden doors.

"Bring out the lion."

"The lion?" Tempest whispered; her words lost beneath the uproar of the fervent, delighted crowd.

Her mind scrambled to latch onto any knowledge she had of the beast. Never in the history of the Trials, had any would-be Hound faced a *lion.* The beasts were bloodthirsty creatures who knew how to rip through a battalion of soldiers with ease. Maxim's scar on his face flashed through her mind. Her uncle rarely spoke about his old wound, but he'd warned her to run the other way if she discovered any sign of a lion.

She took a step toward Madrid and spoke in an undertone, panic rising in her throat like bile as she stuttered out, "Tell me this isn't true—why am I facing—"

"Hush, Tempest," he muttered back to her, careful to hide the fact that the two of them were talking. "This was not my decision. Just keep a level head, think on your feet, and you'll be fine."

Tempest felt anything *but* level-headed. A finger of dread ran down her spine as the wooden doors rattled and shook in front of her. She could hear the beginnings of a growl, low and rough and angry.

Wicked hell. They sentenced me to death.

Tempest steeled herself as Madrid lifted the table, along with its three bottles, out of the fighting ring. She slowly pulled her sword from its scabbard and braced herself for the demon that would soon be unleashed upon her.

Nobody would be around to help her. If Tempest failed, then it wouldn't be the healer's tent she would be visiting—it would be her grave. The solider retreated into the stands as the doors containing the lion finally swung open, leaving Tempest as the only person standing on the dirt-covered platform facing one of the realm's deadliest creatures, besides the ever-elusive ice dragons.

Her gaze flickered to the king. For one moment, they locked eyes. Hers was accusing, his smug.

The bastard.

He didn't want a woman to succeed. She clenched her jaw and concentrated on the task at hand. All thoughts fled her as Tempest caught sight of a jaw full of snapping teeth.

Bloody hell. The monster was more enormous and terrifying than she'd anticipated. The lion would bat her sword from her hand like a cat playing with string.

"A spear!" she cried, locking eyes with the soldiers. "Give me your spear!"

One of them acted as if he had not heard her, and Tempest hated him for it. But the other one—younger than his partner, handsome, blue-eyed and sandy-haired—tossed his double-ended spear into the arena, and Tempest skittered across the ring to retrieve it just as the lion prowled from its cage. Quickly, she sheathed her sword and clasped the spear in her shaking hands.

The beast was huge, with a thick mane the color of King Destin's hair protecting its neck. *A male, then,* she concluded as he crept toward Tempest, each of his movements sinuous. His sharp, feline eyes flitted from her face to her spear, as if trying to decide which part of her was the biggest threat. Tempest kept her stance wide, holding herself low to the ground should she have to roll away to escape the lion's snapping teeth.

She scrutinized the beast. He was clearly not a native lion since his coloring was too red. In fact, Tempest had seen these ones depicted only in books, and Aleks used to tell her stories of his travels in the exotic south when he was training as a healer. There were rust lions there, Tempest knew. Lots of them.

Tempest appraised the lion and tried not to let the majestic creature distract her. She'd only ever heard of the fable creatures in stories and lessons designed to teach children never to wander into the forests alone—but she doubted many people in Heimserya had seen one before. In the past, the kingdom was altogether too cold for the creatures. Too windy. Too snowy. But over time, the lions had adapted, their fur turning a snowy white to blend in with their surroundings.

Virtually impossible to detect until they set upon you.

A snap of its tail was all the warning she received before the lion lunged forward, swatting at Tempest with a paw that was larger than her head. She'd been right to stay low to the ground; with a simple shift in weight from one foot to the other, she rolled away with half a second to spare, aiming her spear at the lion's paw in the process, to force him to withdraw. The creature retreated, clearly reassessing the risk Tempest posed to him.

Sweat beaded on her brow as she got a good look at the lion's side. Her lips thinned at the sight of his ribs sticking out from beneath his fur. They'd starved him. Rage ignited in her gut. A simple spear wouldn't keep him down. She'd have to fight dirty.

Or die trying.

It truly wasn't fair. A starving lion was different from a man.

They really do mean to kill me.

Tempest shuffled a step to her left and spun the double-ended spear in front of her to keep the lion momentarily at bay. She risked a glance at the king, who despite his earlier disinterest was now watching Tempest—and the lion—like a hawk. Was the man really going to take his dislike of female Hounds so far that Tempest would have to die for it?

"I think not," she muttered through gritted teeth, though her own words were swallowed by the roaring lion and deafening crowd.

But Tempest had never been quiet. She'd never been soft-spoken, meek, or demure. If the lion wanted to roar at her then *she* would roar at him.

"Come and get me!" she bellowed at the beast as she twirled her borrowed spear before flinging it toward him.

The lion just barely avoided the weapon, but Tempest had expected that. All she'd needed was his momentary distraction—a long enough pause for her to pull her mother's bow from her back and nock an arrow. She sent it flying into the lion's flank.

He yowled as she struck true, and Tempest darted forward to collect her spear once more. But just as she turned to deliver a second blow, the lion knocked her to the ground. Her bow skittered across the ground just out of reach.

She screamed as he raked his claws across her bare back. Searing pain caused her eyes to water, and Tempest barely had enough time to roll onto her abused back and brace the spear in front of her, keeping the lion's teeth at bay. He gnashed and growled around the wooden shaft, intent on breaking it to pieces.

The wood groaned and her arms trembled as she fought to keep the beast from tearing her apart.

I don't have the strength for this.

He snarled, his fetid breath washing over her face. She blanched when the lion swiped at her bicep, tearing through her skin with his razor-sharp claws. His eyes narrowed at the scent of her blood, truly lost to his instinct to hunt and kill.

Her arms strained and in the back of her mind, Tempest realized she should feel more fear and pain than she actually was. A dull buzzing filled her ears and drowned out all the sounds around her. All she could see was the poor, starving beast above her. She pitied the creature. He was as desperate as she was.

I'm going to die, but at least I'll go out fighting.

She mustered her strength and roared into the creature's face once more, then kicked at the arrow lodged into his back leg with enough force to cause the lion to yowl and lunge away in pain—but not before he yanked Tempest's spear from her grasp and snapped it in two. She crawled away, across the dusty arena floor, pure panic and adrenaline urging her to stagger to her feet.

Blood dripped down her arm and back, the remnants of her shredded cape fluttering in the breeze. She pulled her sword from her scabbard and a wickedly long dagger from the sheath at her left hip that Dima had gifted her.

She said a little prayer, thankful that Maxim had taught her to dual wield. Before she could talk herself out of it, Tempest grinned wildly and attacked the lion before her pain and terror froze her in place.

Time slowed as Tempest closed the gap between herself and the lion. Sound faded in and out—the crowd screaming, and then only the sound of her own heartbeat pounding in her ears. She palmed the blade and made a split-second decision.

Please let this work.

She slung her blade, and it struck true. Bile flooded her mouth as her dagger sunk into the left eye of the lion. He screamed a horrible sound—one she was sure would haunt her nightmares—and wildly clawed at her. Tempest ducked beneath what would have been a killer blow to her head, but, instead of darting away, she swung beneath him, slamming her sword upward into his neck.

Tempest gritted her teeth and held on as the lion gurgled. He swayed, and she scrambled back as he collapsed onto her, his massive head on her chest. Her stormy eyes met his dulling amber ones. But sadness overwhelmed her, and she couldn't find it in her heart to let the poor creature suffer. With a flick of her wrists, she ended his pain. A clean death.

THE HUNT

Several agonizingly long seconds passed, and the lion slumped against her, all light disappearing from his fierce eyes.

"I'm so sorry," she choked out, tears thickening her voice as buzzing filled her ears.

He didn't deserve to die. Tempest stared at his still form, feeling like she'd just lost a part of herself. With care, she wiggled her legs out from under her opponent and pulled her blades free.

She staggered to her feet and then fell to her knees, her bloody palms pressed against the earth. Tears threatened to burst free, but Tempest battled them back. She refused to give anyone else in the damn arena another part of herself.

Tempest lifted her head, the chants of the people starting to make sense.

"Tempest! Tempest! Tempest!" the people screamed.

They were chanting her name.

Sheer disbelief washed over her.

She'd defeated a *lion*.

And she'd passed her third test.

I just became a Hound.

Chapter Five

Tempest

Time halted, and the world turned watery at the edges. It was almost as if she'd taken a plunge into the sea—her senses had completely cut off from the surrounding universe.

She slowly blinked as a shadow covered her, and Madrid's handsome face floated above her. Vaguely, Tempest realized he'd pulled her to her feet, not that she could feel them. The people in the stands moved like undulating waves, their arms swaying back and forth in celebration of her victory.

"Please welcome our Kingdom's newest Hound!" Madrid's deep voice bellowed.

The ground lurched beneath her feet, but she managed to hold steady. Just barely. A dull ringing filled her ears, drowning out the screaming crowd as deep-red blood dripped down her pale skin and onto the dirt floor. A tremor worked through her body, and her hands began to shake. If she didn't make it to the healer's tent, there was a good chance she'd pass out. Tempest knew that was a bad thing, but she couldn't find it in herself to care as Madrid put pressure on her wounded shoulder.

"Bow," he muttered underneath his breath.

Painfully, she bowed again to King Destin, who was watching her with an unreadable expression that made the hairs on the nape of her neck stand on end. He was her sovereign, and, yet, there was something she didn't like about him.

"Mother of Darkness," Madrid swore. "Drop your gaze, Tempest, before the king notices your disrespectful sneer."

"Sneer?" she murmured, dropping her gaze nonetheless. Temp didn't even know she was sneering. She needed to work on that.

Her eyes grew heavier as Madrid escorted her from the arena and toward the healer's tent. Tempest gagged as a sickeningly sweet smell greeted her, so cloying that she staggered out of Madrid's grasp and banged her hip against a sturdy wooden table, jarring glass bottles. Her lip curled as she got a good look at the bottles. The ones from her Trial.

"My dear—Tempest, just lie down," Aleks soothed, apparently mistaking her imbalance for injury.

It was probably both. Her hurt and the world was tipsy.

The man grinned at her, pride and delight plain as day on his face. Tempest couldn't help but return the smile, even though her adrenaline was wearing off and the pain was really setting in.

"You bested a lion, lass. A *lion*. You must be mad."

Tempest choked on a laugh, another tremor wracking her body as Aleks helped her to lie belly-down on a rickety cot. He had no idea how mad. She almost hadn't made it out.

"Whoever set it as the final task must be mad, you mean. Another few seconds and the beast would have broken my skull in two!" she joked, as she pressed her cheek to the cot so she could watch her uncle buzz around the tent as he gathered supplies.

"And, yet, here you are, almost entirely in one piece."

He gently lifted the cloak from her back and a deep unpleasant throb worked its way up to her shoulder. His expression pinched and then smoothed out as he noticed her watching him. That wasn't a good sign. Her back must be a bloody mess.

"No worries. We'll have you fixed up in no time." He glanced at someone over her head. "Now hold still—Mimkia stings when applied directly to wounds."

A set of masculine hands on her other side pinned her arm and hip down. Her eyes widened.

Oh Dotae, no. This is going to hurt.

Tempest clenched her jaw and spoke through gritted teeth. "Can't possibly sting more than a lion clawing through—oh, hell!" Her body bucked against the restraining hands. Tears flooded Tempest's eyes, and she panted as fire licked up and down her wounds.

"The worst is almost over," Madrid's deep voice rumbled from her right side.

She slowly turned her head and stared up at the Hound master, not ashamed in the least by the tears dripping down her cheeks. Aleks had healed many men with Mimkia as she'd grown up, and most screamed bloody murder until they passed out. A small smile pulled her lips up a touch.

"What are you smiling about?" Madrid asked, eyeing Aleks over her shoulder as the healer continued to work.

"Just something one of my friend's mums said once."

"What was that?"

He was trying to distract her, and Tempest appreciated it. She hissed as Aleks probed her arm, but she forced herself to continue. "That men are babes when it comes to pain, and that women can bear almost anything."

Aleks snorted. "That's the truth if I ever heard it. Many a man pass out when they experience pain, let alone witness a woman giving birth."

Madrid smiled at her. "There's a reason why women bear the children. The all-knowing understood that we couldn't handle such pain or such glory. We're wicked, vain creatures as a whole. Could you imagine how men would act if they actually had the power to create life?"

"Unimaginable. You lot are difficult enough to live with," Tempest muttered as a needle pierced her skin. "So I need stitches?"

"Only a few. The Mimkia will do the rest. Just a bit longer, Temp," Aleks murmured softly. "Madrid, will you rub this over the lacerations on her other arm?"

Tempest's eyes drooped as she watched Madrid lift her arm and liberally slather a pale paste on her bicep. A tingling sensation ran across her skin and her aching bruises, scratches, and sore muscles disappeared.

"That's amazing," she slurred, realizing her pain was completely gone. In fact, she could only feel pressure from Aleks working on her wounds. "So, this is Mimkia, huh? I understand why people fight over the stuff."

It was bloody glorious.

Madrid studied her arm and glanced away, doing his best to turn into a stone statue. Tempest had wondered when he'd distance himself. He was a Hound, but being *the* Hound set him apart. And he liked it that way.

"I suppose you've never had cause to use it before. It can be used to heal almost any injury, though it's no good for fevers and sickness," Aleks responded, breaking through her thoughts. "Which is too bad, because you sure could have done with a one-drug-heals-all approach to the multitude of illnesses you had as a child."

Tempest said nothing and allowed herself to drift, her weary body shutting down.

There was something relaxing—nostalgic, almost—to have the man looking after her in such a way. Once more Tempest indulged the idea that he really was her father. He'd always been the one to look out for her practical concerns, the one to heal her, the one to make her eat even if she didn't want to.

You don't need to know. Knowing he cares for you is

enough. Who cares who your sire is?

"Dotae be good, that was incredible!" Maxim exclaimed, his heavy tread giving away his excitement.

Tempest's eyes snapped open, and she turned her head, flashing a smile at her favorite uncle. He dropped to his knees and placed a kiss on her sweaty temple.

"You did good, girlie. Real good." Maxim glanced at her back and whistled. "He got you good, didn't he?"

"He tried."

Some of her uncle's excitement melted away, revealing a glimmer concern. "When Madrid—" He shot an icy glare over her head, "—made the announcement, I swear my heart stopped." His brown gaze dropped back to her face and warmed. "You fought as a true warrior today. Not many get to lay eyes upon a lion and survive to tell the tale."

She swallowed hard. She didn't feel much like a warrior. Killing that lion had been self-defense, but it still felt wrong. The poor creature didn't deserve to die like that. "Will you make sure the beast is buried? He was a worthy opponent. He shouldn't be discarded like rubbish, and I can't stomach the idea of using his pelt."

Maxim nodded. "By law he is your kill. I will do as you wish."

"Thank you," she whispered.

Maxim pulled away from Tempest and stood to roughly pat Aleks on the shoulder. "Fix her up quick, Aleks. We all need to be presentable in time for the celebration feast, and something tells me Tempest will not want to show up covered in blood and guts and—"

"We get the picture," Aleks said good-naturedly. He looked at Tempest. "Your servant friend—Juniper—is waiting in the barracks with an outfit for the evening, I believe."

Tempest's stomach lurched in a way that had absolutely nothing to do with her Trial or the pain. "Do I really have to wear a dress?"

Maxim laughed. "*Really* really. And who knows? You might actually *like* being a lady of the court now that you're eighteen. For all we know, you'll fall in love tonight and never pick up a sword again!"

Madrid rounded the cot and all three of her uncles stared at her in silence and then simultaneously burst out laughing. Every member of the Hounds knew how ridiculous Maxim's claim was—and Tempest most of all.

"Never," she sputtered, horrified. Not in a million years would she put her sword down for a man.

Tempest fingered the ravaged purple cloak laying on the floor. They could laugh all they wanted, even play matchmaker, but she wasn't having any of it. Her life was just beginning. The stained purple silk slipped through her fingers like water.

Hell. She'd rather wear what was left of her ceremonial cloak than a dress. Her lips pinched. And if it was anything like the king's gift that morning, Tempest was guaranteed to hate it.

"It is a shame this has been destroyed," she murmured. "I rather like it, now. Especially compared to a *dress*."

Aleks took the material from her and tossed it into the wicker bin. "I'm sure it can be replaced. Now, the Mimkia did its job. You won't feel any pain for a few hours, so you'll be able to get through the celebration feast tonight and fall asleep before the pain returns." His light brows pulled together as he frowned disapprovingly at her. "Your wounds are sealed for now. Don't get wild or you'll ruin all my hard work."

He helped Tempest sit and the room spun. She pushed her left hand against the cot to steady herself.

"Anything else, worried one?" Tempest asked sarcastically.

Aleks rolled his eyes. "Get along to your room and clean up. Mimkia paste takes an hour or two to fully seal the skin, so keep it dry as long as you can before washing it off and binding the wound."

Tempest nodded, slowly getting to her feet and testing that she was strong enough to stand. Now that the heady, addictive rush of adrenaline was leaving her body, she felt like she might faint where she stood.

"All right," she said. "I'll keep it dry. Do you think I could get away with having a nap before—"

"Don't you *dare*," Maxim cut in. "You and I both know that if you fall asleep that'll be you out for hours and hours."

"Yes, and that would be the point..." No one would *really* miss her once they started in on the spirits.

"You're coming to the feast, and you're wearing the damn dress, girlie. Now, get to it."

And here I thought becoming a Hound would give me more freedom. Lies.

Tempest slowly skirted around her uncles who watched her like a hawk as she shuffled toward the entrance of the tent like an invalid. She paused and pulled herself together. It was time to put on a brave face for whoever might be lurking outside.

"Hold your head high," Madrid said.

She cast a glance over her shoulder at the Hound master before pushing through the canvas flaps into the cold air, a smile upon her face.

She had won today.

She'd accomplished step one of her goal. If reaching step two involved wearing a dress and acting like a lady for the evening, then so be it.

How bad could it be?

"I've never seen such a conflict over whether everyone should be celebrating or not!"

"Won't stop anyone getting riotously drunk, regardless of their stance on the matter."

"What do they care, anyway? A Hound is a Hound. And Tempest more than proved herself today."

"Thanks, Uncles," Tempest muttered into her wine, flushing furiously. She did not need to hear Maxim, Dima, and Aleks defending her right to belong in their ranks. She *had* won her position fair and square, the king had acknowledged her, and that was the end of it.

Or so she'd thought.

And yet, as she eyed the snickering gossipmongers who whispered among themselves in the feast hall, the attitudes of many around her were beginning to more than simply grate upon Tempest's nerves. Going by the reaction from the crowd during her Trial, Tempest had assumed the people of the court were not strictly making fun of her because she was the first female Hound. They had been more than supportive in her fight against the lion.

Which means they're making fun of you for being you.

Tempest looked down at the silver dress Juniper had finally wrangled her into wearing. It was tight in the bodice and hung low on her shoulders, exposing Tempest's collarbone and the top of her breasts. Split sleeves of white gossamer fell to her elbows. The skirt was long and sweeping and threatened to trip Tempest up wherever she walked.

Though she knew the silver fabric perfectly complimented her hair and suited her skin well, wearing something so figure-hugging, revealing and outright unsuitable for moving about in made Tempest feel incredibly self-conscious. She hated anything that hampered her movements, let alone her breathing. She bowed her head, her gaze dropping to the indecent neckline again, and her lips thinned.

One careless move, and she'd fall right out of the top.

Ridiculous. Utterly ridiculous, that's what it was.

It was probably a man who designed this dress. The bastard.

She finished her goblet of wine with a sigh and allowed Maxim to pour her another.

"If only I could have worn trousers," she lamented, shaking her head at her own body. "There's far too much fabric going on in all the wrong places. So restrictive."

Several women nearby were audibly shocked by the comment. They stared at Tempest, wide-eyed and rosy-cheeked, then tittered when a finely dressed man said, "If you want someone to make things *less restrictive* for you, my house is but ten minutes away from the palace!"

Tempest's cheeks grew even redder than the court ladies in all their rouge and lipstick. Dima stiffened to her right, and she placed a hand on his leg beneath the table to still him. He arched a brow at her.

"I'm fine," she muttered.

Tempest winked at her uncles as she stood as gracefully as she could in a dress that threatened to suffocate her, abandoning her wine to the table.

"I think I'd rather have ale," she said in an undertone, rushing off before anybody could try and stop her.

Tempest found that despite having been thrilled that she passed her Trial, no amount of excitement and pride could allow her to simply enjoy the evening's celebrations. It wasn't that she didn't enjoy a party, but the people one spent it with mattered greatly. And no one in this room was her friend. She was either an oddity—which meant she was to be studied or to become the butt of the joke—or a conquest for a man who decided he wanted to tame the warrior girl, which was the worst of the two in her opinion.

Subconsciously, she drifted to the edge of the great room, searching for anything out of place. Women spoke secrets behind their fans, men smoked and eyed the women, lush for their pickings. She hid her smile as a small hand darted from beneath one of the banquet tables. Little ones were stealing snacks, and yet, she couldn't find herself comfortable.

Perhaps you can find Madrid and ask him about Tomas. The poor boy had been terrified earlier. What has become of him?

With a purpose in mind, she glided through the throngs of people, keeping a sharp eye out for the Hound master. Tempest breathed a sigh of relief when she exited the ballroom and found a bunch of men drinking ale; they happily handed her a tankard and allowed her to lean against the wall and drink in silence, with only a few curious glances tossed her way.

They were of a rougher, poorer class than the people from the court Tempest had only just run from—the palace and its grounds had been opened to the public for today and today only. At least around merchants and soldiers and ordinary folk Tempest could be herself... dress or no dress.

"It's getting worse in the south," a man with grizzled hair and a thick, foreboding scar across one of his hands said. "By the mountains bordering Talaga. My brother nearly lost his life last week on the road. Lucky he only lost his horse instead."

"Aye, I've heard it's gotten further out of hand than anyone is aware of," another man said. He eyed up a soldier, who Tempest at last recognized as the handsome palace guard who'd given her the spear she'd used to defeat the lion. "Rane here has been hearing all sorts since he was promoted to the palace. Ain't you, Rane?"

Rane glared at him. "It'll be on my head if anyone knows I've spoken of such things." But the men around him merely waited for him to relent and tell them more, so, with a furtive glance around them—which lingered on Tempest, who smiled slightly in return—he elaborated. "There's a... sickness... spreading through the kingdom. A deadly one. It's wiped out whole villages, all along the Talaga mountain range. More bodies are piling up by the day."

Tempest stilled. She had not heard word that the Talagan rebellion had gotten so far. In truth nobody had even called it a rebellion yet, since no official attack had been made against the rest of the kingdom yet. The Hounds were like a group of older gossiping women. Surely if one of them knew something, then all of them would?

This damn well feels like an official attack *against us. Just what is the king doing about it?*

Tempest sipped her drink and quietly melted into the shadows, leaving the men to their discussion to search for a bathroom, or a storage room, or literally any kind of empty, quiet space she could make use of. She needed to *think* away from all the noise and bustle and alcohol of the feast. Her mind raced. How deadly was the disease? Was it spreading through the mountains from the former shifter kingdom? Was it an act of war? If the Talagans were making their move against Heimserya, this could be Tempest's opportunity to find her mother's killer. Vengeance was so close she could almost taste it.

She just had to figure out a way to get permission to look into it all.

"How odd, to see the person for whom this entire feast was organized for standing all alone in the dark."

"I simply needed a moment to breathe," Tempest replied, irked by the stranger's audacity and his ability to sneak up on her for precisely two seconds before she turned to see who had spoken.

King Destin stood there, resplendent in gold-and-ruby finery accented his long, tawny hair and amber eyes. Those lion eyes locked onto Tempest's, preventing her from bowing or backing away.

Damn.

"Y-Your Grace," Tempest stammered. "I did not hear you approach. I—"

"Needed a moment to breathe," he cut in, smiling. "I understand. However, I have been looking for you for quite some time. Won't you spare your king a few minutes of your time?"

Tempest knew she couldn't say no. Destin was the *king*, after all, and a tall, powerful man to boot. Really, she had no reason to refuse him. He hadn't done *anything* to her. Yet.

Her attention homed in on his fingers gloved in midnight silk. Huge jeweled rings adorned his gloved hands, the stones catching in the lantern light.

He could crush your windpipe with his bare hands, and you'd have to let him do it.

She inclined her head slightly, hoping it would suffice enough as a response until her voice came back to her.

"You were quite wonderful during your Trial today. Tell me, have you ever faced a beast as large as a lion before?"

Tempest had to assume he knew she hadn't. Who else could have set her up against a lion than the king himself, after all? Which meant she could only conclude that King Destin was testing her—to see what she would say in the face of such an obvious attempt on her life.

"No, Your Grace," she said, forcing a smile to her face. "Never. A wolf once, in the woods, but that is all."

"You did not seem frightened by it."

"I would not make a very good Hound if I displayed all my emotions on my face."

Thank you, Maxim, for your training. She was putting it to use right now.

King Destin smiled, and amusement glinted in his amber eyes. He waved a hand back toward the center of the party. "The people clearly adore you. It is good that you secured such an outstanding victory today."

Tempest snorted in derision before she could stop herself. "I am but a novelty to them. A female Hound. Soon the novelty will pass, and I'll be naught to them." How she prayed for that day.

"You give your opinion freely, even to your king," Destin said, cocking his head to one side as he regarded Tempest. There was something akin to admiration in his gaze that had been decidedly absent during her Trial. "It is a good trait to have in a wife, if one wishes the marriage to be fruitful. And you are quite beautiful. Truly, any man would be lucky to have you. Any man indeed."

Wife? Marriage? Fruitful?

Tempest felt as if a spider was crawling up her spine when the king reached forward and stroked the back of his huge gloved hand against her cheek.

Do not flinch. Do not flinch. Do not flinch. He is testing you. He never wanted a female Hound. He is seeing if he can scare you. Fear does not rule you.

"You are kind to say so," she replied, curtseying slightly. Relief rushed over her as his hand fell away. "However, I must profess to finding myself not at all ready for marriage quite yet. I have only just embarked on my future as a Hound, after all. I will not lay my sword down for hearth and home for quite some time, if ever," she tacked on, not able to help herself. What would he make of that?

There was a long, drawn-out pause. And then King Destin said, quietly, "You are a fascinating woman, Tempest. I would very much like to discuss your *future* as soon as possible, in a setting a little more private than a corridor. Come up to my chambers in an hour—I shall have a servant escort you."

Tempest stared at him, torn between dread and

curiosity. If there was ever a time for her to use her new-found position to begin looking into the Talagan shifter, now was that time. But she wasn't stupid. The way King Destin was looking at her… well, he wasn't thinking of the kingdom.

"Of course, Your Grace," she said eventually, careful to keep her voice as level as possible. She could not allow the man to know she was afraid of him, nor could she refuse him. He was her sovereign, and she had to obey, whether she liked it or not. And she had chosen this path. "I look forward to continuing our discussion." *Lie.*

Tempest wanted nothing more than to run away from the grin he flashed her way, but she forced herself to stay rooted to the spot until the king turned and left her, blessedly, alone.

She'd never thought she'd wish to be back in the arena with the lion, but there was a first time for everything.

Chapter Six

Tempest

It wasn't until the servant calling her name was practically standing on Tempest's toes that she finally broke from the panic clinging to her heart. Truly, it was a testament to just how nervous she was—and, perhaps, a sign that she'd had one glass of wine too many as she had not sensed the servant's presence.

She eyed the silver goblet distastefully and set the wine on the table to her right.

King Destin was even quieter when he crept up on you. Get your wits about you.

"The king will see you now, Lady Tempest," the servant said, inclining her head politely. "If you would follow me?"

"I'm not a lady," Tempest mumbled, following the woman from the hall. Temp had been raised with crass, rambunctious men. The ladies of court would have swooned at some of the things she'd seen growing up.

Tempest had been to the palace just once before, when she was five. Dima had taken her to see the king so the Hounds could work out what to do with her. Much of that time had been a blur. The bizarre thing was that the king looked the same today despite the passing thirteen years. Her lips curled as she remembered how he'd ordered her to be placed with a governess of the court, a fine lady who'd preened like a peacock. It hadn't taken long for the woman to throw Tempest out. She'd complained that all Tempest did was cause mischief and mayhem—that she was too unruly to become a lady of the court. She might have Madrid blood, but she was just as wild and crass as the poor she'd been raised with. Now that Tempest was older, she had a sneaking suspicion the woman had been his mistress because it only took one or two words and Tempest had been thrown in with the Hounds.

It would have helped her nerves to know the layout of the palace better. She glanced over her shoulder and hiked up the silver silk of her skirt before catching up with the servant. They wound their way up a helical staircase lit by torches set into recessed sconces. The shadows writhed and danced like pagan wraiths and put Tempest on edge. The staircase was too dim and narrow to be a main access point to the king's chambers. It felt too confining. It was either reserved for servants or... Her gut twisted.

For the women sent up to see the king under the veil of night.

Tempest gulped.

Don't dwell on such things. You're not here for that.

Humor your sovereign and then you'll leave with your honor intact.

It was a good plan. All she had to do was keep up a strong, self-assured front during her meeting with the man, lest he take advantage of her. It was *Tempest* who would get something out of their talk about her future, not him.

Living and being raised by men should have prepared her for this moment, but each step closer to the king's chambers made her question her decision to visit.

There was never a question of obeying.

"The lion was *definitely* easier than this," she mumbled, only narrowly avoiding tripping up over the skirt of her dress in the process. The servant turned her head slightly to raise a questioning eyebrow.

"Pardon, Lady Tempest?" she asked politely.

"It's nothing. Just talking to myself."

"My lady, may I offer a word of advice?"

"Yes," she drawled.

"Do not let King Destin know that the lion was easier to handle than him."

Tempest hesitated before responding. That wasn't what she expected. And it was a gross breach in protocol, not that she cared. "And why is that?"

The servant sighed. "He will take it as the highest of compliments. So, please, keep in mind that less is more in some situations. It will be to your benefit."

Translation: don't talk to the king more than you have to or you'll encourage his attentions.

Tempest's gaze locked with the young woman. The servant was bold and her words alone could get her a lashing.

"And why would you tell me this?"

The woman didn't look away. "You're our champion, my lady. A warrior never lets anything take her by surprise."

Tempest studied her blankly as she came to a realization: the servant was on her side. Going by the bead of sweat on the woman's brow and the way her hands twitched slightly, she was not happy about having to show the kingdom's first female Hound up to the king's chambers so late at night.

That didn't bode well for what the king had planned.

Tempest pasted a smile on her face. "Very wise words. I'd be a fool not to listen."

The woman sighed in visible relief, her shoulders sagging as she continued to lead them through several more minutes worth of winding, smooth-stoned corridors covered in richly woven tapestries of knights, battles, kings, and shifters. The servant stopped in front of perhaps the grandest, most ostentatious set of doors Tempest had ever set her eyes upon. They were carved from a ruddy wood—mahogany, perhaps—which was shot through with impossibly intricate gold scrollwork.

She squinted and leaned a little closer, trying to make out the words inscribed on the door. Odd. It was a language she'd never seen before. Tempest straightened and lifted her chin when the servant knocked upon the door softly and opened it a fraction a moment later.

"Your Grace," the servant said, bowing her head. "Lady Tempest is here."

A pause. And then: "Send her in," a deep voice rumbled from the other side.

Even though she'd prepared herself, the sound of his voice alone caused her stomach to drop. So unlike herself, she reached for the young woman's hand and squeezed, inhaling deeply.

You can do this. Come on, Tempest. You're stronger than this. You passed the Trials.

"You're a lioness," the servant whispered and squeezed her hand once before stepping away.

Tempest's fingertips pressed against the door, and then she entered the king's chambers. The heavy wood closed behind her with barely a sound, though Tempest had expected it to thunder back into place. The silence of it was deafening.

It took her only one glance—thanks to her Hound training—to pick up on all possible escape routes and potential weapons should she need them. Flames roared in a massive fireplace on the left-hand wall, surrounded by various, ornate tools covered in suitably pointed and jagged edges. For a moment, Tempest entertained the idea of skewering the king with one of them and fleeing back down the corridor.

Morbid, Tempest, very morbid. Keep those thoughts off your face.

Her second sweep revealed much more. Over on the

right-hand side of the room was perhaps the largest four-poster bed Tempest had ever seen. It was made of the same wood as the door, with heavy, draping curtains of burgundy fabric obscuring much of the interior. *Winter's bite*, it could sleep her entire barracks. Not that the men would ever be caught dead sleeping in such an atrocity. At least a dozen pillows and embroidered, claret-colored, velvet cushions decorated the mattress. To top it all off, a gaudy matching coverlet had been thrown over the bedsheets.

She took another step into the room, and her slippers sank into the plush carpet. If she'd been barefoot, Tempest imagined it would have felt wondrous between her toes.

Stop that train of thought right now, missy. Focus.

Directly in front of her, moonlight shone through an immense stained-glass window, showing the entire kingdom of Heimserya. A handsome wooden table with a carafe of amber liquid—possibly fire whisky—and a blue, crystal goblet set beside it.

Finally, she turned her attention to the other inhabitant of the room. The one she'd been ignoring.

Right in front of the window, bathed in silvery light, was King Destin himself, lounging in a throne-like chair as if he didn't have a care in the world. Tempest cast her eyes from the spirit and took him in: barefoot, leather trousers, no shirt, and a blood-red robe. The king's long, bronzed hair was braided and tossed over one shoulder.

Tempest's mind blanked. *Oh Dotae, be good.*

The man might have been years older than her, but he

sure didn't look it. Tempest would hazard to say she'd never seen a more attractive man, and she'd seen her fair share of the male form having lived with men most of her life. There was absolutely no way she'd be able to keep meeting with King Destin if he'd deigned to greet her half-naked. How many women had he tempted into his bed with such a look?

He beckoned for Tempest to come closer with a finger. "My Lady Hound. I am glad you did not run away from the palace with your tail between your legs."

She took a steadying breath before walking a few careful steps forward, keeping her calm façade in place. "My king called for me. Of course, I must oblige." She curtseyed, the picture of courtly manners.

He smirked. "Indeed, you must. Come, take a seat on the bed. You must be tired, especially since you are not used to wearing such uncomfortable shoes."

Damn him. That was one of the only things he could have said to entice her to break propriety. Well, more than she already was. She was skating on thin ice as it was. But even if her tight, restrictive slippers were killing her feet and all she wanted to do was tear them off, burn the infernal contraptions, and curl up someplace comfortable, she would not sit on the bed. *Must* not.

She looked around for somewhere else to sit—a look the king noticed immediately with an arched brow.

His smirk became a grin. "Smart girl. Intelligent, capable and beautiful. You really could have everything you want, you know. You need only ask for it."

She had everything she wanted, except vengeance for her mother's death. But she kept that thought to herself.

Tempest inclined her head politely and phrased her words carefully, "All I want is to serve my kingdom to the best of my ability. My lord, I have heard distressing murmurs of the brewing Talagan rebellion, which I was hoping to discuss with you this evening."

King Destin quirked an eyebrow and slowly placed his tumbler of spirits onto the table. He stood up, worked out a crack in his right shoulder, and closed the distance between himself and Tempest with lazy strides. It was like watching the lion prowl toward her again, his intense gaze pinning her to the spot. She bristled despite herself. If there was one thing she hated, it was being backed into a corner or having her space invaded; both led to her coming out swinging.

You can't hit your sovereign.

"What about the rebellion is it that you wish to *discuss*, Tempest?" King Destin asked, amusement plain in his amber eyes.

She stood her ground. "You know of my history, of my past with the shapeshifters." Her lips curled in distain. "I wish to investigate the truthfulness of what is going on."

"Such a serious issue to discuss so late at night."

"Those who seek to tear down our kingdom never rest." She licked her dry lips and ignored how the king tracked the movement. "May I speak plainly, my lord?"

"You may, Temp."

His use of her nickname caused her to freeze, but she

continued. "I'll be frank. It's high time a few Hounds were sent out there, anyway. If the Talagan shifters are making our people sick, then we need proof of their treachery in order to quash them."

And they needed quashing, once and for all. The Talagan shifters had been making trouble in their kingdom for decades and someone needed to take a stand.

King Destin studied her, never losing his smile. "Why don't we entertain ourselves in another way and, then, when the sun is up, we can return to the subject of the rebellion? Won't you have a drink, my Lady Hound?"

She eyed the spirits. If the king didn't listen to her now, he never would. And once spirits were involved… Well she'd seen how it loosened many a man's morals. His déshabillé was proof of his intentions for tonight. Unease churned below her belly button at the heated challenge in his gaze.

Over the course of the last several years of her training, he'd made his distaste of her apparent.

He tried to have you killed today. Why make nice now?

Her unease deepened. What did he *really* want?

"I will have a drink," Tempest said slowly, "but only after we have discussed the rebellion properly. You did wish to talk about my future, did you not?" She gathered her courage. "It's known that you grant a new Hound a favor once he has passed his Trials. May I be so bold as to ask you to consider this my one and only request as a new Hound?"

For a moment, it looked as if he would argue with her.

Something dark flashed across his face, and he stared at the bed for far too long. Her breathing turned thready as she waited for his patience to snap. The king wasn't weak by any stretch of the imagination. It wouldn't be a big leap to say she could find herself knocked down onto the gargantuan four poster bed whether she wanted to be there or not.

She slipped her left foot back and prepared for an attack. Tempest would go down fighting.

"Most Hounds ask for wealth, prestige…" A smirk followed. "Or a wife. But not you. You want to be sent into danger."

"I'm not like most men." A thin smile. "I'm not a man. But I am a Hound."

Instead, the king turned back to her and laughed. "Fine, have it your way, sweet. What makes you think you have anything to bring to the cause that I don't already have?"

Chapter Seven

Tempest

The dagger strapped to her thigh seemed to burn her skin as Tempest compelled her muscles to relax. Out of the two outcomes she foresaw for this evening, this option was the one she least expected. Men had been around her for almost her whole life, and while she loved her uncles and fellow Hounds fiercely, they'd also shown her the terrible side of the male population.

Men could be vile, degrading, and violent.

But it seemed the king was going to humor her.

She blinked back her disbelief and tried to sort her thoughts into something a king could get behind.

King Destin wandered over to his bed and leaned a hip against the mattress, staring at her expectantly as she continued to gape at him.

"Sooner rather than later, if you will," Destin said,

amused. He crossed his arms over his muscular chest and arched his eyebrows. "I would rather like to crack open the fire whisky."

She glanced at the amber-colored liquid in its blue crystal carafe, innocuous on the table beneath the window. Tempest very much did not want to *crack it open* at all. She'd had enough wine as it was. Smoothing out the front of her dress, she ran over the speech she had been rehearsing since King Destin had announced he wished to speak to her.

"My Trial today showed how adept I am with poisons," Tempest began, "so if the Talagans are using any to cause the sickness by the mountains, I'm qualified to look into it. I also demonstrated my skill at gaining the trust of strangers, which lends itself well to asking questions in numerous villages. And, of course, I can more than serviceably defend myself against any shifter threats—as well as those of wolves and other large animals in the forest. I would be an excellent solo candidate for exploring the unrest by Talaga." Damn. She sounded like an overexcited child.

King Destin smiled good-naturedly. "Anything else?"

Might as well continue.

"Yes, in fact. You mentioned yourself that the common people adore me, for I am one of them, Madrid blood or not," she pointed out. "That means I can blend in well to investigate the matter properly. All I need to do is dye my hair, so they don't know I am a Hound. I can look into this discreetly without raising the alarm of the Talagans. And once I have proof of what they're doing... Well, I'll bring it back. And then—"

"And then might you entertain the idea of my advances?" King Destin cut in, a calculating glint in his eyes.

Wicked hell.

Tempest didn't like it, no matter how attractive he was. But she nevertheless knew how to handle it—unlike the man's advances themselves. Maxim had trained her to be an expert in bartering.

"Yes," she replied, though she knew she would use everything in her power to refuse the king upon her return, "but if I *am* successful—*if* I find solid proof that the Talagan shifters are responsible for this new wave of sickness—I want a position on your war council."

Bold, Tempest Madrid.

Destin considered her for a moment, then nodded. "That is fair. After all, providing the proof that begins the war certainly warrants one being part of the war itself. However, regardless of whether you are successful or not, you must still return to my side when your *research* is done. Do not make me look for you."

A chill ran up her spine. That was a direct threat. He was shrewder than she'd like him to be. But one didn't become king without being brutal in attaining what he desired.

"Yes," Tempest said, keeping her tone even. "I will come straight to you. Can you tell me anything about the rebellion that I'll need to know before I set out?"

King Destin walked over to the stained-glass window

and waved a hand at her, indicating for her to join him. He pointed to the Talagan mountainside, where several kinds of shifters were portrayed in tiny, shimmering fragments of color.

He pointed to a gold-and-orange fox. "There's a kitsune who is in charge of the entire rebellion. He's known as the Jester."

Damn. The Jester was the monster that parents taught their children about at night to keep them from bad behavior. The Jester had a hand in everything from drugs and poison to women, murder, and rebellion.

Ice seeped into the king's tone. "He's not to be trifled with. Make no mistake, he is one of our deadliest enemies." Tempest swallowed hard as the king turned and brushed his thumb along her bottom lip. "If you can find him and infiltrate his base of operations, I have no doubt you'll eventually dig out the proof we need."

Merde. She'd planned on some reconnaissance, not taking on the bloody Jester.

Tempest stared at the glass fox without saying a word. The king had caught her in a crafty trap. She almost wanted to laugh. Too focused on the rebellion and her revenge, she hadn't even noticed he was setting her up for failure. Many a man had tried to destroy the Jester—and failed. Some even considered him immortal.

"Tempest?" King Destin whispered. "Do we have a deal?"

She nodded once. "I will find him," she said. "I'll find the fox. And I'll get the proof you need."

The king smiled. "Good. Then you'll leave first thing in the morning. I suggest you return to the barracks now to pack for your journey—it can be cold by the mountains."

Tempest blinked, taken aback by his suggestion. "And that drink you insisted I have?" she blurted like a total idiot. Could she really get away so easily? There had to be some sort of trickery afoot.

"I am the king, my Lady Hound. What you wish to do for my kingdom is more important than indulging my desire to have a drink with you just now. However…"

He reached for Tempest's hand, and she could do nothing but let him take it. Destin circled the pad of his calloused thumb against her skin, watching her face carefully for her reaction. His astute, amber eyes never left hers as he brought up her hand to his lips. A bolt of anxiety ran right through Tempest, but she knew better than to recoil and run away. The soft kiss wasn't disgusting, but she didn't have a choice in the matter. And she hated that.

King Destin broke away from her hand with a grin, all sharp canines and white, gleaming teeth. "However," he repeated, "once you return to me, things will be different. You can expect my full attention when you come back from the mountains, just as I shall be expecting yours in return."

Silence stretched out between Tempest and the king. She did not know how to fill it; no words would form in her throat for her to vocalize. But she knew she could not rescind her acceptance of his terms—it was that or openly defy him.

"I will return to your side whether I succeed or not," she said softly. "But I won't promise anything further than that. My life is devoted to being your Hound." Maybe deference would soften him.

"Bring me the Jester's heart, my sweet," the king murmured, shifting his blood-red robe just enough to reveal the full extent of his well-defined abdominal muscles and powerful chest. "And we'll discuss this further when you return."

He slipped his arms around her waist and pulled her against him. Tempest stayed ridged as he brushed his nose along her cheek.

"Leave while you can, my Lady Hound, or I'll quickly find myself unable to let you leave."

"I... best be off, then, Your Grace," Tempest said, pulling back to put space between their bodies.

"Sleep well, Temp," he whispered, smiling in a way that was all too knowing as she tried not to run to the exit.

Tempest cursed out loud as she tripped on the skirt of her dress, most definitely tearing the hem of the expensive garment.

"My apologies," she muttered and glanced over her shoulder.

King Destin chuckled and smirked. "I like my women a little crass. I'll see you soon, sweet."

With a red face and a hammering heart, Tempest yanked open one of the doors and walked at a clipped pace down the corridor before it even had the chance to close properly behind her. That was what she told herself anyway. But who was she fooling? She was running away. Never in her whole life had she run from something that scared her. Tempest supposed she should have counted her blessings that she'd got what she wanted without having to give the king anything outright.

But as she fled the king, Tempest felt anything but blessed.

She felt hunted.

Chapter Eight

King Destin

Destin caught the door before it closed and watched as Tempest practically sprinted down the hallway, away from his chambers, her silver dress trailing behind her like a satin extension of her periwinkle hair. She hadn't been comfortable wearing such garments, that much was clear. He imagined removing the dress to make her more *comfortable* and couldn't stop grinning.

His new Lady Hound, as King Destin was beginning to think of her, was certainly an interesting woman. Tempest seemed both far more mature than her eighteen years *and* woefully underdeveloped. Perhaps that was because she'd grown up around coarse, brash men without the company of the ladies of the court. It meant she was simultaneously bold, fearful, certain, *and* unsure.

It was a wonderful mix.

Easy to manipulate.

Destin hadn't relished the idea of a woman joining the ranks of the Hounds. Indeed, until he'd witnessed Tempest's Trial he had been sure she would be a failure—an example to the entire kingdom that women were not fit for such work.

Now that he'd met Tempest properly and seen her in action, Destin was happy to rescind his previous assertion. For this particular young woman, at least. But it wasn't simply that Tempest was clearly going to make a good Hound.

He had much bigger plans for her.

Destin clucked his tongue and stared down the darkened empty hallway. She'd entered the dragon's lair and there was no escape for her now. It would have been better for her if Tempest had never crossed his path.

A dark smile teased his lips as he leaned a shoulder against the doorway, musing over her reaction to him. All he'd done was kiss her hand and she'd practically ran from him. She was as skittish as a wild horse. What would she think if he told her of his plans to strip every piece of clothing from her fair body?

A deep rumble of laughter spilled from his lips. His Lady Hound might faint outright for the first time in her life.

In any other situation, he would have been offended that Tempest hadn't outright accepted his advances. No, he *should* have been offended. Women fell at his feet all the time, for who wouldn't want to engage in an affair with the king? And if anyone dared to refuse him, well...

All it took was a prettily worded threat of imprisonment to change their minds.

But it rarely—if ever—came to that.

Destin wasn't wanting for women companionship even as he entered his forties. His tawny hair held no trace of gray, his amber eyes had not deteriorated in the slightest, and the rest of his senses were just as keen. He was in good physical shape. There was no risk that he was going to drop dead from poor health any day or year or decade anytime soon. With his late wife having tragically passed away three years prior, any woman who caught Destin's attention for long enough was in a prime position to become the new queen of Heimserya.

Or so they thought.

There weren't many women who would turn down such an opportunity.

Women were fickle, tactile creatures. Most you could ply with gifts and vague promises. But somehow, he knew Tempest would be different. She'd be a challenge, and his life had been boring of late.

Slight irritation burned in his chest at how she'd fled from him. He would have liked to have played with her a little more. Sleep was still a long way off and he would've liked some company.

He snorted and moved into his chambers. His Lady Hound had been raised by men and yet he had the feeling she didn't know how to handle them. Part of his ire melted away at that thought.

It had been a long time since he'd broken a woman in.

The thought alone put a cheerful smile on his face. The young woman may have turned him down but little did she know she'd made the hunt all the more sweeter. Tempest had more potential than any other lady Destin had met over the past few years, and he wasn't about to squander that by losing his temper at the first hurdle.

He'd be calm and careful and plan his seduction of his Lady Hound properly. After all, it really was high time he married again. The kingdom longed for it.

Closing the door to his chambers, Destin let out a satisfied sigh and wandered over to a mahogany table that stood beneath a stained-glass window portraying a stylized map of Heimserya. The table was varnished to a high shine; the king could almost see his reflection in it. He unstopped an intricately crafted carafe of blue crystal and poured out a liquid the color of molten gold into a matching crystal goblet. Fire whisky, from Talaga.

One of the few good things to come out of that damn country.

That wasn't completely true.

Destin took a sip of the fiery concoction, and his throat and belly heated as the spirits settled.

The shifter lands had made his kingdom rich: fertile lands and large stores of minerals and oils were just the icing on the cake. The Mimkia plant was the true treasure.

All the country's riches belonged to him now, but there were drawbacks. His grandfather had invaded the country and placed it under his rule nearly one hundred and thirty years ago. There had been quiet, prosperous peace for a few decades, but then the Talaga shifters rose up in rebellion. It had been quashed, of course, but forty years later there had been another one. Heimserya had once more won the fight, but it had been much harder than the first time.

His lip curled. Now there were rumors of yet another uprising.

Destin hated the shifters. He wanted them gone. If he had his way it was only a matter of time before they *were*. And yet the Talagans were just one of several problems he currently had to deal with.

His spies had revealed to him the whisperings of discontent all across Heimserya in every village and town not within immediate walking distance of Dotae, the royal city. Even within the city, there were well-off merchants and members of court alike who were spreading rumors that Destin preferred they would not spread. The worst potential betrayal he'd heard of had been from within his Hounds; not even his most loyal guard dogs were immune to the rumblings of unhappiness that were spreading throughout the country.

He needed to make a stand—and soon.

It wouldn't do to have so many people angry and dissatisfied with their king. It would only lend further credence to the Talagan rebellion, if Destin did not manage to extinguish the dissent before it grew too large. But even if he *did* eliminate the shifter threat—which Destin was certain he would do before the year's end— that didn't change the fact that his own people were unhappy. Many of them were too poor, over-worked, and under-fed. They needed a distraction from their dreary, pointless lives.

And Destin knew just the solution to this problem. His little Lady Hound.

"Tempest is a commoner," he told his fireplace. "One of the people," he mused.

The flame lunged up the chimney, licking at the smooth stone until it was blackened and charred. It struck Destin that Tempest herself had been found covered in soot by his Hounds. They had placed her with ladies of the court to raise her, but she had been untamable, so the men had raised her. Destin had not thought much of it at the time. Tempest had been but an unruly child. An annoyance. He'd been thrilled to have the little heathen gone from his home, along with the complaints of the ladies of court.

How the times had changed.

Who would have guessed she'd make the perfect candidate for his queen? She was young enough to be molded, unlike his previous wife.

"Traitorous wench," he muttered. The heavens had been kind to him when she'd died.

King Destin had never been fond of his previous wife, though they put on one hell of a show for the kingdom. He had his own life ruling the kingdom, and she had hers raising their children.

He chuckled. The woman was a shrew and not much of a mother. Her ladies had more of a hand in raising their children than his deceased wife ever had. She'd concerned herself more with her appearance and position.

Destin threw back the rest of his fire whisky before pouring himself another. Just thinking about her made him want to down all the spirits. Even now, he swore he could hear her shrill voice screaming at him for his dalliances.

If she'd wanted me to remain faithful, she could have tried to act more... palatable.

Three children the woman had borne Destin. Two sons, now seventeen and fifteen, and one daughter, now eleven. The king doted on his daughter, for she too adored him and had spent the least amount of time under the influence of her mother. His sons, on the other hand...

"Foppish, entitled, useless boys," he muttered, scowling as he thought of them. They hadn't even inherited Destin's bronzed hair, instead exhibiting their mother's pale blonde coloring. Even the eldest acted more like a child than a man. "And he is just one year younger than my Lady Hound!"

My Lady Hound.

He liked the sound of that almost as much as he liked collecting treasures.

Destin thought about how the woman had looked during her Trial, fierce and fearless against the lion. *A lion.* She had used that double-ended spear like an extension of her own arm. Her fighting style was elegant and efficient, with not a single ounce of energy wasted as she prowled the arena. And when she had screamed in the creature's face, daring it to attack, even Destin had to admit he was impressed.

"*That* is what my sons should be like," he asserted, once more talking to the fire. "Strong and frightening and handsome."

She'd no doubt produce fine, strong sons. Or beautiful, fierce daughters. Satisfaction filled him at the idea.

Tempest was no doubt beautiful, both in her silver dress and her fighting gear. Her periwinkle hair—a sign of a connection to the noble Madrid line at some point—was thick and lustrous, and her gray eyes were like a storm at sea in which many a sailor lost their lives. Her lips were full and stained barely red; Destin had sincerely wished to possess her the moment he laid eyes on her earlier today.

She was taller than he usually found attractive, but her legs...

Heat moved through him.

Her training should have made her more masculine, but it did the opposite. It turned what would have been a bountiful figure into one with lithe, sensual curves he wanted to trace his hands along. And hell, her thighs and hips... One word came to mind: sinful. He loved a woman with wide hips.

She would have no problem in childbirth.

It wasn't only Tempest's physical attributes that made her an attractive candidate for queen, though they were certainly important. But what was perhaps the most important was that people *loved* her. The poor people from every village and town on the outskirts of Dotae viewed her as one of their own. A girl raised from the ashes themselves, who'd grabbed an opportunity with both hands and Madrid blood to prove herself—and succeeded. To witness such a member of their ranks become queen would boost their moral and faith in the crown.

The court loved her, too. Tempest was a novelty to them—a lady who was not a lady, who could just as easily outdrink the soldiers at their table as she could be the object of their desire. The women did not see her as a threat, because of the way she acted, so they liked her, too. They rarely turned her into the source of their amusement. Even the servants seemed to enjoy her presence. Destin knew of at least three within the castle who regularly snuck out extra food for their favorite Hound.

The Hounds.

Of course the King's Hounds loved Tempest. They doted on her. She was their daughter, after all, in almost every way that mattered. If Destin took her as queen then that would put a stop to any and all potential betrayals from the men, for they would just as equally worry over her safety as they would be pleased that one of their own had become a member of royalty.

Yes, Tempest was definitely the best candidate for queen that Destin had come across. She couldn't have shown up at a better time.

"And she is interesting," he murmured, swirling the contents of his goblet around and around. He grew tired of the same tedious women and conversations.

Destin squinted at the amber spirits that were stark against the blue crystal; both colors were beautiful individually but viewing the whisky through the glass made it a very ugly shade of brown. Would that be his future with Tempest?

"You're being maudlin," he growled.

Destin tossed the goblet into the fire in distaste. The alcohol caused a momentary flare of white-hot fire to spring up, temporarily dazzling him.

But Destin was not blind to the goings-on of his country nor to Tempest's reluctance to accept his advances. He'd thought it a genius move on his part to approve her request to research the deaths within the kingdom. He knew exactly why the deaths were occurring, and who was to blame for the crimes. Now he only needed her to confirm it.

Either Tempest would succeed and get her seat on Destin's war council, giving him means to fully crush the Talagans once and for all. Or she would fail and crawl back to his side anyway, hoping that her patient king would give her another assignment as a Hound.

Either way, she'd have to fulfil her side of the deal—she'd have to entertain his advances without running away. Destin was going to make damn sure she was in no position to refuse him this time.

"My Lady, it's your turn," he whispered to the empty room.

Tempest could fight all she'd like. He liked the hunt and with careful planning, she'd be bound to him by the end of the year and fat with his babes.

And, with any luck, he wouldn't have to kill a second wife.

Chapter Nine

Tempest

Tempest shivered and wrapped her arms around her stomach in an attempt to keep warm. Not only was she chilled from her encounter with the king but it was so cold, and her silk dress did nothing. She gazed up at the sky, her breath fogging the air, and admired the diamond-like stars scattered across the black velvet of night. It wouldn't be long until the first snow blanketed the king's city. Already, the storms raged in the mountains.

Warm light beckoned from the barracks' windows, and she picked up her pace, entering what she'd called home for most of her life. Relief flooded her as she closed the door and eyed all the empty beds and the roaring fireplace on the far wall. At least no one would question her as she was packing.

A fist seemed to squeeze around her heart. How was she supposed to tell her uncles? Sure, they would be proud of her for passing her Trials but as for the assignment…

She'd planned on only reconnaissance, but the king had ordered her to bring the Jester's heart to him.

Unbidden, the hair at the nape of her neck stood on end. Tempest was confident in her skills but other Hounds had tried and ended up dead. She swallowed. She wasn't necessarily afraid of death. Death was a part of life. But there was a special sort of torture reserved mostly for women that terrified her. Her uncles had taught her well, but they'd drilled into her mind that she would *always* be a target to dangerous men.

And the Jester was the most dangerous of all. When he wasn't murdering and selling weapons, he was dealing poisons, elixirs, and women.

Now, rebellion.

What was his motivation? Her lip curled as she kicked off her painful slippers and wiggled her abused toes against the stone floor. Money, no doubt. War was lucrative for those selling the weapons.

She pushed away from the door and stalked to her bed. The Jester was just a man. A man who could bleed like any other. A small chuckle escaped her as she yanked open the trunk holding her clothes. Tempest leaned forward and brushed her hand along her mother's bow nestled among the garments. He wouldn't even see her coming.

Hopefully.

She packed in a flurry, tossing necessities onto her bed without taking her dress off first. She huffed and tied the dress up by her hip to keep from tripping on the material. As much as Tempest wanted to rip the contraption off her body, she was too tense to remove it and—in reality—she was not entirely sure *how* to unlace the damn bodice all by herself.

"Stupid dress," she muttered to herself, carefully folding her clothes in neat squares.

Tempest eyed her weapons, the clothing, and her knapsack. There was no way it would all fit in the faded leather bag. Her gaze wandered to the gorgeous Hound uniform laying on her bed. Unable to help herself, she ran her hand over the butter soft leather and touched the sturdy corset inlaid with an intricate metal mesh, then the deep royal blue cloak. It was stunning but too bold for her task. Chagrined, she repacked most of her Hound uniform, only keeping out the elaborate corset and leather pants.

She needed to keep her clothes as plain and inauspicious as possible. Most women didn't wear trousers, so she had to take a skirt. Fingering a roughly woven forest-green skirt, she smiled and added it to her pile. It would help to keep her hidden among the evergreens and as much as she was loath to wear a skirt, it would also serve as a blanket as she traveled. Humming her mum's lullaby, she packed underclothes, a loose linen shirt, and a tunic into her bag alongside medicine and a wound kit.

"Thank you, Aleks," she whispered, throwing in a spare dagger, a length of rope, and her waterskin.

She laid out another set of clothes and a dull, worn gray cape—one Tempest threw over herself when she did not want to be noticed in Dotae—on the chair by her bed. Her sword, dagger, bow, and quiver of arrows sat on the floor by the chair, ready to be strapped on at a moment's notice.

"What else do I need?" she murmured for nobody but herself and the flickering lantern. Maybe Aleks was right and lists really meant life and death. Holding up her right hand, she ticked off what else was needed for the journey. "I have to drop by the kitchen for food rations..." She winced. If her uncles discovered she left without saying a word, they'd thrash her.

Tempest glanced outside at the dark, silent night. It was cold, and it would only get colder outside of the bustle of the city. It would not serve her to catch a chill on her very first day as a Hound, not to mention the fact that Tempest might trip and hurt herself in the pitch black of rural Heimserya. It made sense to sleep first and travel with the first light.

Plus, she was exhausted. Her wounds were mostly healed thanks to her uncle but her body ached something fierce. Tempest reached back and tugged on the laces to her dress. After twenty minutes of fighting with it, she was sweating. Tossing her hands in the air, she yelled and then snagged the dagger from the chair and sliced through the delicate fabric. The silk fluttered to the floor, and she unceremoniously kicked it away once she was finally free of it.

She washed her face with water from a basin and freshened her teeth with mint before collapsing onto her bed. She had so much to think about—so much to process—but now that her head was sinking into her pillow, Tempest found she could barely hold coherent thoughts at all.

"Sleep first, think later," she breathed, the words lost to the air as she drifted into sleep.

"You are not—Tempest, you only *just* became a Hound!" Aleks exclaimed the moment he spied Tempest in the courtyard of the barracks, dyeing her periwinkle hair black with a thick, woody-smelling mixture of coal and lotion.

She gave him a grim smile. "Morning, Aleks. I guess you must have heard about my assignment."

"We *all* have," Dima said, appearing from behind Aleks so suddenly that Tempest jumped in surprise.

Bloody quiet man.

"How did you wind up taking on such a job?" he demanded softly.

Tempest didn't want to tell them about King Destin and the predatory way he'd looked at her, or how she'd used her information about the rebellion to hold him at bay. It was a recipe for violence, death, and disaster.

She shrugged. "The king was impressed by my skills in the Trial. This is just an information-gathering assignment. I'll likely only be away for a few days, so relax, uncles. I'll be fine. You've taught me well."

Aleks looked anything but relaxed. Tempest bit her lip when she realized Dima wore the same tense expression as Aleks, and she frowned. It wasn't like Dima to be so outwardly concerned—he trusted Tempest to make her own decisions and had always been the first one to push her to try harder.

Her gaze narrowed in suspicion when Maxim—with a surly-looking Levka in tow—showed up with an equally troubled look upon his face. Tempest scowled at her family. "Do you think I can't do this? Have I not proven myself—"

"Dotae be good, lass, of course we think you can do this!" Maxim cut in.

He moved forward to give her a hug, and she held her dye-covered hands out to the side and inhaled her uncle's familiar smoky scent.

"We're simply worried for you. We're allowed to be, aren't we?" Maxim rumbled and released her. He stepped back and crossed his arms over his barrel chest.

Dima nodded his agreement, his lips puckered like he tasted something sour. "Hounds don't typically go off on a solitary assignment two days after their Trial. It was folly of you to have accepted."

"It wasn't like I could refuse our king," Tempest replied, bristling.

She caught Levka's gaze, expecting him to be glaring at her or generally annoyed that she was already off on an official assignment before he'd even had a chance to complete his Trials. But, to her surprise, he looked almost contemplative. Quiet. Wariness flooded her. It was odd to see him like that, when he was so often just as loud and brash as his father.

Levka's lip curled, and he averted his eyes, before

stalking away toward the training grounds, leaving Tempest with her three worrying uncles. She stared after him in puzzlement.

That was odd.

She rolled her neck and turned her attention back to the men impersonating thunder clouds and gave them all a reassuring smile. "I will be all right. I swear. I won't do anything rash. I'm just gathering information."

Liar, liar. She kept her expression placid even though she wanted to puke. Tempest had never lied to her uncles, and she hated that she did so now. It made her feel dirty.

"Gathering information is often more dangerous than combat, Tempest," said a deep voice full of ice.

She stilled and fought not to fidget. *The* Madrid. No one knew what his first name was. Tempest squared her shoulders and turned around to face the man that still inspired fear to run up her spine.

Madrid stood there, arms crossed over his chest as he stared down at her. "You should not have taken this assignment," he said. "You should have come to me first."

"I couldn't," she protested softly, keeping her voice down. Hounds were the worst sort of gossips. No need to spread her business everywhere.

It was on the tip of her tongue to come clean about the deal she'd struck with the king, but her tongue stuck to the roof of her mouth, and the words remained trapped inside. King Destin hadn't said to keep their conversation private... but she got the feeling it was better to keep silent.

Tempest stood as tall as she could make herself and matched Madrid's frigid stare. "Ultimately, I am obliged to the king. And, while I respect you, this isn't something you can change. I serve my king, first and foremost. I'm a fully-fledged Hound—a weapon for our majesty to use as he sees fit. It doesn't matter whether you like it or not. I'm going on this assignment."

Madrid studied her and eventually sighed, shaking his head before rummaging through a pouch attached to his belt. He pulled out a pale blue ring carved from agate; it depicted the snarling face of a hound. "For you. All Hounds have them. Keep it hidden while on your journey, though."

She snorted and held up her dye-covered palms. "What do you think I'm coloring my hair for? I can't exactly go undercover with blue hair that screams I'm born of the Madrid line, now can I? Because I'm certainly not doing this for fun. This stuff is disgusting."

Maxim's face relaxed. "Just listen to us all and be careful, Tempest. I don't want to have to face Levka's joy at hearing you've been mauled by a wolf or kidnapped or something."

"Such wonderful words of encouragement." She cracked a smile.

"Don't venture too close to the mountains," Aleks admonished, still looking dead serious.

A chill ran down Tempest's spine and she thought about the strange smell in the healer's tent the day of her Trial. She gave the man an encouraging smile and nodded.

"If all things go well, I won't have to go anywhere near

them."

"And try to limit your travel through the forest, too, if you know what's good for you," Dima added.

If they knew what she was really doing—hunting the Jester—they would become unhinged.

"I'll be ever on guard," she said carefully, not wanting to lie. "You've trained me well. I'll be back before you know it."

She hoped. The Jester wouldn't be an easy adversary.

Tempest rinsed her hair and hands in the closest barrel of frosty water, the excess color clouding the water. She stood and faced her uncles who stood silently watching her. A lump lodged in her throat. It was time to leave them, and she wasn't sure if she was ready.

It was now or never.

She sidled up to Maxim and hugged him once more, then Dima, then Aleks, bidding them all farewell in the process. She did not look at Madrid, who watched on silently if the scratchy feeling between her shoulder blades meant anything. Tempest left them all to pick up the rest of her things from her room and leave the barracks, her wet hair seeping through her thin linen shirt. Their concern warmed her heart. To have them all looking out for her—even the impassive, intimidating Madrid—meant more to Tempest than she'd ever admit.

Tempest wove her long hair into a thick, black braid and double checked to make sure all of her weapons were secure. She scanned the barracks one last time before sneaking past the sparring ring and into the flow of morning workers heading to their assignments. She peeked over her shoulder, barely able to see the roof of her home.

"I'll be back soon," she promised.

Twilight warmed the sky by the time Tempest reached the edge of the forest that surrounded the mountain range dividing Heimserya and Talaga.

She patted her horse on its sweaty shoulder. "Such a good boy," she murmured as they picked their way through the forest.

She'd ridden at a hard, unforgiving pace in order to reach the first of the trees before night truly fell. At each village, she'd hired a new mount, and the black beauty she currently sat astride was her favorite so far. He responded to each command she gave flawlessly and the way he galloped was almost like flying.

"Some apples for you when we get to the next village." His ears twitched at the word apple, and she smiled while keeping a sharp eye on their surroundings.

Tempest was the first to admit that she wasn't perfect with a weapon—her swordplay was sloppy and lazy at times—but she was a good tracker. Excellent, even. After long range combat, it was her best skill; with a year or two of on-the-job experience she had a feeling her tracking would surpass combat, too.

She tugged on the reins, and her eyes narrowed on a freshly trampled leafy plant and a bare footprint in the mud. The hair along her arms rose and the warnings of her uncles rang in her ears: *be on guard at all times*. The forest was rogue shifter territory, and they tended to attack anybody who trespassed into the woods. Her lip curled at the thought. The bloody woods didn't belong to *them*. They were criminal interlopers who refused to work and hid in cowardice.

With utmost care, she swung from her mount and landed on the spongy ground without a sound. She brushed her fingers along the footprint, wet earth clinging to her fingertips. The track was fresh. Tempest inhaled softly and strained to pick out any sounds as she scanned the lush forest.

Where did you go?

She examined the area around them for any more signs of shifters. Nothing.

Tempest soundlessly crept around the base of the tree, the horse trailing behind her, and smiled as the set of footprints led to the stream. What a clever little shifter, hiding their tracks. She studied the growth around the banks of the creek and grinned when she found a snapped reed. Maybe not so clever after all.

Her mount huffed, pulling her attention from the broken reed. Tempest looped the reins over a branch and gave the beast one last loving pat before she started tracking.

"Stay here," she murmured softly. "I'll be back soon." His ears twitched again, and he began nibbling at the low plants covering the ground. That was as good of an answer as anything she supposed.

A chill seeped through her boots and numbed her toes when she waded into the clear water. Tempest gritted her teeth and picked her way upstream, careful not to make too much noise or slip on the moss-covered rocks beneath the water's surface. The ash trees on either side of the creek leaned toward one another as if embracing.

It would be a magical sort of place if it weren't occupied by scum. Disgust filled her as she fingered another broken reed. It was reasonable to believe her mum's killer hid somewhere in the immense forest. Now, that she was older and understood the dynamics of their kingdom, she hazarded that the shifter her mum had helped had run away from his assignment. While she and her mother had plied him with kindness, he'd given Tempest nothing but heartache and betrayal.

Tempest hated all of them.

She sucked in a sharp breath and held it. Well, not *all* of them. Juniper was her friend and a good person.

The tall grasses around the stream opened. Tempest slipped toward the bank and studied the mossy ground. There weren't any footprints, but a smirk curled her lips. The shifter had avoided the mud and had tried to use the grassy patches to hide his steps. The footsteps were too large to be female, so she assumed the shifter was male.

Her feet whispered across the undergrowth as she followed the tracks to a clearing. Tempest hesitated to investigate the clearing. In an open space, her back would always be turned toward potential danger. And not for the first time, she wished the king had given her a partner.

As he should have. He wants you to fail.

She rubbed at her forehead and found she was squinting. Tempest looked at the sky, noting that the last of the day's sunlight was bleeding out across the horizon, behind the trees. Damn. In a few scant minutes, the forest would be too dark to traverse without a lantern. Only idiots traveled at night alone. Tempest gazed mournfully at the meadow. The trail wouldn't be as fresh tomorrow, but at least the nearest village was only fifteen minutes to the north, situated beside a mill that made use of the strong river current running past the outskirts of the forest. She would rest there for the evening and start her search anew at first light.

She backtracked toward the creek and stiffened when a faint sound reached her ears.

Footsteps.

Tempest rotated slowly, desperately trying to work out where the hushed noise had originated from, only for a second set of footsteps to join the first, and a third, and a fourth.

Wicked Hell.

Tempest silently swung up into the boughs of the closest tree as the footsteps drew nearer. She climbed higher and higher until she spied the group; two of the clan had long, pointed ears held high on alert. The other two were shuffling close to the forest floor, noses twitching as they tried to catch her scent.

Winter's bite. Of course, they'd be shifters. The only people dumb enough to be in the forest at this time of day were shifters and criminals. And not only that, but they were ones of power. Only the most powerful could partially shift.

And you. Time to disappear.

Without another glance at the shifters, Tempest jumped over to the next tree nimbly, then the next, thankful for her balance and flexibility. She gritted her teeth when a branch beneath her boots groaned. Tempest pressed herself against the tree trunk, praying that the babble of the nearby creek drowned out any sound she made, and continued on. Staying in one place guaranteed that they'd discover her.

Sweat sprang to her brow as she traversed the forest in this way for the next ten minutes, following the rush of the river until it was so deafening that nobody—not even a shifter—would be able to hear Tempest above it. She climbed back down to the forest floor with slow, careful movements. She hissed as her foot slipped and the underside of her bicep scraped against the rough bark.

Her arms quivered as she lowered herself to the ground beside her mount who blended into the descending night. Tempest quietly pulled the reins from the branch, placed her foot in the stirrup and hauled herself onto the tall mount.

She pressed her heels gently into the horse's sides and nudged him forward. Goosebumps erupted along her arms as they moved through the darkened forest. Every deepened shadow and moan from the trees set Tempest further on edge. The tension in her shoulders drained when the trees thinned, and she reached the outskirts of the village.

That was too close. Even now, it felt like someone was watching her.

Tempest glanced over her shoulder and shot a furtive look at the forest. She jerked as she saw a pair of eyes reflected in the light.

"It's just your imagination. Calm down," she muttered as she swung back around and spied an inn.

But the uneasy feeling didn't dissipate. She was damn lucky they hadn't caught her. If they had found her ring... it wouldn't have gone well for her. The fact that she hadn't noticed them before they were so close was troubling. Clearly, she needed to work on self-awareness more than any other skill.

Her gaze darted to the woods and then back to the inn. Even if the clan had caught her scent, being surrounded by others would mask her scent if the shifters decided to come into town. She handed her horse to a wide-eyed stablehand and smiled shyly at him.

"Please make sure he receives some oats and apples."

Tempest scratched the horse above his nose and massaged his ears. "You did good, my friend." He nickered and bumped his head into her chest. She smiled and gave him a few more scratches before collecting her pack. She yanked out the skirt and tied it around her waist, ignoring the blushing boy.

She adjusted the skirt and placed a coin into the boy's palm. "It's our little secret. Riding in a skirt is never fun."

He gave her a toothy smile. "I wouldn't wanna ride in skirts."

Tempest ruffled his hair and sauntered to the inn.

Time to see how good her acting skills were.

Chapter Ten

Tempest

Tempest's ears rang from the sheer volume of chaos inside the inn, and she glanced at the door over her shoulder. Her heart still thundered in her chest after the close call in the forest and the safest place to hide was the inn, but all she wanted to do was curl up and nap in the barn with the horses where it was nice and comforting. But that wouldn't get the information she needed. Surreptitiously, she studied the room from beneath the hood of the cloak. Maybe she could get the knowledge she required this way. Especially if she hovered by the door like a gargoyle.

Get started.

She wound her way across the busy room and pushed back her hood, a secret smile curling her lips at the bawdy shouts assaulting her ears. Any woman of good breeding would be shocked at the lyrics, but Tempest found herself humming under her breath. Being raised with men didn't give one delicate sensibilities.

"What can I get you?" a pretty, large-chested barmaid asked Tempest when she pushed her way to the front of the bar. She admired the wench's observational skills as she did not tear her eyes away from the drink she was carefully pouring.

"A pint of ale, please and thanks," Tempest replied after a moment, inclining her head politely toward the barmaid despite the fact she still hadn't once looked at Tempest.

Tempest planted her feet as the many men standing by the bar jostled her and brazenly ogled the young serving woman in her pale blue, low-cut dress without an ounce of shame. Tempest had seen many of the Hounds react in such a way to women before, but it didn't make it any easier to witness the twitch in the barmaid's brow as she swatted a customer's hand away when he tried to grope her breasts. Her fingers inched toward the blade hidden underneath her cuff. It would be so easy to show that man a little respect.

Tempest leaned an elbow against the bar and ignored some of the attention that had been turned her way.

"What's a young and pretty thing like you coming in here alone, hen?" a middle-aged man with graying hair and a scar across his jaw asked. He smiled easily at Tempest, clearly intending it to be disarming. She smiled genuinely at his antics and the desire in his eyes as if he had announced out loud that he would like to bed her.

Cheeky bastard.

"I'm just passing through," she said, reciting the answer she had invented that morning. "Visiting my grandmother. She's sick."

"Nearly everyone is sick round these parts, these days," another man piped in. His voice was gruff and hoarse and barely coherent. When Tempest took in his appearance, she noticed a scarf hanging around his neck that he immediately coughed into. It was stained with speckles of a dark, poisonous-looking red.

Blood. So much blood.

Looking around, Tempest realized the man wasn't the only one with a scarf covering his mouth or neck. At least half of the customers were wearing one in some form or another, all of them pale-skinned and fearful. Clearly, they knew what awaited them at the end of their sickness if they did not get better soon.

Winter's bite. Too many on death's door.

It wasn't too difficult to bring tears to her eyes as she played her part. She gulped slightly, and the men by the bar all looked at her with expressions of sympathy.

"Might be better for you to turn back, lass," the first man said. "If your grandmamma is sick chances are, she might not be around by the time you reach her. I'm sorry."

Tempest didn't say anything. She paid for her ale when the barmaid handed the tankard over the scratched dark bar to her. She sipped bitter brew in order to appease the men who were watching her, to keep up her nondescript, devoted granddaughter act in order to keep their suspicions at bay, for a lone traveler—a woman, no less—was rare to see close to the forest.

Not that she expected too much trouble.

The men at the bar might have been friendly with the serving wench, but they'd backed off when she'd given them a firm swat. They understood no, meant no.

And for those who didn't care to be polite Tempest was sure she could introduce them to a few of her favorite weapons hidden on her person. Her sword, two daggers, a container of poisonous darts, and her bow and arrows hidden from sight by her heavy cloak.

She surveyed the room over the rim of her ale and noted a few dangerous lecherous looks some of the men were giving her. Once again, she hid her smile as she took a sip from the tankard, and knew that by far *she* was the most dangerous person currently presiding within the inn.

Raucous laughter rang from a round corner table full of men and women playing cards. That's where she wanted to be. Tempest said her goodbyes to the men by the bar and struggled through the crowd until she reached a dusty, blue-and-red stained-glass window. She leaned against it, the chill seeping through her cloak, listening carefully to each and every conversation she could make out.

A group of elderly women were complaining about the lack of various herbs used for healing in the forest. Three men a few feet away from Tempest were mumbling about a pair of women who could not have been much older than

Tempest herself. The women, in turn, were completely ignoring the men, instead devoting all their attention to gossiping about a handsome man in a wide-brimmed hat who was dealing the cards at the loud table.

Tempest almost laughed when the man in the hat glanced in the young women's direction and they puffed out their chests and preened like peacocks. People were so predictable and peculiar. Everyone was dying around them and yet they kept on with their gossip and flirtations as if nothing was awry.

What were they supposed to do?

Death was a common part of life, and life waited for no man. If she was in their position, she supposed she would pick up and leave and find somewhere that the sickness hadn't spread yet. But if it *were* that easy, everyone would have done it already.

Her thoughts screeched to a halt as a juicy bit of information reached her ears. She scanned the room to work out who had spoken, listening hard as she caught another bit of the conversation.

"The fox is up to his old tricks again," a thin man at the card table muttered.

Taking a deep breath, Tempest took a fake swallow of her ale before plastering a lovely smile to her face and sauntering over to the men, her heavy skirt rustling around her legs.

"What are you playing, gentlemen?" she asked, running a hand through her hair in order to hang it over one shoulder, her smile widening when the man in the top hat glanced up and grinned.

"A game we created ourselves," he said. His voice was soft and low and lilting—the kind of voice that inspired thoughts of sin and silk. "Care to watch and learn, luv?"

Oh, he's good.

Beneath the shadow that the brim of his hat cast across his features was a sharp, handsome face, with a pointed chin and the kind of cheekbones Tempest had only seen illustrated in books of legends and fairy tales. She thought his eyes might be brown, but then he shifted slightly and they caught the light, and Tempest realized they were gold. Not amber or topaz or citrine. Pure, molten, unrelenting gold. They were perhaps the most astonishing eyes Tempest had ever seen.

Wicked Hell, the man was handsome.

"I—I would love to watch you play," she said, ashamed that she had lost herself to the sight of the man in front of her for even a moment. What was worse was that he knew he'd caught her attention and was pleased.

He whispered in the ear of the man to his left. The man vacated his chair and the man with the hat stood and pulled out the seat. "Here, have a seat."

She smiled and sat as ladylike as possible, coyly glancing at the other men staring at her from around the table. "Thank you." Tempest bit her lip and frowned when his hand lingered by her shoulder for longer than was polite.

He sat in his chair with a flourish and glanced at her from the corners of his startling eyes. "Where are you from, lass?"

"Dotae," Tempest replied, taking but half a second to compose herself as the man began shuffling his cards and dealing out new hands for his companions. She had already decided that a vague retelling of her actual history was the best story she could give strangers. "Though I lived outside of the city when I was very young. In the forest, in fact. But I barely remember life from back then."

"So, what's the royal city like these days?"

"Very loud. Very busy." Tempest tilted her head slightly, raising a curious eyebrow at the man as if he was the most interesting person in the world. He eased against the back of his chair with the confidence of a person who clearly believed the same thing about himself. "Do you visit the city often?"

The man's resultant laughter was genuine in its amusement. The sound was akin to a stream over pebbles—if Tempest thought a young woman would never tire of his voice, his laughter was another level entirely. Her cheeks flushed at the sound, and she barely kept from rolling her eyes at herself.

He's just another flirtatious rake. You've dealt with handsome men before. Don't lose your composure.

"I haven't visited Dotae in a few years, I must admit." The man chuckled. "Let's just say I don't much like cities and leave it at that."

Tempest didn't know how to interpret his statement. Clearly, he had a reason for avoiding Dotae that she couldn't possibly work out, given that she'd only just met him. She watched his hands as they deftly placed a few cards face-up in front of his friends. Hmmm... Quick fingers were always dangerous. Was he a thief or just a card enthusiast? The former, if she was to hazard a guess.

"You prefer villages, then," she said, choosing her next words very carefully. "I always thought they'd be cleaner than the city. This sickness seems to be proving me wrong, though."

"Aye, well, this *plague* has nothing to do with how many baths the villagers have had this year," he muttered, almost to himself. He placed the last of his cards on the table. "And this round is mine. Care for another?"

One of the other men threw down his cards in frustration. "Bloody *no*. You've decimated us all evening, and you know it."

"I concur. I think it might be time to call it a night before it gets too cold," said the second man.

"Another fire whisky for Fox, as requested."

Tempest stilled at the voice of the barmaid, who had appeared at the table while Tempest's back had been turned.

The man with the wide-brimmed hat looked up at the barmaid, grinning his sharp-toothed grin as she handed him a glass of amber liquid. Tempest inhaled and noted that it smelled the same as the fire whisky from King Destin's chambers.

That was out of place. Fire whisky was extremely expensive.

Tempest took a tiny sip of her ale and slid her gaze

down Fox's throat as he took a heathy swig, noting just above the chain of his forest-green cloak there was a scar that seemed to stretch across his entire throat. A person didn't come by a scar like that without consequence. The dashing dealer—Fox—wasn't all that he seemed.

"Many thanks, Lil," he crooned.

Lil, the barmaid, blushed in response, beaming at Fox before sauntering back to the bar. Apparently, he'd caught the eye of every woman in the entire establishment.

Tempest kept her thoughts from her face as Fox began collecting his playing cards, whistling a melancholy tune to himself as he did so.

"Fox is a strange name," Tempest said while swirling her ale, adding a smile and a flutter of her eyelashes when her tone ended up being far more pointed than she'd intended.

Fox looked at her from beneath the brim of his hat, smirking. "You do not like it? Too exotic for your city sensibilities?"

Tempest snorted before she could stop herself. "I think you speak too highly of both of us."

"A difficult thing to do, indeed. Does the lady have a name to go with her pretty face? Or is it part of your mystery?" He smirked, flashing his white teeth. "I love a good mystery."

I bet you do. Time to get him alone.

"Juniper," Tempest lied easily, thinking of her best friend. She fished a pipe out of her cloak, and held it out, deciding to take a risk in order to push for more information on the *plague* Fox had mentioned. "Would you like to go outside and join me, Fox? I must admit to being wary of venturing outside alone now that it is truly dark." She cast a furtive look toward the window for good measure.

Fox plucked her pipe from her fingers and grinned at her. He picked up his glass, downed his fire whisky in one gulp, then stood up to pull Tempest's chair out for her.

"Lead the way, my lady," he whispered in her ear.

Chapter Eleven

Tempest

"So… you mentioned something about a smoke, my lady?"

"You do not have to call me that," Tempest said as Fox twirled her ebony pipe between his thumb and forefinger. In truth it was Maxim's pipe; she figured he'd forgive her for pilfering it in due time.

Out of a small pouch attached to her belt, Tempest pinched a measure of herb leaves, dropping them into the pipe when Fox held it out for her.

"On the contrary," he said. "Every woman should be treated like a lady."

"If only the rest of the male population thought the same," she muttered, searching for her flint and steel.

"Allow me," he said with a roguish grin.

Tempest jumped when light flashed across her vision, lighting up the dark night around them for one moment. She blinked slowly at the pipe as it began to smoke and burn, unease skittering across her skin. "Are you some kind of magician…?" she asked, pushing some awe into her voice.

"Not really," Fox laughed. He pulled out a satchel from his coat pocket and shook it. "Flammable powder. A mere parlor trick. It does look impressive though, does it not?"

"Only if you don't explain how you did it," she retorted, her mind whirling. Flammable powder could cause a lot of damage in the wrong hands.

The man continued to chuckle as he held the pipe to his mouth and took a long draw from it, then handed it over to Tempest. She did not like smoking, in truth, but she knew how to handle the bitter leaves, so she took a practiced draw from the pipe before passing it back to Fox.

He nodded at her, clearly impressed. "Not every day you see a young woman who can handle her vices, *Juniper.*"

There was an inflection on her friend's name that suggested to Tempest that Fox had rightfully concluded that it did not belong to her.

No matter. He obviously isn't what he claims to be either. It would be a battle of wits and then I'd be on my way.

"You must not know very many women if you think we can't hold our own." Tempest blew a ring of smoke so perfect that she couldn't quite believe she'd managed it. *Thank you, Maxim.*

The grin on Fox's face grew even wider. "I never said that. You're putting words in my mouth."

She cocked a hip and arched a brow. "My apologies. Let

me clarify. I think you underestimate city girls if you are surprised. I can handle my vices."

"Okay, *city girl*. Tell me this: why are you out here in the middle of nowhere? Past this point all there is are trees and mountains, and then Talaga." He appraised her. "And if you were smart, you'd be traveling with a companion or two. It's not safe to journey alone these days."

Even though his words were a casual warning, they felt more like a threat. Was he suspicious of her?

"Not all of us are given a choice in which pathway our life takes," she said carefully. "We can't rely on the protection of others, only on our own capabilities."

Fox hummed but didn't comment.

She studied him as a comfortable silence settled between them. He held out the pipe but she waved her hand for him to continue. The man tipped his head back and gazed into the night sky, the glimmer of the lanterns highlighting his strong jaw and the warm skin of his neck.

Another anomaly.

Dotae was a cold kingdom by nature. Most direct descendants had pale skin of some variety like Tempest, and, yet, his skin was almost russet in color. So he either was a foreigner or spent significant time working outside.

"If you look at me like that any longer, I might draw the wrong conclusions and start to believe you wanted me alone for another purpose."

Tempest smirked. *Over her dead body.* Handsome he may be, but trouble he definitely was. But it wouldn't hurt to play it up a little. Just a little.

"I'm trying to work out where you're from," she admitted. She flipped her dyed hair over one shoulder and batted her eyelashes.

"Clearly not from here." Fox laughed easily. "But I asked you a question first: what are you doing out here? You *are* alone, aren't you?"

If another man had asked her that question, she'd have been suspicious of his intentions, but despite the way Fox flirted, she doubted he had any designs on creeping into her bed. He clearly was after information so she'd feed him a lie like everyone else.

She nodded. "I'm alone. I'm visiting my grandmother. She's taken ill. Though, going by what I heard by the bar, I should turn around before I get sick myself."

Your move, Fox.

He grew serious. Fox puffed on the pipe and blew out a narrow stream of smoke in lieu of a sigh, leaning against the stone wall of the inn as he did so. His wide-brimmed hat cast his face in shadow. She kept her irritation from showing as she could not work out the expression on his face. His strange, golden eyes glinted in the moonlight.

"You really should turn back, city girl. I wasn't joking when I called this *sickness* a plague. If something isn't done soon, it'll decimate almost every village in the forest and along the mountain range."

"Does... does anybody know where it came from? I never heard anything about a plague in Dotae—"

"Well of course you wouldn't," Fox said with a humorless laugh, his empty, hollow tone causing shivers to run up her spine.

Tempest edged away from him just a little and slipped her hand into her skirt pocket, her fingers brushing a dagger. Fox hadn't made any aggressive moves toward her, but the air seemed charged with violence.

"Nobody in the precious royal city could possibly know of anything going on outside the walls that protect them," he continued, lips curling into a bitter smile around the ebony pipe. "Imagine if *His Royal Highness* actually did anything about the problems that ail his people. That would involve him caring, and you and I both know those who are high-born rarely look at the dirt beneath their boots."

"To say such a thing is treason," she said softly, leaning against the wall to mirror his stance.

"And who will tell him I spoke such treason?" he asked, tipping his chin at her. "Will you?"

"Of course not." *Lie.* "I don't desire to go to an early grave." *Truth.* "I'm concerned about this plague, though. Do you know any more about it than what you've told me? Is there truly nothing that can help?"

Fox quirked an eyebrow and scanned her from head to toe. "And what could a slip of a girl like you do to help stop a plague?"

More than you'll ever know.

Her gaze narrowed. "My business is my own," she replied, straightening her back and fixing her eyes on the strange man in front of her. "My grandmother's life hangs in the balance. If you know something, you need to tell me." Tempest took a step closer and boldly placed her hand on the sleeve of his jacket. "Please."

He eyed her hand on his jacket. "Personal boundaries aren't something you adhere by, are they?"

"You didn't strike me as a prudish man."

Fox gently brushed her hand from his arm and stepped into her space, heat radiating from his body. Her breath hitched and the fingers of her right hand curled around the dagger in her pocket. He trailed his finger down her cheek and neck, then across her shoulder. He picked up a lock of her hair and twirled it.

"Luv, you really shouldn't play games you know nothing of." His molten gaze ran over her cheeks, and a slow sensual smile spread over his face. "Information doesn't come cheap," Fox whispered in her left ear.

Tempest's pulse quickened, but she didn't back down, not when she was so close to getting a firm lead on what was going on outside of Dotae, and getting one step closer to the Jester too. She turned her head and brushed her nose along his jaw and pulled a small purse laden with coins from her left pocket and twisted so there was more space between their bodies. "I can pay you for the information, if that is what you're looking for."

The look Fox gave Tempest then was entirely unreadable. But he shook his head and chuckled humorlessly. "You must be wet around the ears, city girl, if you think that'll—"

The sound of shattering glass interrupted Fox's sentence. He turned in the direction of the sound, head tilting up as he did so. For just a moment, Tempest spied the furred edge of a fox ear beneath his hat.

Bloody hell. A shifter. Right under her blasted nose. It took her approximately two seconds to decide her next course of action. Fox was too smooth and cunning to be a run-of-the-mill gossip. The male had to know *something.*

Simultaneously, she pulled the dagger from her pocket and another blade sheathed at her left hip. "I won't play games with you. I only want the information, and I'll be on my way."

Fox turned his attention back to her, almost lazily, and removed his hat with a slow, careful hand. "Information can be a dangerous thing, luv. You sure you're able to handle it?"

She smiled sharply and didn't hide the fact she was staring at the two pointed, black-tipped ears poking through his wine-red hair, though a single streak of white broke through the hair that grazed his forehead.

"Enjoying the view?" he purred.

Tempest tracked his hand as it lowered to the dagger at his hip, but he didn't pull it out. He was waiting. Waiting to see what *Tempest* would do.

He was playing with her. He didn't take her seriously.

The air around them seemed to crackle, tense and charged. For a long moment, neither of them did anything. Then, as if deciding that Tempest was harmless, Fox began to smile—the bastard.

"Clearly there has been some misunderstanding here." He held up the hand holding his hat. "Why don't you tell me—"

A patronizing bastard.

She darted forward and grazed her dagger across his right shoulder and jabbed the pommel of her other dagger hard into his stomach. Pain lanced up her arm. It was like hitting a brick wall. Tempest danced out of his reach.

Fox fingered the shallow cut to his shoulder, but the smile from his face did not disappear, if anything it deepened. She fought a shiver of trepidation as his gold eyes glittered with something much darker than revenge.

"So you *do* know what you're doing, city girl," he said, his voice a low growl. He tossed his hat on the ground along with the pipe and pulled two wicked-looking daggers from inside his coat. "Let's see just how good you are, then."

Tempest had barely a second to prepare for the man's attack. He brought his dagger down low, as if to slash her thigh, but Tempest kicked the blade away before twirling out of the way, her heavy skirt flaring out around her. She responded with a strike of her own aimed at Fox's back.

He bent low, avoiding the attack, then swept out a leg in an attempt to unbalance her. A chuckle slipped from her mouth. It was the oldest trick in the book. With light footsteps, she jumped out of the way, then threw a dagger that pinned Fox's handsome green cloak firmly to the ground. He unclasped it, the fabric billowing to the ground to reveal a lean, muscular frame encased in a tailored jacket that was too fine for someone from the village.

Fox leapt forward, and now he had both of his

daggers—one short, one long—aimed at Tempest's throat. She parried them away, careful to keep in control of her breathing so that panic and adrenaline did not make her careless.

"Is this the best you can do, luv?" she taunted.

He winked at her. "You haven't even had a taste of what I can do. You'll never be able to go back once you've experienced my skills..."

"That's what every man says," she huffed, circling him. "Find something a little more original."

Fox laughed; it was simultaneously a brutal and beautiful sound. His eyes were bright, his canines exposed and his entire body taut with the power to spring upon Tempest at any given moment. He was enjoying the fight—that much was clear. Tempest had no problem admitting to herself that she was enjoying it, too.

"I have much more in me than this," he taunted. "But I would like to know the real name of my foe before I best her."

"You—"

"*Where is she? We can smell her.*"

Both Tempest and Fox froze. His inhuman ears pricked up to attention, drawing her focus like he was listening carefully as the sound of growls and rough, demanding voices edged closer and closer.

"We know she came this way. Where is she?!"

Tempest stared at Fox in horror. They'd tracked her scent even with all her precautions.

It was time to make a run for it.

Chapter Twelve

Tempest

Tempest kept her gaze pinned to Fox and quickly masked her expression, even as her heart thundered in her chest. She strained to pick out how many voices there were. A trickle of fear ran down her spine. Five! Five bloody shifters hunting her. She bared her teeth at the male in front of her as he pressed toward her. Make that six. Tempest bit the inside of her cheek as she tried to think of a way out. She was good, but six against one wasn't good odds.

There wasn't a choice. She had to run, or she'd die.

Run, run, just run as fast as you can.

"We know she came through this way!" a man growled again from somewhere down the cobbled street. "Use your damn noses and find her bloody scent. He won't like that one of her kind is roaming around."

One of her kind? What the hell did that mean? Were they referring to her gender or race? Tempest barely hid her flinch as another idea wormed its way into her mind. Had they somehow discovered she was a Hound?

Calm down. You haven't given yourself away. Panic is your enemy.

She'd taken every precaution to protect her identity—dyed her hair with charcoal and doused herself in a scent-masking solution Aleks created.

"You in some sort of trouble, luv?" Fox drawled.

She glared at the man, who lazily flicked a piece of lint from his jacket with the tip of his dagger. He shifted his longer blade so it pointed over her shoulder, toward the direction of the voices.

"Nothing I can't handle," she managed to say evenly.

Liar, liar.

Fox kept his careful eyes on her. "You chose a bad time to pick a fight with me when you're on the run."

"I wasn't picking a fight. You weren't cooperating."

"And you were the one who pulled a blade first."

"Because you're not who you're pretending to be."

Fox chuckled. "Don't we all do that?"

Tempest tightened her grip on her blade and took a step closer to the Talagan. "All I need is the information and I'll be gone. I'm worried about my grandmother. If I don't help, who will?"

"That's the way of the world, *city girl*. Now, I suggest you make a run for it before those unsavory fellows find you. I'd hate to think what they'd do to such a tasty morsel."

"They'll taste the kiss of my blade before they touch me."

Fox laughed roughly. "Now, that I do believe. What did you do to them?"

"Nothing. Not a bloody thing. I don't even know them. I spotted them at a distance in the woods and made sure to give them a wide berth."

"Which part of the woods?"

"The green part," she retorted sarcastically.

The shapeshifter scowled at her. "Did your parents teach you nothing as you grew up? You never travel alone in the woods. Trespassing is a death offense."

"I wasn't traveling alone," she huffed irritably and moved farther into the shadows. How much time did she have until the shifters discovered her? "I had a horse."

Fox snorted and his lips quirked. "While amusing, that's not what I meant, and you know it." He waved his dagger carelessly toward her. "We're at an impasse. I don't like it when someone pulls a blade on me so you shan't be getting any information. Weapons don't make friends, luv." He scanned the darkened street. "And you can't possibly best me *and* escape those who are hunting you. So, what are you going to do?"

"I don't know," Tempest muttered, panic beginning to creep up her throat like bile. Time was short and, at any moment, the pack of shifters could find her. Her gaze moved back to the woods. It wasn't possible to hide in the village so that left the forest as her only option. She hated to leave empty-handed, but she couldn't fulfill her mission if she was dead. If only she had a bloody partner.

"You know, I'm not the enemy. I could help you."

She flinched. Had her thoughts been so obvious that a stranger could read them from her face? Her dagger wavered for a moment. "No one does things for free."

With one swift movement, Fox sheathed the long dagger and readjusted his stance, his keen eyes peering into the darkness as he searched for the pack of shifters. "True," he repeated. "There are five of them and only one of you, and I happen to enjoy protecting a damsel in distress."

Tempest faltered and almost accepted. *Don't be an idiot.* He was a liar and a cheat if she went by anything she observed at the table. She'd more than likely end up stabbed in the back. Her eyes flicked to his ears. A kitsune was never to be trusted. Ever. They were tricksters by nature. And then there was the matter of him hiding his ears and, thus, his identity as a shifter. Only somebody who had something to hide did that. No, Fox was not to be trusted.

You are one to talk, lady imposter.

"Thank you, but no thank you."

He shrugged and tucked his other blade away before she could see where it disappeared to. "While this has been a stimulating rendezvous, my lady, I believe you have somewhere to be."

He walked over to his cloak and yanked Tempest's dagger from the fabric. Fox clasped the rich forest-green cloak to his neck, plucked his hat and the pipe from the ground, and sauntered up to her.

Tempest lifted her remaining dagger and pressed it against the base of his throat. "That's close enough."

The kitsune flashed a smile and surprised her by holding the hilt of her dagger out to her. "You'd better take this." She took the weapon from his hand, never taking her eyes off his peculiar ones. "All you have to do is ask, and I'll help."

"Tempting," she murmured with a sharp smile.

"Suit yourself," he said simply.

Then, with a flourish of his cloak and just the slightest of smiles, Fox leapt on top of the inn with one impossibly high jump, creeping along the tiled roof until he reached the next building. She gaped as he launched to the next roof and kept running without a sound.

"What a bastard," she muttered. How bloody unfair. The kitsune made it seem easy. And he stole her pipe.

Fox disappeared just as the glint of lanterns closed in on the street. There was no escaping that way. Up it was. Tempest ran over to the stone walls of the inn, tucked one of her daggers away, and held the other between her teeth as she spotted promising handholds. She tucked up her skirt and began to climb. Sweat beaded on the back of her neck and her legs trembled as she neared the roof. The barely healed claw marks across her back and arm ached something fierce as she scrambled over the edge of the roof, her breath puffing between her lips in little, white clouds of steam. She stifled a groan and rolled to her feet.

Where did Fox go?

Tempest rotated her sore shoulder and snuck across the roof. She inhaled deeply and took a running jump and landed on the far roof without much of a sound. A thread of pride warmed her as she jumped to the next roof without incident. *You've got this.*

Her eyes widened as she got a good look at the next gap between buildings. She gritted her teeth and sprung. The night air whistled past her ears as she caught the edge of the roof, her feet scrambling for purchase. Her arms shook as she pulled herself up onto the roof and rolled over and laid there, white-hot pain lancing up her back and through her shoulder.

She peeked over the edge of the building at the stone cobbles below. That had not been fun. But breaking her legs would have been worse.

"Maybe I should have let him help me," Tempest whispered.

In the very least it would have stopped Fox from running off. But on the other hand, she got the feeling he'd been toying with her the entire time and he didn't do anything he didn't want to. Tempest caught her breath and thought about their interaction. The stars above blurred as she thought about his luxurious cloak and fine clothes. That certainly didn't add up. For a shifter, he'd been dressed remarkably well which wasn't something a person saw every day, but that didn't make him a bad person.

"What are you hiding?" She rolled her eyes and silently

crawled to her feet. Probably not as much as she was. What would he have thought if he'd seen her in Hound garb? Molten gold - amber eyes flashed through her mind, and Tempest wanted to slap herself. He was a damn shifter for Dotae's sake.

She shook her head in an attempt to clear it. It was a death sentence to get distracted. She needed to concentrate on what was happening in the present—the shifters in hot pursuit of her and how she was going to find a safe place once she entered the forest. Her skin prickled as if someone was watching her. Tempest froze and scanned the rooftops. Nothing. She did another cursory sweep and snuck to the far edge of the building that faced the woods.

Careful to put most of her weight on her uninjured arm, she swung down from the roof and sucked in a lungful of air once her boots touched solid ground. Now for the next round of hide and seek.

She ran as silently and as swiftly as she could toward the forest. With any luck, she could lose the men trying to find her between the dark boughs of the trees. It would be easy to climb one and stay hidden for the night.

Her breaths formed little puffs of mist in the cold night air. When she reached the edge of the forest, she scanned the ground for any sign of humans or animals but spotted nothing. Tempest cursed under her breath at the darkness and rushed through the trees as fast as she dared. In truth, she could barely see five feet in front of her now that she'd left the village and its lanterns behind.

A twinge in Tempest's back sent a shocking wave of pain through her nerves. She stumbled, knocked her shoulder into the trunk of a tree, and would have caught her balance if it hadn't been for the root that tripped her. A squeak of pain escaped her lips, but it was enough. Tempest swallowed down the agony, already compelling herself to her knees. Mistakes like hers cost people their life. A cry like that would send every predator in the area sprinting in her direction.

Her jaw clenched as she knelt, tears of pain pricking her eyes.

Get up! Get up before they find you. You've suffered worse.

She fought the pain, adrenaline, and panic warring in her system and forced herself back to her feet and clawed her way forward, deeper into the forest.

Just a little farther. Find a good tree. The trees will save your life.

A wolf's howl sliced through the still night, and goosebumps rose along her arms. She picked up her pace, damning every unclimbable tree she passed.

"There she is!" a voice called.

Hell. She hadn't even heard them approach.

On instinct, she veered to the left, running parallel to the forest in an effort to find the best opening for her to lose her assailants. If she could double back and crisscross her trails, she would confuse them. The barn with the horses should mask her scent, but she was losing speed.

The shadowy shape of a man stepped from behind a

tree to her left. Tempest veered closer to the edge of the forest and pushed her legs harder, her arms pumping at her sides. In the space of a few seconds, two more shifters made their way to her right, blocking her path back into the village.

Damn it.

Tempest came to a rapid halt, breathing heavily as she turned to see the remaining three shifters cutting off all other escape routes. She positioned herself so a large tree was at her back, pulled out her sword, and shifted her cloak over one shoulder so she had access to her bow and quiver.

You cannot fight them all.

The pain burned away while she observed her attackers stalk closer. If she wasn't careful, she could cause permanent damage to her back and arm. Tempest schooled her expression as the shifters approached—all were male—and going by the looks on their faces, their little tête-à-tête would be a bloody one. But what were a few scars compared to a shifter's sword embedded deep in her heart? Or their teeth in her flesh?

She shut that thought down and held her sword up in warning. "A nice night for a run, is it not, gentlemen?" Her voice rang clear throughout the forest, but the men stayed silent as they circled her like a pack of animals. "Cat got your tongue?"

"You'd best watch your mouth," snarled the burly man to her immediate right.

Tempest tightened her grip on her own sword even

though every instinct inside her said to get as far away from the predators as possible, but that wasn't who she was. She was a bloody Hound.

"It's my best feature, so I'm told," she remarked. "Now, if you're quite finished staring at me, why don't we get down to it?"

"You're surrendering?"

She smiled icily. "There will be no surrendering you giant arses."

"Sharp tongued twit."

"I assure you my blade is even sharper. Come closer and let me introduce you."

Chapter Thirteen

Tempest

Sometimes, she really needed to shut her mouth. Maxim always said she was too blunt and that diplomatic words went a long way.

Tempest smiled thinly and pushed her shoulders back, deciding to withdraw her earlier challenge. "I've no quarrel with any of you despite the merry chase you led me on. Let me pass, and I'll be on my way."

She had a feeling that her words were pointless. Even though she didn't have a shifter nose, Tempest could practically smell the aggression pouring off them. They were spoiling for a fight. A lanky, young man stepped closer to her right, his sharp smile setting her further on edge.

"Now, why would we let a pretty little skirt like you scurry away?"

Tempest bared her teeth at the man in a poor imitation of a smile. No, she would not get out of this encounter unscathed. Her heart thundered in her chest, but maybe she could attempt to stall them—if only to get her breath back and become accustomed to the pain in her back. She should have taken something more for the blasted pain.

A man with pointed, black ears sneered at her. He swung his sword round and round in his hand. Tempest hid her amusement at his cheap parlor trick. Any swordsman worth his salt knew that such a showy display was a useless endeavor. He clearly hadn't been trained well. All the better for her.

"We don't want your kind here. You should never have set foot in the village."

"And what kind is that?" Tempest asked, keeping an eye on all the men.

"Don't play dumb, wench. Everywhere you go, misery follows. We won't have you disrupting our homes with your mischief."

Tempest stiffened. Were they referring to the fact that she was an outsider or a Hound? There was no way they could have discovered the latter part of her identity. She ground the soles of her boots into the dirt, feeling for the best stance to keep her steady against the inevitable attack.

"I have no interest in disrupting your homes or families. I only seek information so I can better help my grandmother."

"Such pretty words from a lying little witch," a fellow

with a long face drawled, his shaggy black hair obscuring his eyes. "She was searching the forest with a fine-toothed comb. There's much more than meets the eye with this one. Her tracking skills are phenomenal for someone without a snout."

The fingers of her left hand trembled, and she curled her hand into a fist as she took a closer look at the black-haired fellow. He grinned, flashing square teeth. It was an equine smile. A horsey smile. *Oh no.* "You?"

His smile grew. "Yes. Those apples were quite a treat." He smacked his lips together. "But not as delicious as the long ride I got to enjoy between your supple thighs."

All around her, the shifters sniggered.

"I think I liked you better as a horse," she muttered. "At least I didn't have to listen to your donkey-like braying." Ass.

His horsey smile dropped. "Let's be rid of her."

"Patience," a cat-eared shifter purred, his inhuman pupils reflecting the light from the lantern he was holding like mirrors. "You see, dearest, we don't appreciate it when outsider come poking around where they don't belong. If you were any other maid, you would have run back to Dotae with your tail between your legs when you first noticed us tracking you, but no." He tsked. "So willful."

You're about to see how willful I can be if you don't get out of my way.

"I can promise you that I plan to leave your woods straight away, if you'd step aside," she said calmly, her sweat-slicked palm heating the pommel of her sword.

Why weren't they attacking? They'd already hunted her down. Were they only here for a bit of sport? Her lip curled at the thought. They wouldn't gain any pleasure at her expense.

The man with cat ears smirked. "Not quite yet, my pet; while you're not welcome in these parts, you've traipsed around our fine home without paying the toll."

"The toll?" she repeated and shrugged a shoulder slightly, lowering her bow until it was an inch away from slipping down into her hand. If she could just get a couple arrows lodged in one or two of the shifters then she might be able to get away. She looked behind her at the other two men, searching for a weakness in their ranks. Damnation. There wasn't one.

"Our fine lord takes the care of his forests quite seriously."

"You mean King Destin?"

The wolf-eared shifter took a step toward her. "Don't you dare speak his name here!" he snarled. "Or I'll tear your tongue from your blasphemous mouth."

"If you keep threatening me, I will have no choice but to use force against you," Tempest replied, her voice hard. "I'll pay your toll and be on my way. How much?"

"It's not that simple," the cat shifter remarked. "You failed to pay the toll upon entering into our fine woods so you've technically broken the law. Disobedience begets consequences."

The men laughed again, a horrible mocking sound.

She snorted, unable to help herself. "And whose law

have I broken?"

His smile turned completely diabolical. "The Jester's."

Bloody hell. Terror filled Tempest as she fully realized whose company she was in. These were not some run-of-the-mill brigands, but the Jester's mercenaries—men without consciences, for they were murderers, thieves, and dealers of everything nasty.

Steel against steel hissed behind her, and only years of training saved Tempest. She ducked to the left, the wolf shifter's sword biting into the tree trunk instead of taking her head. The world turned silent as she dropped her sword and slid her bow down to her hand, grabbed for an arrow and aimed it at the wolf-eared shifter. The arrow whistled through the air and lodged in the man's thigh. He yowled in pain.

The horse-faced fellow threw an axe at Tempest in response, but she darted away in time for it to become embedded in a tree trunk instead of her skull.

She drew another arrow and fired, before snatching her sword from the ground and fleeing through the trees with the shifters hot on her heels.

The cat man's delighted laughter floated through the trees. "Don't let her get away!"

Branches tore at her clothes and stones tried to trip her, but she didn't slow. Tempest was fast, but her legs were short. If she didn't get to safety, sooner or later they would catch up to her. She pulled another arrow from her quiver and spared a glance over her shoulder to let loose another arrow at one of her assailants. She cursed as her shot went wide and disappeared in the darkness.

"Come here, my pet," a voice crooned as footsteps approached from her left. "The longer you run, the worse it will be."

Her jaw clenched and sweat dripped down her back as branches broke to her right. They were circling her again.

Don't let them get ahead of you. You can do this. Push hard.

Tempest focused on her breathing as she fought the searing pain in her stomach and the iron grip of her lungs from sprinting so hard.

Use the pain. Madrid's voice echoed in her mind. *Fight.*

Tempest caught movement to her left and managed to parry an attack in time. A man with huge eyes and snowy hair—an owl shifter, no doubt—slashed at her with a thin, wicked-looking rapier that could easily carve through her skin like butter. She grunted as the man's blade sliced open her left forearm. *Damn it, that hurt.*

She batted the blade away and took advantage of the heavier build of her own sword and slammed the flat side against his hand. He screamed and dropped his weapon, clutching his shattered hand to his breast. Tempest kicked him squarely in the chest, satisfied when he tripped backward over a fallen log and crashed to the ground.

Though her body protested, Tempest wasted no time in sprinting away before any of the other shifters attacked, her legs and arms burning from exertion. The stream rushed up to meet her, and she jumped, not quite managing to leap over the breadth of the shallow creek.

Freezing water stung her ankles, and her feet scrambled for purchase among the slippery pebbles below the surface. Her legs came out from under her, and, in a blind panic, she grabbed for a nearby branch.

Pain shot down her left arm as she righted herself and yanked at her sodden skirt that had come loose in the chase. Tempest cut the useless piece of fabric from her body and slogged toward the other side.

"She crossed the stream!" a man yelled behind her.

Tempest quickened her stride, not knowing where the strength came from, and crashed straight into a clearing bathed in moonlight, her boots squelching with each step. Her eyes darted wildly around—which way did she go? She inhaled a desperate, shallow breath and crept toward an area where the trees were the thickest. She grinned when the heavy scent of pine and animal feces lingered in the air. With any luck, her scent would be masked and she could swing into the boughs and hide high above the shifters' heads.

Frantically, she searched the trees for the perfect escape route, keeping her footfalls as quiet as possible. She continued straight on through the forest for close to a minute with no indication that anybody was following her. Goosebumps erupted on her arms at the continued silence. It was like the forest was holding its breath. Just because she didn't hear the shifters, it didn't mean they weren't there. Tempest was sure they were hot on her heels so she kept up her unforgiving pace while she looked for a promising tree to climb.

Tempest almost cried in relief when she spotted a suitable tree. She wanted to collapse against its trunk but she knew she had to sheath her sword and climb before she could rest. The smooth bark was slick against her hands as she heaved herself upward. Tears sprung to her eyes as she tried to pull, but her injured arm refused to hold any weight. Tempest crashed to the forest floor in a heap, and a jagged stone pierced through her cloak, digging into her spine.

"Bastard!" Tempest huffed, staring at the bark of the trunk. Not one bloody foothold. Unbelievable.

She barely had the strength to roll onto her front and stagger to her knees when she heard a branch crack behind her. Much too close.

Run. Just run, Tempest. You'll find another tree. If you stay here, you're dead.

She stumbled through the shrubbery and continued the search for another tree. Even if they knew she was in a tree, they wouldn't be able to get her. She'd have the high ground, and if they had any arrows, surely they would have already shot her in the back.

This is what you wanted.

Tempest scowled at the thought. She'd never wanted to be hunted through the woods in the middle of the night by barbarians.

Your uncles warned you to be careful.

She winced. They'd warned her, and she'd dismissed them. Tempest never planned to get up to any mischief, and they'd trained her well. She was a Hound, after all. But she wasn't prepared for this. She had no clue what she was doing. She spied another clearing, smaller than the first one, and cut toward it.

With leaden feet and a throbbing heart, she forced her way onward, barely able to see through the tangle of coal-dyed hair obscuring her eyes and the blackness of the night air around her. Tempest spied the flash of a sword to her right, and then to her left, so she pushed herself even harder to break through to the clearing and—

The very ground beneath Tempest's feet caved in, and she fell, fell, fell into darkness.

A scream caught in her throat as the darkness rushed up to meet her.

Fox was right when he said she was wet behind the ears. She'd panicked and this was her own fault. She was just a city girl.

I know nothing at all, was her last thought before she blacked out.

Chapter Fourteen

Pyre

The city girl was spunky, he'd give her that much.

Pyre had been following Juniper's—which he doubted was her real name—escape from the pursuing shifters from the very beginning. Call it a hunch, but no one had a name that earthy who wasn't Talagan. Then there was the matter of her creamy skin—it screamed human.

After disappearing across the rooftops of the village, he'd dropped down to hide behind one of the stone houses, witnessing with his keen night vision the moment the girl was corralled into the woods by the men. *His* own men. It interested him that she'd gotten past them in the first place. Chesh, Pyre's lead man—a wily cat shifter—rarely had the rug pulled out from beneath him. Pyre grinned at the thought of the girl pulling one over on his old friend. It probably wounded his pride. The bastard deserved it. Chesh was too smug as it was.

Pyre crept through the trees as the girl led his men on a merry chase. It wouldn't be long before they cornered her. She wasn't at full strength if he had to hazard a guess. Pyre had noted a weakness to her arm and back while they'd been fighting; well she'd been fighting, he'd been playing. It was rare that he got to spar with a woman. It was impressive that she'd managed to keep up with him. There had been something sensual about it that had got his blood racing.

He ghosted through the brush with a smile as he thought about her brash touch. No one touched him these day without his say so. The darkness inside him had purred in contentment when her scent of pine and lemon had teased his nose. Even now, his mouth watered at the memory. But delicious scent or not, where had she come by her skills? Talagans taught their women to fight from necessity, but those from Heimserya discouraged the females from such endeavors. *Idiots.* Women were the most dangerous creatures to walk the world.

And his little city girl had a bit of fire.

The notion should have unsettled him. Instead, it excited him. The mysterious city girl—whose name was most definitely *not* Juniper—was strong, smart, and attractive.

Dangerous.

She might have been playing the dutiful granddaughter, but he'd eat his own hat if there was an actual grandmother. No, the city girl was after something—

information about the plague. It was possible she was a spy—King Destin had been changing up his tactics recently. Pyre's lip curled at the thought of the king. He didn't mind their games, but the stakes had changed when hundreds of people had begun to die.

"How do you fit into all this, Juniper?" he whispered to himself.

Chesh's laughter cut through the night as Pyre crept closer to where his men had caught the girl. He hid himself behind a tree and watched as the little, maudlin play progressed. The girl's pale face was red as she caught her breath. He'd expected screaming, maybe even a little begging, but she did neither. Her calculating gaze tracked each of the men with precision.

How stimulating. And the plot thickens.

Juniper was most definitely not who she said she was. She blew a wayward dull onyx strand of hair from her face and changed her stance.

Intrigued, Pyre leaned closer as Brine—his wolf—pulled out his sword. The girl mysteriously produced a bow and shot an arrow at Brine, dodged an axe, and fled into the forest within a matter of seconds. He rubbed his chin and listened while the shifters chased after her, disappearing into the darkness.

Chesh glanced his way. "Are you coming?"

"How is it you always know where I am even though no one else can?" Pyre asked.

His friend flashed a wicked smile. "I can smell the girl on you. Have a little fun, did we?"

"Not in the way you think."

The cat shifter tipped an imaginary hat. "Those fools will lose her without me. You hunting tonight?"

Pyre grinned. "Let's just say I'll be observing."

"Suit yourself."

Chesh loped off into the trees, and Pyre took a moment to really listen. The girl was pulling ahead of them. Curious, he tracked her, keeping to the darkest parts of the shadows and inhaling her faint scent: lemon and pine with a touch of coal. That alone was telling. She'd dyed her hair. What was she hiding, or more importantly, who was she hiding from?

He frowned and paused when he caught a whiff of something else. Blood. Pyre didn't mind blood, but he did take offense to damaging perfectly good property. And that's what the city girl was.

She'd traipsed into the Jester's lands without consent and that didn't go unpunished.

Pyre stalked through the woods, following the stench of fear and blood. Too much blood. If it were a mere flesh wound, there would have been less. He picked up his pace in order to get to the girl. If only she'd accepted his help when he'd offered it. Her evening could have gone quite differently.

So headstrong.

Whoever the girl was, whomever she worked for clearly had sent her out too early. She might have had training, but she was a new recruit and had inexperience in gathering information. He smiled at the thought of luring her to his side. There wasn't anything he enjoyed more than turning a spy into a double agent. Doing so was one of the most satisfying things in his life.

She won't be easy.

He didn't like easy. Tough nuts were his specialty. It might take a little time, but she'd warm to him. They all did in the end.

Pyre shook his head as he reached the large clearing ahead of the girl and found a good spot to observe. It was what he liked best. To watch. To study. He hid in the opposite end of the clearing as the girl broke through the trees. Her hair was a mess around her pale, terrified face, likely obscuring her vision and tangling with the arrows in her quiver. Her eyes darted around, passing over him and taking in her surroundings before she swerved to her right, exiting the clearing through the densest part of the forest.

Clever. I'd have done the same.

But his men were not far behind her—Brine was in the lead and Chesh brought up the rear. The group grinned at each other and split up. *Divide and conquer.* Chesh twitched an ear in Pyre's direction, clicked his heels together, and slunk off into the forest in a slightly different direction.

Pyre rolled his eyes at Chesh's antics and followed his men. His gaze narrowed on the surrounding area as he realized what their plan was. They were going to trap her. In the pit.

Damn.

Pyre didn't spare another moment before rushing off in pursuit of the girl, the wind whistling and roaring past his alert fox ears as he noted every minute noise in the woodland. Capturing her had been the idea, but the pit... The pit meant death.

He growled and his eyes narrowed on the small clearing ahead when an agonized cry pierced the air.

"Bloody hell," he snarled as he burst through the tree-line and angrily prowled to the edge of the pit. Pyre peered at her crumpled figure in its deep, dark depths. His lips thinned as he stared at her chest for any signs of life. One second. Two. Three.

She took a breath.

Not dead. But the way her arm lies at an odd angle probably will make her wish she was.

Chesh materialized by his side and blankly gazed into the pit. "There's quite a bit of blood. Do we leave her?"

Should they leave her? It would be the simplest thing to do. No one would question a disappearance in the woods. But then again... It would be a shame to waste all of her talent.

Pyre fished through his bag obscured by his cloak for a length of rope, taking a step toward the pit.

"Fox, don't."

He turned to Brine, whose ears were twitching just as much as his own were. Blood ran down Brine's leg from where the girl had shot him, dripping onto the ground. "She's trouble, and you know it. We don't need her kind."

"I don't know anything because you lot ran my source

of information into a death pit," he said softly.

Brine paled and busied himself with removing the arrow embedded in his flesh.

Chesh crossed his arms and tipped his chin toward the girl. "What do you want us to do? We don't usually make exceptions."

"We usually don't get women who can outrun shifters, sneak through their woods, and wound some of their best."

"Touché," Chesh murmured. "I can say for myself that I'm intrigued." He flashed Pyre a smile. "Plus, you know how I love all that creamy skin." He smacked his lips. "So delicious."

"I should let her die just to spare her your attentions," Pyre muttered, but he could not help but notice her legs indecently encased in leather. Delicious, she was.

Chesh pouted. "You wouldn't be so cruel."

Pyre ignored his commander and glanced at Brine and then back to the pit again. She'd hurt one of his own and had trespassed. Those were things he'd couldn't let go. She had a lot to answer for, and he wanted to slowly unravel her, bit by bit.

"Bloody hell," Pyre cursed, dropping down into the pit and checking her pulse. It was faint and fluttering, like a bird's.

Pyre ran his finger along her willowy neck. He would hardly have to do anything at all to kill her. Instead, he shifted the girl into his arms as gently as he could, taking a moment to watch her impassive, unconscious face highlighted by the pale moonlight above them. She had fine features by human standards, though they were a little plain for his taste. He gazed at her closed lids. It was her stormy eyes that had arrested him earlier—so serious and yet, they held myriads of secrets.

"Fox, it's a mistake to save her," Brine insisted, peering over the edge of the pit.

"Noted," he replied. "If she causes problems, I'll sell her. No one believes anything a slave says."

Warm, thick blood seeped through his jacket and trickled down his leg. That was not a good sign. She needed the attention of a healer.

"She'll be useful, mark my words." He held the girl above his head, and Chesh gingerly took her from his arms.

"Winter's bite. Where is all the blood coming from?"

Pyre hauled himself from the pit and brushed the dirt from his jacket as he stepped next to Chesh. He scowled at the blood the girl had left behind. She'd ruined his favorite jacket. He frowned at her and leaned closer to her ear.

"I don't know if you can hear me, but you owe me your life *and* a new jacket. Don't be difficult when you wake. I haven't the time for it, and I don't relish selling you. Understand?"

"She can't hear you," Chesh said wryly, adjusting the girl in his arms.

"Life works in mysterious ways." He glanced at Brine. "Where are the others?"

"In the trees."

"Send them back on patrol. I want to know if there are any other irregularities."

Brine nodded and limped from the meadow.

"Let's go," Pyre said.

"It's about time. I'm hungry," Chesh complained.

Chapter Fifteen

Tempest

Tempest had been taught that death would be peaceful, a void of unconsciousness and nothingness.

She'd been lied to.

Heat licked at her skin as awareness filtered in. Shivers wracked Tempest's body, and dots flashed across her vision when she tried to open her eyes, the bright light assaulting her. A familiar crackling reached her ears, and Tempest jackknifed upright. She screamed as agony crashed over her, one miserable wave after another. It was so much worse, by far, than the pain the lion had inflicted.

What had she done to deserve such torment?

She shuddered as tears gushed down her face in a torrent. Tremors worked through her, and sweat dripped down her face and neck as the temperature increased.

Movement flickered to the left, catching her attention.

What the bloody hell was that and why won't the pain stop?

Blurrily, she peered through her tears to locate the source. Terror seized her, and her blood froze in her veins despite the heat pressing down on her. Flames taller than the castle writhed around her, their wispy edges disappearing into a void of inky darkness.

A fire giant crept forward. Black eyes and teeth appeared, forming a face. Bile burned the back of Tempest's throat, and she tried to scramble backward. The giant lashed out and fire curled around her right arm. Her mouth bobbed, and a scream caught in the back of her throat at the torture. It was too much. Too damn much.

Tempest sucked in a deep breath and *screamed*, the anguish too much.

"Help me," she begged, her voice going hoarse as more fire giants crept closer, searing her skin. "Please!" she yelled as blisters ran up her arms. "Someone."

No one came.

Fiery heat ran up her legs, and she sobbed when, no matter how much she ran, the flames just consumed more of her body. "Why?" What had she done to deserve such treatment? Such torture? Where was the blessed nothingness she was promised?

As if some deity had heard her prayer, cool fingers brushed across her forehead. Tempest moaned and desperately sought out the relief, trying to press farther into the loving caress.

"Please make it stop," she pleaded.

The cool touch ran down her arm, and the fire giant retreated with a hiss. For a moment, some of the pain abated.

"Thank you," she croaked gratefully.

But it was too good to be true.

The touch tightened and then crushed her arm in its grip. Tempest choked on her pain, and the flames seemed to lean closer in anticipation as the world blinked out into darkness.

Chapter Sixteen

Tempest

Tempest wanted to weep bitterly.

Could she not just go in peace?

Agony radiated up and down her arms and legs, and liquid heat rolled down her cheeks. Where was the deceiving touch? She'd take that over the continuous torture. Her bottom lip trembled as she debated opening her eyes to see what nightmare Death had waiting for her.

Being blind is being vulnerable.

She cracked open her crusty, swollen lids and squinted at the wavering room around her. Nothing made sense. Ghoulish strangers hovered around the hot room, their reflective eyes locked on her. Tempest whimpered and attempted to lift her left hand but her fingers wouldn't move.

"... can't believe she's woken up in this condition," a

voice that was equally familiar and strange muttered.

Tempest tried to look through her hazy, unfocused eyes. A creature stepped forward, his skin as dark as pitch black night. She marveled at the beauty of him as he approached, his form towering above. For such a large being, he moved with a grace she longed to possess. He bent to pick something off the floor, giving her an unobstructed view behind him. The shifter from her dreams stood behind him, his expression bland.

My mother's murderer.

A snarl curled her lip, and she lunged toward him, but pain crippled her. Tempest let out a wordless cry, and spit dribbled down her chin, her gaze locked on the murderer staring her down.

"I'll kill you," she hissed, her voice as dark and twisted as the Jester's soul. "I'll kill you!"

"That's enough of the drama for now." The person who had previously spoken clucked his tongue in disapproval from her left side. "I didn't drag you out of the pit for you to die right now, city girl. How can you possibly escape with all your injuries? Just lie down. This next bit is *really* going to hurt."

She jerked to the left and snapped her teeth at the creature who had crept up on her.

The man's face came into focus just before his hands touched her right arm and yanked her.

Fox, she thought uselessly, managing to hold eye contact with his startlingly gold irises for but a moment, before passing out.

Tempest woke slowly. Her tongue stuck to the roof of her mouth, and everything ached. She licked her dry lips and opened her eyes despite her throbbing head. It felt like she'd been on a drinking binge for months.

She blinked sluggishly as the room slowly came into focus. Rustic lanterns hung around the small stone room of a house she didn't recognize and scattered soft light in the darkness. No windows. Was she in a cell? What time of day was it? Where was she?

Her breathing accelerated as a thread of panic wound itself around her chest.

Calm down. You're not in chains. Use your mind. Think your way through this.

Tempest slowly inhaled and exhaled to regulate her heart rate. A modicum of calmness settled over her. While the pain was awful, it wasn't the agony she'd experienced before. She twitched her fingers on her left side, and a twinge of pain ran across her skin. Tempest had dealt with pain like that only once before.

I must have dislocated it when I fell into the pit. But who put it back into place?

Onyx skin and gilded eyes floated to the forefront of her hazy memory.

Shifters. *Fox.*

"Finally awake?" a deep, sinful voice whispered.

She jerked, wincing at the whoosh of breath that rattled her ribcage, and schooled her expression as Fox appeared in the darkened doorway followed by a mob of other creatures. Tempest struggled to sit upright, but it was useless; her body was too broken.

"Don't move," he murmured without looking at her.

Though Fox's hat was nowhere to be seen, his face was still obscured by shadows, punctuated only by the occasional flicker of torchlight across his features. But it was enough for Tempest to notice that he was beginning to shift more toward his kitsune form—his cheekbones had grown even sharper than before, and there was a slant to his eyes that was distinctly inhuman. When Tempest glanced at his hands, she saw Fox's nails had grown longer and thicker.

Fear skittered up her spine.

Claws. He had bloody claws. He could puncture her skin in a half second and watch her bleed to death if he wanted to. So why had he kept her alive? She kept her face carefully blank as she realized there would be only one reason why he would want her alive.

They had discovered her identity.

Numbness seeped through her fingers at the realization of what came next. Torture. Her left cheek twitched while she fought to keep her emotions intact. Her gaze ran over the small group of shifters, some of whom had already half-shifted. Only the most powerful of the Talagans could partially shift. A show of power.

She pressed her lips together as she took stock of the danger creeping into her room. Winter's bite. Eight partial shifters. So much power.

Fox sauntered closer to her bed and ran a claw over the

blanket covering her left foot. He flashed a fang in a mocking smile as she jerked her foot away from his touch, her skin crawling. His smile deepened.

"Is my lady shy?" he crooned.

Tempest swallowed, cursing herself for falling into the damn pit in the first place. Her nightmare still lingered fresh in her mind, and, while she wouldn't go back to that fiery place for anything, she wished she was still sleeping. The situation seemed quite unstable—if the energy in the room was any indication. She needed to tread lightly if the looks on their snarling faces were anything to go by.

"Not at all, I—" she tried to reply, but the words caught in her parched, scratchy throat as if she had choked on them.

"Don't speak," Fox said in a dangerous undertone. Gone was all his previous easy-going arrogance—including even the vicious delight that had been plastered to his face when Tempest had fought with him.

She snapped her mouth shut and carefully kept her contempt at his commands hidden. Being completely under his control didn't warrant a smart mouth. If she wanted to make it out alive, she needed to be very careful in choosing her words. Everything she said or did had to be calculated.

The hulking man from before stalked to Tempest's side and shocked her by placing his massive palm over her forehead. His brows slanted together, and his deep red lips pursed.

"The infection may still take her yet." His baritone voice

was so deep it was like two rocks being rubbed together. "Her fever is high."

Mutely, Tempest watched the healer as he checked her pulse and then ran his hands down her left arm. The size of his paws made her arm look like a doll's. His palm alone could smother her. Even though her instincts screamed for Tempest to pull away, she held perfectly still, aware that he could tear her arm from her body.

She shot a scathing look in the kitsune's direction, hating that her life rested in his hands.

Fox watched impassively and leaned a shoulder against the wall next to the bed. His gaudy jacket and linen shirt were wrinkled, smudged with dirt, and covered with blood, and yet he still managed to look like an indolent prince. What a bastard. Pretty boys made her sick. How much time did he spend staring at the looking glass to achieve such a look? Probably more than she had in her entire life.

He arched a brow at her when he caught her appraisal, his chest puffing up. "Find something to your liking, luv?"

Tempest bit the side of her cheek to keep from retorting with a scathing remark.

His playful façade melted away. "So you're one of those." He leaned closer and inhaled. "You can hate me all you want but you won't ever be able to keep your emotions from me. Look your fill, luv. I'm not impartial to your kind."

Her kind.

For Dotae's sake, she was too tired for this. As it was,

171

her eyelids were drooping, and sweat pooled between her breasts. She shifted uncomfortably on the mattress and instinctively stiffened when the wolf shifter she'd shot in the leg stepped away from the silent group.

His luminescent eyes clashed with her eyes. His gaze narrowed when she didn't look away. The corner of her mouth twitched as she fought to stop herself from smirking. The man was clearly an alpha. Her direct eye contact was probably driving him crazy, but she wouldn't be the first to look away. Her body might be weak but not her mind or her will.

He bared his teeth, and a growl rumbled from his chest. The hair along her arms rose but she didn't look away.

"Don't be foolish, girlie," the healer chastised. "Drop your eyes."

Tempest ignored him as the Talagan wolf moved around the end of the bed and placed his hands on the mattress near her hips, his lips still pulled back from his teeth.

"You shot me," he snarled.

"You attacked me, and I'm sure you're healed already," she said softly, keeping eye contact. She should have poisoned the arrow tip.

He leaned farther into her space—his nose almost touching Tempest's—as the others in the room looked on in silence.

"Do you want to die?" he demanded.

"Death is inevitable, but honor is easily lost," she whispered, her fingers curling into fists to keep them from trembling. It would be so easy for him to tear out her throat.

He froze and then huffed, the sound one part amused, the other part irritated. "Just because you know the words of my people, it doesn't mean a damn thing."

"True."

With one last snarl, he pulled back, crossing his arms to glare down at her. "I don't like it," the wolf barked at the kitsune.

It? Well, that was rude.

"For a moment, I thought you were going to run away with her, Brine," Fox commented, blasé.

Brine—the Talagan wolf—eyed her in disgust. "Only to show her who her master is."

A flash of rage burned through her, but the pressing danger reeled her emotions back into check. No one was her master.

Another shifter stepped forward, and Tempest recognized him. His long face marked him as her former mount. Heat burned in her cheeks at the thought of riding another person for hours. He crossed his arms and lifted his chin, tossing his waist-length, thick, black hair.

"Let us kill her, Pyre," the equine Talagan demanded, stabbing a finger at Fox.

Tempest tucked her smile away at the bossy subordinate's use of the kitsune's real name. *Pyre.* She filed away the information and continued to listen.

The kitsune stripped his bloodstained jacket from his body and tossed the soiled garment into the corner. He meticulously rolled his bloodied sleeves up to his elbows, revealing swarthy, corded forearms covered in dried blood.

Her blood.

Nausea rolled through her belly. Tempest was going to be sick.

Pyre produced a dagger and flipped the blade in his hand with calm indifference. She knew the trick well; when she was nervous or afraid in front of the older Hounds she, too, had found objects to 'appropriately' fidget with. Ones that would make her nerves appear obsolete and, in turn, make Tempest look as if she was completely in control.

Had she mistaken the situation? Was Pyre not the one in command?

"She will be useful," Pyre told the shifters simply.

Pyre's eyes moved across the group, his sharp gaze touching on each and every one of them before turning his unearthly attention on Tempest. Her belly flipped, and she stared impassively back. No, she wasn't mistaken. Power clung to him like a second skin. She studied the loose laces of his shirt and pondered over Pyre. He wasn't old enough to be the Jester... but maybe a son or relative? Peering through her lashes, she scanned the Talagans. Many appeared to be older than the kitsune.

"Whoever you are, city girl, you'll bring us good luck. I know it."

She highly doubted that. If she had her way, they'd be the ones bringing her good luck as they led Tempest to the

Jester.

Rich feminine laughter teased the air from a petite, cloaked Talagan. "She's very good at keeping her expression bland, but I'll bet my blade she'll be a fun one to break."

Tempest stiffened. *Just try.*

The woman laughed again. "Be cautious, not everyone wants to kneel at your feet, Pyre."

Pyre leaned a hip against the bed and hooked a clawed finger underneath Tempest's chin. With gentle pressure, he tipped her head back so she met his darkly amused gold eyes. He cocked his head, and a smile touched his mouth fleetingly.

"You're not going to cause me trouble are you, luv?"

Wisely, she remained mute.

Pyre ran his thumb along her cracked bottom lip. "We are not killing her," he said softly, his tone laced with steel. "We will heal her wounds and let her stay with us, then she will pay us for our generosity."

His *or else* was implied.

Tempest fought not to shiver at the absolute silence of the room. Her heartbeat pounded in her ears as Pyre bent closer to nuzzle her right temple.

"I have a feeling she's exactly what we've been looking for," he hummed.

"Is such a risk worth it?" the horse man asked.

"*I* am the one who takes such risks," Pyre murmured, pulling back to study Tempest's face. "I would not expect any of you to put your life on the line to deal with her."

Inside, Tempest trembled, and her mask began to crack at his close scrutiny.

"If you know she's a liability, then why even risk helping her?" Brine asked.

Pyre straightened and released her face with a glint in his eye. "It is precisely *because* she's deadly that it makes helping her worth the risk." He smiled warmly at Tempest. "It's that kind of danger that intrigues me."

"Don't be a fool!" the equine Talagan burst out.

The temperature in the room dropped, and Tempest's eyes rounded as every person in the room froze.

Pyre picked up his dagger from the bed and brushed his sleeve off with his opposite hand. "Do I strike you as a fool?" His tone was soft but dangerous.

Goosebumps ran down Tempest's legs.

The blood drained from the horse man's face, but he held his ground, his square teeth grinding together. "This is all foolish. All for a bit of skirt."

Pyre laughed. "A bit of skirt, eh? Pick up your blade, Timo."

Timo plucked his blade from his waist and gripped it between his teeth, and then tied back his black hair. "As you command, my liege," he gritted out. His gaze flicked to the left for one second and then he attacked.

Another shifter moved from the group and attacked in tandem with Timo.

The kitsune only grinned in a bloodthirsty way that chilled her very soul. Tempest watched with begrudging awe as the kitsune shifter dodged both assailants by leaping high off the ground, and launched a snapping kick at Timo's jaw. Timo fell into his companion, snarling with rage, before turning to find Pyre standing there, ready and waiting to punch him in the face.

That Pyre chose not to use any weapons but his own body was inspiring. He avoided his opponents' knives with ease, as if he himself was made of water, then responded with kicks and punches and elbows and knees that almost always made contact with his targets. In a manner of minutes, both men were on the ground, breathing heavily, bleeding from various places and clutching their stomachs in pain from where Pyre had kicked an unforgiving metal-toed boot at them.

"Do not test me on this," Pyre talked down at them, his voice steady and unwavering as if he had not spent the last three minutes locked in a violent fight. And then, aimed at the entire crowd, he said, "Is there anyone else who doubts me?"

No one dared even breathe, Tempest included.

"I've not failed you before, nor will I fail you now."

Nobody said anything. Tempest watched the faces of the crowd carefully, looking for any sign that they would revolt against Pyre. He had the air of the bloody king, standing there addressing the people—*his* people—as if ruling had been in his blood from the day he was born. She could see why he thought he could get information out of her. But she wouldn't be swayed by him. Tempest had a job to do.

Eventually Brine muttered, "I hope you are right, Pyre.

For the love of us all, I hope you are right."

"Now, leave us," the kitsune commanded.

The crowd dispersed, leaving Tempest in the care of the silent, giant of a man still tending her arm... and Pyre.

The kitsune sheathed his unused blade and rubbed the back of his neck. "I think Timo bit me."

"You never stated any rules," the big healer at her side said gruffly. "How does your arm feel, girlie?"

"It hurts," she rasped.

"I don't doubt it." He smiled at her, his teeth blindingly white against his dark skin. "You look like you're about to pass out again which I wouldn't advise against as your healer. Try to get some sleep."

Tempest nodded. "Thank you."

The healer blinked slowly. "You're welcome."

She turned her attention to Pyre who stared at her, expressionless. Tempest did her level best to respond in kind.

A moment of silence passed. Two. Three.

Then Tempest said, very quietly, "Let me go. I do not wish to be here, and your people do not wish it, either. I just need to get to my grandmother."

"No," was all Pyre said in reply, though the smug, victorious smirk that crossed his face told Tempest everything she needed to know.

There was no way she was escaping the shifter's clutches tonight.

Chapter Seventeen

Tempest

"Mind how you hold her," a deep voice admonished.

Tempest snuggled into the blankets and sighed at the pleasant, spicy scent tickling her nose. The bed vibrated beneath her cheek, chuckling.

Her brows furrowed together. Beds didn't laugh. Tempest opened her eyes and stiffened. Everything was dark. Absolutely *everything.* She was bloody blind.

"You're not blind, and stop squirming or I'll drop you," Pyre muttered.

Tempest stiffened even more as she became hyperaware of the arms wrapped under her legs and around her shoulders. She blanched as she realized the shifters had tossed a sack over her face, and, to make matters worse, she'd been snuggling into a shifter's embrace.

"What are you doing?" she barked.

"Taking you somewhere safe."

Safe. What a joke. Everyone knew if a knave took you to his lair, you were surely going to die.

A door creaked, and frigid wind ruffled her blanket, cutting right to her bone. She shivered and began to wiggle even though it hurt. A lot.

"Put me down," she clipped out, her hot breath heating the sack and almost making her gag. When was the last time she brushed her teeth? Three days maybe?

"No," Pyre said.

"Where are you taking me?" A twinge ran up her side, and she gasped at the pain.

"Nowhere you could get away from, given your condition."

He had no clue what she was capable of.

Pyre's arms tightened. "You're going to hurt yourself, and Briggs will blame me. Settle down or I'll hog-tie you. See how that'll feel with all your blasted wounds."

Tempest silently cursed her inability to see his expression. But if she went by his tone and past actions, she didn't doubt he would follow through with his threat. She settled in his arms and glared at the dark, rough-hewn-like sack blocking her vision. Her fingers twitched as nerves jingled through her despite her exhaustion. Death would be easier than torture or prison.

"You seem like a man who speaks his mind and appreciates candor. If it's all the same to you, I'd rather die sooner than later if that's your plan," Tempest said baldly.

Silence met her statement, and then another person

sniggered.

Wicked hell. There was another shifter walking with them? She closed her eyes and strained to hear his footsteps. Nothing but the wind and the kitsune's soft breaths. Her lips thinned. The bloody shifters had every damn advantage.

"If I wanted you dead I would have left your pitiful carcass in the pit to rot." A pause. "Or to be torn apart by the beasts."

A tremor worked through Tempest. What kind of beast—man or shifter?

She hissed as some of her hair was caught when the brute yanked the sack from her head. Lifting a heavy hand, she rubbed at her smarting scalp and scowled at the shifter. Pyre looked down at her, the smirk on his face making her distinctly wish to punch him.

"Don't look at me. It was Briggs."

Her attention darted over the kitsune's shoulder to the hulking healer. How in the blazes did he move so quietly? Briggs—the healer—returned her regard, his brown eyes reflecting an animal glow in the darkness. Tempest kept her expression neutral no matter how much she wanted to cringe. It was unnerving how unnatural his gaze was.

"My apologies," he rumbled, his deep soft voice almost blending into the night. "Your breathing was uneven, and I worried for your health."

"Appreciated," she replied. *But you were the ones to put it on my head in the first place.* Tempest kept those thoughts to herself. It was clear she didn't have any friends here, but when she escaped, Briggs would likely be her out and she needed to be nice to him.

She allowed herself to relax in Pyre's arms and internally berated herself for being so weak. Even now, she was scarcely capable of staying conscious. And it wouldn't do her any good to waste strength on fighting an uphill battle.

Skeletal trees surrounded them creating an ominous feel, their outstretched branches looking like claws. Using her peripheral vision, Tempest searched for landmarks and anything unusual that would allow her to wind her way out of the trees and back to Dotae. But the forest was too dark to see much of anything, and the weak moonlight only revealed enough to ratchet up her nerves. The woods were unusually quiet. Not even a woodland creature dared to stir or call out.

Unconsciously, Tempest's fingers curled around the blanket swaddling her, and she pressed closer to the kitsune. She peered up at his shadowed face and then back to the trees, irked. His keen fox eyes could see through the blanket of night as easily as Tempest could see during the day. It was bloody unfair.

The man tightened his grip on her and let out a low chuckle. "What's wrong with you now?"

"Nothing." She wanted to kick herself at her surly tone. *You won't win over anyone acting like a shrew.*

"I've spent a great deal of time among women—"

Tempest snorted.

Pyre's strange, inhuman ears twitched in amusement

as he continued, "—so I know nothing is never really *nothing* with a woman."

"You're not afraid to show off your shifter abilities," Tempest eventually said, changing the subject.

Pyre shrugged his shoulders as best he could without jostling Tempest. "Well, why should I be?"

"Because it's dangerous. Why mark yourself as a... as a—" She faltered, not wanting to offend him.

"As a shapeshifter? As a slave? As a Talagan? What, city girl?"

His tone was soft, but it still made the hair at the nape of her neck stand on end. It spoke of violence and rage.

"I meant no offense," she offered and then chose not to speak more.

I'm way over my head. She hadn't even discovered the whereabouts of the Jester's court, and she was already failing horribly.

Pyre accepted Tempest's silence with a satisfied kind of smile she was coming to quickly associate with the arrogant man. It riled her, but it wasn't like she hadn't dealt with arrogant men her entire life. If he thought to bait her by being an arse, he'd have to try harder. Although, his prideful mien filled her with the desire to fire off a razor-sharp quip in response—the kind Maxim encouraged her to use growing up—to cut him down a size.

She bit her tongue and counted each of Pyre's footsteps to stay awake. Her lids drooped farther, and it seemed like a losing battle. Tempest lost track entirely of where she was, which wasn't surprising given that she had no idea how long she'd been passed out or where the hell they actually were. Surely, they hadn't traveled too far from where she'd been attacked.

Hopefully.

A few minutes later, the trees began to thin, and a few neglected cottages came into sight. They were constructed of rough stone walls and thatched roofs—Tempest could tell, even in the darkness, that they were made from stone that had to have been mined from a nearby river.

Thank Dotae for Dima's geology lessons. She'd never figured that the lessons would be useful for something as important as an escape from a band of shifters, but she was glad to be wrong. They must be near a river. There was only one large river near the Azul province. Once she had time to search for the river, it would only be a matter of following it south until it reached the coastline of Heimserya. It would be easy traveling from there on. Reaching the capital of Dotae would be simple.

Feeling altogether better about her secret escape plan, Tempest managed to gulp down her nerves as they passed the abandoned homes and pressed into the trees once again. Her breaths puffed in the air in little white bursts of steam, and the air seemed to cool even more. It wouldn't be long until winter raged war upon them.

A lone cottage appeared in the gloom, and Briggs stepped ahead of them to unlock the door of the isolated cottage—which was hidden from sight of the other houses by a small ring of hazel trees. Briggs stepped inside the dark building. Pyre followed and crossed the creaky wooden floor, gently placing Tempest upon a bed. The frigid air seeped through the blanket, and her nose twitched at the dust. Briggs moved around the room silently and lit a lantern, then another.

Tempest was glad for the light even if her eyes watered the tiniest bit. She hadn't enjoyed the fact that Pyre could see everything when she could not. But now that she *could* see...

"I'm a mess!" Tempest cried, looking down at herself to see that much of her clothing had been torn and ripped by branches, blades, and sharp rocks, and that what remained was soaked through with dark, crimson blood. She swayed where she sat, struggling to keep upright. Blood had never bothered her, but that much of her blood... Her stomach rolled and she became incredibly light-headed.

How am I alive? When a man lost that amount of blood in Aleks's infirmary it almost always meant death.

"Careful, city girl," Pyre said wryly. "Or you'll fall on your face."

The room wavered, and a hand settled on her shoulder to steady her and then tried to push her back onto the bed. Tempest shrugged the hand away, her lip curling. No one was putting her to bed.

Pyre laughed and leaned into her face. "Something tells me you don't have the strength to fight me right now, so let me help you. Had you only accepted my help earlier, you wouldn't have ended up this way in the first place."

His gaze wandered over her face. "I don't offer my help often, luv. So be grateful."

"As if I would trust you to actually help me," Tempest bit out testily, wincing at the pain in her back. "I would however be more inclined to believe you if you'd give me back my weapons."

His gaze sharpened. "They are very fine weapons. Where did you come by them?"

"My mother," she answered immediately. It was partly true at least. "I would like them back, please. It's all I have left of her."

"When we're through, you may have them back."

When? How long would that be?

Briggs bustled around the room and tossed bandages and other medical tools onto the bed. Tempest paused as she noticed a scalpel. Her hand itched to snatch it up off the mattress. Her gaze slid to the kitsune who watched her with an unreadable expression.

"Try it," he whispered softly. "You won't even be able to touch it before we're on you."

Tempest blinked slowly, hating that he'd read her so well and that he was right. She didn't stand a chance in her condition. But a small part of her wanted to try anyway. It didn't suit her to sit idly by and wait. Patience was not her virtue.

"I don't know what you mean."

Pyre shook his head, grinning. "You're a little liar."

So says the pot to the kettle. Her arm throbbed, and she rolled her left shoulder. Agony lanced up her back, shoulders, and neck. She hissed and cradled her injured arm against her chest. Tempest dropped her head and tried to work through the pain when she noticed fresh blood leaking from the bandage wrapped around her left thigh. They'd cut a section of her pants away but hadn't stripped her. The knot in her chest loosened a tiny bit. The world was a dangerous place for a vulnerable woman. At least her innocence had not been stolen.

Briggs tutted in disapproval as he nudged Pyre out of the way and frowned at Tempest's leg. "You're a bloody mess."

"Literally," she joked.

The healer snorted and fussed about Tempest, pulling away the shredded remains of her cloak. His full lips thinned as he eyed her leg. "Why did you go and do that?" he grumped. "You don't want to put stress on your wounds."

She hadn't done anything but sit on the mattress. Tempest swept her gaze over the room under the guise of curiosity, looking for anything that might be of use to escape. All in all, it was pretty bare. The cottage was an open plan style. Two small windows to her left graced either side of the door like beady eyes. The far wall hosted a fireplace and in the right back corner of the room sat a woodstove, accompanied by a dusty, ancient-looking table that butted up against the back wall. Shelves that had seen better days had item scattered about them in disarray and also hovered precariously above the table. A ladder rested two paces to her right, against the wall, and led to what

Tempest assumed was a loft.

She'd seen worse places. The place was old and sparse, a tad dirty, but it wasn't human filth. Tempest would deal with dirt over piss any day. Briggs bustled over to the hutch in the corner and yanked open the doors, its contents rattling.

"It's colder than a witch's tit in here. Start a fire, will you?" the healer grumbled.

Her eyebrows practically flew to her hairline as the kitsune obeyed without comment. That was a first. Since she'd met him, he'd had something to say about everything.

Briggs hummed as he discovered what he was hunting for and moved back to the bed. He gestured to Tempest's leg wound. "I need to cut your pants away."

"And?"

"Do you give me permission?"

"Yes," she said slowly. "I don't know why you need to ask. You've already helped me."

His serious, deep-brown eyes met hers. "I make it a habit to always ask. You weren't conscious before, and I left what I could of your clothing." Something bitter entered his expression. "Humans are fond of taking advantage of a shifter's help and then crying foul."

Did he mean…? "Are you insinuating that women—"

"I insinuate nothing. It is experience that has taught me to be cautious. Your kind enjoy the thrill of the exotic, but the consequences of such encounters usually yield imprisonment for males of my people."

She felt sick. "That's not right. Everyone should be accountable for their actions, Heimseryan or Talagan," Tempest said heatedly. "If both parties were willing, then there was no crime."

"You would think," Briggs said, his hands gentle on her thigh as he unwound the gauze. "But that is not the way of the world, my lady. Talagans get the brunt of blame."

"I am sorry for it." And she was. While she hated what the Jester and his minions stood for, and what had happened to her mother, Tempest had also experienced the love and friendship Juniper had offered over the years. "And I am no lady. Just a girl on her way to her grandmother's."

Briggs nodded, his white teeth flashing in a smile, a sharp contrast against his gorgeous midnight face. "As you wish."

Tempest glanced in the kitsune's direction. He knelt and blew on the small fire, the flames beginning to grow. His shirt pulled taut against his back, revealing a tapered waist and muscled shoulders. Heat stirred in her belly, causing her to frown. Growing up, she'd seen many nude male bodies. It was a fact of being raised by a plethora of men. Never had she responded to any of them. The worst part of it was that Pyre was the enemy. She didn't know how he was mixed up with the Jester, but, deep in her gut, she knew he'd lead her to him.

Pyre stood and was smirking once more as he turned to her. His eyes glinted with a knowing smugness that Tempest couldn't stand. Any attraction she felt disappeared like a puff of smoke. Cockiness wasn't attractive. It made her want to stab something or gag.

"You act as if you know everything, but you don't," Tempest commented, keeping sullenness from her tone. Just barely.

Pyre regarded her from beneath the strands of his wine-red hair that fell across his eyes. "I suppose I don't."

She hid her surprise but noticed that his lips curled into the smallest of smiles.

"For instance, I don't know your real name, for one. Since you know mine, I feel that it's only fair that you tell me yours."

"Life isn't fair," she retorted. Dima had said that so many times it was practically engraved in her mind.

"Very true. Tell me your name, anyway. I can't keep calling you *city girl*, can I?" He brushed the dirt off his hands. "Well, I *could,* but you furrow your brow every time you hear it. Do you hate being reminded that you're from our glorious capital that much?"

"That's because I *wasn't* born in Dotae," Tempest said. "I lived in the forest until I was five or so. I was taken to Dotae after my mother was—after she died."

Careful, Tempest. You almost told him she was murdered. Don't show him your entire hand. You know better than that. Just give him enough to trust you.

There was something about his easy-going mannerisms—about the way he was moving around her and helping Briggs clean her wounds without a word of complaint or judgment, all the while engaging her in conversation—that made her think that it wouldn't be so bad to trust him, which was saying something because logic told her otherwise.

Her lips twitched in a ghost of a smile. Oh, he was good. The kitsune was one of the best actors she'd met. With his skills, one could almost think of him as a courtier. In fact... his speech was very gentle for a laborer. She leaned against the headboard and watched the flames dance as the men silently worked on her leg. If she was to get anything out of the kitsune, it was high time she gave a little more of herself to him.

"Do you remember where exactly in the forest you lived, nameless girl?" Pyre asked, ignoring the fact that Tempest had clearly retreated into her own head for the past few moments.

Tempest thought about his question with a frown on her face. "I don't—I've never really thought about it, if I'm honest. Near the mountains. But the mountain range is pretty large, isn't it? So, in truth, I don't know. I was just a child."

"So, was your father not around, if you moved after your mother's death?" Pyre prodded, just as he plucked a small tub of sweet-smelling paste from the bed and handed it to Briggs who began applying it to Tempest's leg.

She growled and flinched away, but Pyre held her leg in place. "*Agh*—you could have warned me before putting Mimkia on me!"

Pyre chuckled roughly. "No amount of warning

prepares one for the stinging. Unfortunately, we don't have much Mimkia paste on hand, so I'll have to use it sparingly. The open wound on your leg takes priority, so you'll have to make do with a sling and good, old-fashioned time to heal your back and arm."

Briggs stood and gestured to her back. "May I check your back?"

"Yes, please."

Tempest gingerly sat up and allowed the healer to lift her shirt. Goosebumps ran across her arms as her back was exposed to the air. The healer brushed her hair over her shoulder and sucked in a sharp breath. She winced when his fingers pressed against her skin; she knew it must be dark with bruises.

"What in the blazes damaged you so?" the healer gasped. Her back twitched when Briggs ran a finger along one of her Trial wounds.

Pyre rose to his feet and eyed her back. He whistled. "That wasn't caused by the pit. What sort of company do you keep, luv?"

Tempest peered over her shoulder at the two shapeshifters. "Life is not always easy. It's dangerous."

"Oh, now you've piqued my curiosity, city girl. How did someone so fair acquire such scars?"

She rolled her eyes. "Flattery won't get you anywhere."

"I think you got that wrong. Flattery *will* get you everywhere."

"Let's agree to disagree."

"So diplomatic." The kitsune tsked. "But you still

haven't answered my question."

"And I'm still your captive. Seems pretty fair to me."

Calloused fingers lifted a piece of her dyed hair and she fought not to back away. The dye was the only thing keeping her safe. If they figured out she was a Hound, it would all be over for her.

"I have a feeling you're going to make my life interesting," Pyre murmured.

"Do you have any more wounds I should know about?" Briggs asked wryly.

"No, I think the rest are internal," Tempest replied, shaking her head as she did so, casually dislodging her greasy hair from the kitsune's grasp. "The wounds were sealed with Mimkia."

"Well, whoever healed you did a remarkable job."

"My uncle has had to patch me up many times. I was a hellion as a child."

"By the looks of it, you still are," the healer rumbled.

Tempest laughed softly, despite herself. "I'm not good with words. I tend to be blunt, and it gets me into trouble."

Pyre moved to the ladder and scampered up into the loft without another word. A series of thumps and rumbles sounded above Tempest's head.

"Is he always like this?"

"He doesn't hold still for long," Briggs muttered and pulled down her ruined shirt.

The kitsune swung down from the loft, landed on nimble feet, and threw a tunic at her. She caught the fabric on reflex and glanced from the man to the garment.

"Your own clothes are ruined," he said in explanation. "Put this on."

"I have spare clothing in my bag," she replied. "If you'll return my things, I'll not impose on your hospitality anymore." Hospitality was too generous a word, but it didn't hurt to play to his arrogance.

Pyre wagged a finger. "What a silver tongue you have, luv. I almost believed you that time. Do you like rabbit meat?" he asked, changing the subject.

"Rabbit? Why—"

"You haven't eaten in hours. You'll need to eat, if you're going to get your strength back."

Tempest frowned in suspicion. "Why should I trust any food you give me?"

"Are you serious right now?" he replied, rolling his eyes. "I spend all that time saving you—cleaning up your wounds and using my dwindling Mimkia supply to heal you—and now you think I'm going to *poison* you?"

Tempest shrugged her good shoulder. "It was a question that needed to be asked. A girl doesn't survive the city without being careful."

Pyre sighed heavily, though he was smiling. "True."

He whistled tunefully as he got to work in the small kitchen, peeling potatoes and chopping carrots and setting water over a fire to boil as Briggs cleaned up the mess they'd made and helped the kitsune cook. It was all very domestic, and it threw her off balance. Regardless, forty minutes later Tempest's stomach began growling insistently at the smell of the stew they were making, despite her misgivings about the food.

But when Pyre handed her a bowl of steaming stew, she passed it right back to him. "You first," she demanded.

"I made enough for all of us, you know. I have my own bowl."

"I don't care. Eat some of this one please."

Pyre's eyes glinted in the light from the cooking fire. For a moment Tempest thought he would refuse her request. "If I planned to poison you, this would be a poor job."

She didn't budge. "Death isn't the only thing a woman fears."

Dark understanding slithered through his eyes. Without argument, he lifted the bowl to his lips and took a long sip of the stew, his gaze never breaking away from Tempest's.

"Satisfied?" he asked her when he handed the bowl back.

Tempest dipped her chin in thanks. "Appreciated."

Pyre moved back to his own bowl and joined Briggs in devouring the stew. In a matter of minutes, both men groaned in satisfaction. The kitsune stood and winked at her as he sauntered to the door.

"Get some sleep," he tossed over his shoulder. "We'll talk more in the morning when you feel better."

"Or you could just leave me alone."

He grinned. "And how on earth could you be useful if I did that?"

For what felt like the hundredth time, Tempest held her tongue and said nothing in return. Silence would be her best friend and only ally in the days to come; she had to learn to keep quiet.

Something told her Pyre would not make it easy for her to do such a thing.

Chapter Eighteen

Tempest

It took hours for Tempest to fall asleep after Pyre had left her alone, despite how exhausted she was. She'd hoped her sleep would be blessedly dark and empty. Restorative. Perfunctory. But, of course, as if on cue, Tempest dreamt of the day her mother died.

Only this time, things were different.

The dream started out the way it always did, with Tempest collecting herbs and flowers in the meadow near her home, shivering slightly from the unseasonably cold spring weather. She smelled smoke upon the air, then spied it, and ran back through the forest toward the sound of her mother screaming.

That's when the dream deviated from its original path. She waited in front of the burning cottage for the shifter to appear, as usual, but this time it was not the memory-blurred man that Tempest remembered.

No, this time it was *Pyre*.

Tempest stared at him with disbelief apparent on her face as Pyre stalked closer to her—closer than the original shifter ever had—with recognition in his golden eyes.

He reached out and ran a clawed finger along her bottom lip. "Things are not what they seem," he murmured, uncharacteristically serious. She gasped and slapped his hand away. Tempest frowned and held her hand up—her very bloody adult *hand. That had never happened.*

Tremors rocked her body when she peered down as blood soaked through her ragged linen dress and dripped down her pale legs. "What's happening to me?" she whispered. Her gaze darted to the kitsune, but, before Tempest had a chance to say anything to Pyre, his form wavered and he disappeared into the wind like a ghost.

Heat from the fire flared and dried her eyes, but she couldn't blink or tear her eyes from the spot he had stood in. What did he mean, things were not what they seemed? Was he speaking of her dream? A sixth sense urged her to search the area.

She ran around to the back of the cottage, forcibly turning a deaf ear to the sounds of her mum's agonized cries as the pull in her chest became stronger. The windows in the rear of the house exploded, and she threw up her arms to protect her face. Little shards of glass rained down on her, searing her exposed skin in their descent.

Her stomach knotted with a sense of foreboding as she searched the area. What was she supposed to find? Her mother's cries reached a crescendo, and Tempest's chest cracked at the agonized sound. She choked back a sob and ran around the cottage as the flames crawled even higher into the sky.

A wall of heat slammed into Tempest when she gave in and crashed through the front door to find her mum. Maybe she could save her mum this time. The soles of her bare feet burned, but she didn't pay any attention to them as she ducked under the ceiling beam and sprinted to her mother's room.

"No!" she shouted when she saw the still form on the floor. Tempest fell to her knees as another beam crashed from the ceiling, the floor shaking from its weight. Her fingers blackened as she touched her mum's pale cheek. "Not again."

The foul odor of singed hair reached her nose, and heat scalded her back. From the corner of her eyes, she saw fire take shape and Pyre sauntered forward, his eyes an unholy red. He ran a fiery fingertip down her right arm and smiled, his face glowing and shifting within the flames. Pain seared her nerves, but she didn't get up, didn't fight it.

If this was what her mother felt in the end, she wanted to feel it too. Perhaps it would melt some of her guilt away for failing to save her only kin.

Pain crept up her legs, her back, then down her arm. Tears blurred her vision, and she pointed a finger toward the image of her mum. "Save her."

The kitsune cocked his head in question.

"Save her!" she screamed. "Somebody save her! Please."

Tempest crawled to her mother and curled over her mum's body to try and protect her. She glared at the vile being studying her with no reaction. "Save her!"

"Juniper," a deep voice crooned.

"Not me! Save her. Save—"

"Juniper, you must wake up!"

Tempest jerked awake, her heart pounding in her chest. Her dream trickled away like ink upon a wet canvas as an unfamiliar face leaned over hers, silhouetted by a dying fire. She slammed her left fist into the giant, rolled from the bed, and sank into a crouch, her body screaming while she stared dazedly at the two males studying her with interest. Where the hell was she?

The larger of the two rubbed his chin where she'd struck him and then held his hands up. "Juniper, you need to calm down. We're not here to hurt you."

Her muscles trembled and awareness began to sink in. "Briggs," she whispered as she studied the healer.

He smiled. "That's right. Come and get back in bed, lass. I'm sure you've hurt yourself all over again."

She turned her attention to Pyre who sat at the table, his elbows resting on the tabletop, one hand covering his mouth. Even though his expression was eerily blank, Tempest didn't like the way he was looking at her. Like he'd just discovered something he didn't want her to know.

Tempest stood and wrapped the blanket around her shoulders like a cape and padded back to the bed, a weak smile on her face as she met Briggs's sympathetic gaze.

"Nightmares are a blight on all people, I suppose," she said lightly and sat on the edge of the bed.

Briggs inspected her arm, his beautiful onyx skin a stark contrast to her own. Her stomach lurched as she remembered her own blackened hand resting on her mum's cheek.

"I'm going to throw up," she whispered and then promptly bent over and dry heaved.

Briggs placed a bowl on the floor and pulled her hair back from her face as she continued to retch, snot and tears dripping down her face. Tempest continued to shake once she stopped heaving, and a masculine hand entered her vision, holding a rag.

"Thanks," she muttered, wiping her mouth and nose, before lifting her head.

Pyre squatted next to the bed. "Are you quite done?"

"I think so."

He stood and exited the cottage without another word. Tempest stared after him and shivered as she remembered his glowing eyes from the dream.

"Time for bed, lass," Briggs urged.

She didn't think she could go back to sleep but she followed the healer's directions and curled into a ball, her gaze focusing on the moonlight streaming in from the windows as a thought more terrifying than her dream occurred to her. What had she revealed to the Talagans?

"Was I..." She cleared her throat. "Was I talking in my sleep?"

"You were screaming," Briggs said softly.

"Oh," she murmured. "Are you sure I didn't say something silly?"

"No, lass."

She didn't know if she believed him, but he didn't have a reason to lie. Although too terrified to sleep, her body succumbed to the blessed slumber of unconsciousness.

"Come now, it's almost noon. You need to eat, and I have to change the bandages on your leg."

Tempest groaned.

"I would groan too if I was in your condition. Looks like you could do with some Mimkia, too." The voice was feminine and lovely to listen to, though her tone brooked absolutely no argument.

Tempest opened her eyes and inspected the newcomer.

By her bed, scrutinizing her leg, was a woman who looked to be perhaps ten years older than Tempest herself. She was beautiful in an earthly sort of way—dark brown, wavy hair, hazel eyes, and sun-tanned skin. She wore a plain white dress beneath a green apron on her curvy frame.

Her attire screamed wholesome and nonthreatening. It made Tempest suspicious. Almost all the shifters of Pyre's clan she'd come in contact with so far displayed their strength by partially shifting. And while the woman was clearly a shifter, she didn't show a bit of her Talagan heritage. Was she merely meek, weak, or was it a choice to deceive Tempest? She had a feeling it was the latter because it was something she would do.

At least she looked somewhat normal. It made it easier for Tempest to look at the woman without wanting to recoil from the touch of her hand on her leg.

"Who're you?" Tempest asked sluggishly. Her throat was parched, the words barely coherent.

The woman smiled, picked up a wooden cup from the bedside table, and handed it to Tempest before speaking. "I'm Nyx," she said. "It's an honor to meet you. What is your name?"

Tempest smiled and cocked her head. "Don't you already know?"

The woman returned the smile, her eyes twinkling in mirth. "I'm not one to always believe the gossips. I'd like to hear it from you myself."

"I'm Juniper."

Nyx tsked. "That is your first lie, but it's no matter what I call you as long as we understand each other. You don't try to harm me or mine, and I'll do the same."

Tempest took a long draught of water. "That seems like a reasonable request."

"Good." The woman patted Tempest's hand. "I'm happy to hear that. Many in the world harbor prejudice for Talagans; I know many who have lost their lives just for being born a shapeshifter." Nyx frowned. "Even those who are sworn to protect the kingdom take part in the violence, the King's Hounds among them."

A Hound would never kill without a cause. She's lying. The ones who follow the laws of the Crown would never be in danger. If Nyx's comment holds any truth, it's because all the shifters around her are bad people.

"I hope you're hungry, Juniper," Briggs called from the front door.

Tempest perked up and turned her head to see Briggs carrying a heavy, steaming pot in both arms with a loaf of bread perched on top. He slammed the door shut with a foot, before lumbering over to the worn, wooden table situated by the kitchen area of the small cottage. He put down the pot with a thump, then regarded Tempest.

"Did you get some rest?" he asked.

"I did, thank you."

"She looks terrible, doesn't she?" a familiar voice drawled from above.

Tempest stilled and flicked her eyes to the loft just as Pyre swung down and landed without one sound. *Bastard.* She'd trained her whole life to gain skills that he had inherently.

He grinned at her. "You really are a fright, if you don't mind me saying. Didn't you sleep at all?"

She turned her gaze downward, not able to look at the kitsune without being reminded of her dream. "Not really," she grumbled while fingering a lock of dyed, greasy black hair. "It was difficult to sleep, all things considered."

"Perhaps we should give you something so you can get some proper rest," Nyx mused, holding onto Tempest's leg tightly while she applied a small dose of Mimkia paste from which Tempest attempted to recoil. Nyx frowned at her. "You won't get better if you don't sleep."

"And eat," Briggs added, pouring soup into a bowl and cutting a thick slice of bread. He jerked his chin at the kitsune and held the plated food out. "Feed the girl."

Pyre snatched the food from the healer and practically shoved a bowl of soup and a large slice of bread into Tempest's hands. She didn't look at him as he did so and sniffed the food for poisons. One could never be too careful.

Pyre clucked his tongue. "So much for gratitude. I could have just let you die, you know—"

"And I told you not to help me," Tempest bit out, all her irritation from the previous night returning in one fell swoop. Slowly, she lifted her head and glared at Pyre, letting loose some of her rage she'd kept hidden since being chased into the woods. "I never asked for any of this."

"There are those pretty eyes," he purred, his grin turning wolfish. "I hate when I'm ignored."

Tempest clenched her jaw and turned to gaze out the small window at the thick, green woods sheltering the cottage from the world. The kitsune had riled her just to get a reaction, and she'd fallen for his act.

Idiot.

"That's the best thing about friendship," he commented, dragging a wooden chair over from the table to Tempest's bedside. "Friends help without an ulterior motive."

He straddled the chair, using the backrest as a ledge for his forearms to lean upon. Tempest forced herself to hold his gaze, if only to prove that she wasn't afraid of a challenge. Pyre was no longer covered in dirt and blood. Instead, in a clean, white shirt, ebony leather breeches, and knee-high boots he looked every inch the gentlemanly scoundrel that he no doubt imagined he was.

"True friendship, maybe. You and I aren't friends. You kidnapped me."

"We can be friends," he offered.

She'd rather be friends with a lion than the tricky kitsune. He was dangerous. The real question was who was he really? What connections to the Jester did he have? Was he a drug runner? A thug? A weapons curator? Someone who marketed the Jester's flesh goods? Who was this enigmatic shifter in relation to Heimserya's greatest threat?

Pyre laughed once more. "Just what are you looking at with so sullen an expression on your lovely face?"

Nyx swatted him around the back of his head, causing Pyre's fox ears to twitch in response. "Our guest is not going to fall for your tricks, you devil."

Guest? "Am I free to go?"

"When you're healed," Nyx replied, redressing the bandages on Tempest's leg before helping herself to a bowl of soup. She leaned against the kitchen table, sighing contentedly as she breathed in the steam coming off the bowl. "We merely want to get to know you while you're still too incapacitated to go anywhere."

Pyre snorted at the comment.

Tempest scowled. "A prisoner by another name, then," she muttered, taking a reluctant sip of soup when her stomach began to growl. It was delicious and warmed her right down to the tips of her toes. She wondered if Pyre had made it just like he'd made the stew the night before.

"So, June," Pyre said after a few minutes of contented, soup-eating silence. "Can I call you June?"

"No—"

"June it is," he cut in, deliberately ignoring her. "Since you won't tell me your real name, why don't you tell us what you were doing in this specific part of the forest? I somehow doubt you were visiting your grandmother."

Tempest stared at her now-empty bowl. "Where is this particular part of the forest?"

Briggs laughed, the sound booming. "I like you, Juniper."

She lifted the bowl up and gave the big man a genuine smile. "Thank you for the soup. It was delicious." She turned her attention back to the kitsune. *Time to give him a bone to gnaw on.* "As I've said before, I was on my way to my grandmother's. She's very ill. In Dotae, we'd heard whispers of a deadly plague wiping out villages. But—" Tempest lowered her voice. "There have been rumors that it doesn't act like a plague. I thought to gather as much information as I could before I reached my kin. There's power in knowledge."

"True," Nyx agreed.

"Why not just ask me outright for the information?" Pyre prodded.

Tempest shifted like she was nervous, putting on a show. "It's not safe to ask questions. Questions have a way of haunting a person. Death sometimes follows closely behind."

"Ain't that the damn truth," Briggs muttered from his place at the table.

"And your reaction when you saw my ears?"

She'd been prepared for this. "I haven't spent much time outside the city, but there are stories of your kind. My life has not been easy, and it's everyone for themselves. Talagans are naturally stronger than those born in Heimserya, and I'm a woman. It was natural that I strike first, lest you take me unaware." Tempest shrugged. "And desperate people do desperate things."

"You're just full of wisdom, aren't you, luv?" Pyre drawled.

"Get smart or die."

"Incredible," Nyx breathed. She laughed, the sound lovely. Bell-like.

Tempest found herself smiling in amusement. Nyx just had that effect. If they weren't enemies, she was the kind of person Tempest could easily be friends with, had they met in Dotae.

But we didn't. This is different. This is practically war.

"You sure do have a way with words." Nyx smiled. "Pyre told me he liked you as soon as he met you. I think you'll change everything."

Tempest frowned. What the blazes did Nyx mean by that? She didn't know. But what Tempest *did* know was she needed her things back and Pyre had promised to return her bow. If she could get to her bag, unseen, she could apply some of her hidden Mimkia paste to her back and arm. Her forced stay among the shifters would be on *her* terms then.

Tempest hid her grin as both Pyre and Nyx questioned her. The duo was something else. Pyre was as blunt as a cudgel and Nyx as sweet as honey. They made the perfect combination for an interrogation. Too bad she knew what they were up to. She loved needling them with short, clipped responses that gave very little away or responding by asking more and more questions of her own, despite the fact neither of her captors gave her any leads whatsoever.

It was a battle of wills, and Tempest *loved* it.

After an hour, Pyre looked so bored that he might fall asleep in his chair. In contrast, Nyx bustled around the room, cleaning and helping Briggs with other small tasks. No one could accuse the woman of being lazy or idle.

Another reason to like her. It was easier to deal with hot-tempered men than with calm and calculating women.

"You're something else." Pyre sighed, running a hand through his wine-red hair to push it out of his face. Tempest wondered if his exasperation was all an act to make her feel more in control—like she was winning. It was entirely possible that he was trying to lull her into a false sense of security, hoping she'd slip up and tell them something.

Such games wouldn't work. She'd been trained by the Madrids. "Thank you, but I'm sure you have it all wrong." Men loved modesty.

The kitsune considered her with a gaze that was far too knowing. It was like he could see right through her mask to the truth inside her mind. "I'm sure I do not. False modesty doesn't suit you. Take the complement."

"Thank you."

"You're welcome," he murmured. "Nyx, I believe our guest needs a bath."

Tempest blinked slowly at the subject change but didn't argue. She could even smell herself.

"Briggs, come alone old friend. The lady is in need of water."

The healer jumped to his feet and followed Pyre out the cottage door. Tempest studied the door like it would reveal the secrets of the kitsune.

"Is he always like that?" Tempest asked Nyx, digging for more information.

"He's a man of mystery. Even I can't gage his moods."

Mystery meant liar—a trickster, a deceiver. Those closest to him couldn't figure him out.

Just what are you hiding, Pyre?

Chapter Nineteen

Tempest

Tempest sighed as she slipped into the bathtub, the hot water stinging and yet soothing her body's aches. "Merde, that feels good," she groaned.

Nyx chuckled and bustled around the metal trough to stoke the fire, her skirts rustling in the silence. "A bath is good for the soul."

The Hounds didn't always believe so. Even though Tempest made it a practice to stay clean, not all the men she lived with saw the appeal, but that was her gain. It meant she always got the first bath when the water was cleanest and warmest. No one ever had to drag her to bathe or dunk her. She smiled softly at the memory and tipped her head back, her hair falling over the rim of the tub as she sank deeper into the water, her eyelids half closed.

The shifter woman moved to the table and retrieved a bar of soap and a bottle of golden oil. She held them out to Tempest. "I can help you, if you'd like?"

Tempest shook her head. While she wasn't ashamed of her body or too worried about modesty, she still liked to care for herself. Helping another person wash was a personal experience, something shared among friends, and Tempest would not give into the temptation of making a friend out of Nyx. There was too much at stake.

"No, thank you," she murmured, taking the soap and oil from the woman's long, graceful fingers. She took a cautionary sniff of the soap and unstopped the bottle—cloves and something a little softer like cardamom, nothing that dangerous there.

With a flick of her wrist, she poured a few drops of the aromatic oil into the water and set the bottle beside the tub on the scuffed wooden floor. She lathered soap between her palms and absentmindedly gazed at the fire as she began to rid her body of the filth from the last few days.

She had another thing to add to her list of suspicious observations: the soap.

Most people only owned lye soap. Scented soap was altogether too expensive, but to be infused with cardamom... it was almost worth as much as Mimkia. Cardamom only grew in the Hinterlands—a southern enemy kingdom of Heimserya—the only way to acquire cardamom was through piracy or the black market.

Tempest lowered her lashes and spied on Nyx as she

hummed a little tune by the table. Her captors weren't what they seemed. Either they truly did think she was a peasant girl, so she'd not know the scent, or they were testing her. If it hadn't been for Aleks's infirmary tinctures, she'd never have been able to place the scent.

"The soap smells divine," she said while scrubbing her legs, careful to avoid the healing wounds. "I don't ever recall washing in such luxury. Where did you find such a treasure?"

Nyx plopped down in a chair, her hands busy stripping thyme sprigs and tossing them into a shallow wooden bowl. "A friend of mine made it."

"I would love to have such friends," Tempest joked. "Did they also distil the oil? I swear I've never smelled something so heavenly."

"It works out well. I distil the scents, and she creates the soaps, oils, and perfumes," Nyx commented.

Interesting.

Tempest looked at the woman in a new light. If she had the training and distilling capabilities, surely she could have created a poison to wipe out entire villages. A coincidence? Most likely not.

"That must be lucrative," she commented, setting the wet soap on the floor next to the oil.

"It has its uses."

Like killing people? Funding a rebellion? Contributing to the Jester's crimes?

"Are you sure you don't need help washing your hair? I know your arm is still bothering you." Nyx smiled in sympathy. "I dislocated my shoulder when I was a young girl. My mum had to braid my hair for weeks afterward."

Tempest mulled it over for a moment and then nodded. She didn't want to become friends with the woman, but it was possible she might glean something from the shifter. Tempest needed proof and soap was hardly evidence of a crime. And, on the practical side, her hair was absolutely filthy, and the dye wouldn't fade for another week.

The woman abandoned her herbs and dragged her stool behind Tempest. "Wet your hair please."

Closing her eyes, Tempest sank beneath the water and emerged, the water in the tub sloshing about. From the corner of her eyes, she observed as Nyx poured a dollop of oil into her palm and then plucked the soap from the floor. A sigh escaped her as the shifter sank her fingers into Tempest's wet hair and began to massage her scalp.

"How did you dislocate your shoulder?" Tempest asked, trying to keep her wits about her, even though her body wanted to dissolve into a puddle of contented goo.

"My mum worked on a farm in Tala and so did I as a girl. I was very sick, and the crop of peas were ready to be harvested. I remember shivering so hard I bit my lip. My mother stopped to hold me just for a moment."

Tempest squeezed her eyes shut, knowing what happened next. The farms in Tala were brutal. No one deserved to be treated the way the servants and slaves were there.

"A lord spotted my mum," Nyx continued, her fingers still working through Tempest's hair. "His Hound tore me from my mother's arms before I even knew what was happening. My mum tried to hold onto me, and the vicious man yanked so hard all I remember is the blinding pain." She inhaled deeply. "It was a miracle I woke up after the beating. But my mum wasn't so lucky. The clan that took me in said my mother never stopped fighting and scarred the Hound with her spade before he killed her in cold blood."

Tempest clutched her knees which poked up from the water and bowed her head. As much as she hated the shifter who killed her mum and those who were actively trying to destroy the kingdom, she didn't hate the Talagans as a whole.

"I'm so sorry," she whispered genuinely. "No one deserves to lose a parent so young. Do you hate the man who murdered your mum?"

"For many years."

"And now?"

"Now, I know that appearances can be deceiving. Even those who have freedom might be as much of a slave as I was. The real problem is accepting it and not trying to make a change." Nyx pulled her hands away. "Rinse please."

Tempest dunked her head under the water and washed the soap away. She pushed her hair from her face and wiped water from her eyes. Tempest froze as she spied the water's color.

Dark gray, almost black. *Damn it.*

The tip of a cold dagger kissed the skin of her throat.

"And it's power hungry zealots like you who keep that monster in power," Nyx whispered. "What a surprise you are, little Hound."

Tempest stared straight ahead and took a shallow breath. *Time to go.*

She slapped soapy water over her shoulder and jerked away from the blade. Tempest launched to her feet and spun in the tub, then slammed her bare foot against the spluttering Nyx's chest. The woman tumbled backward and rolled smoothly to her feet, wiping the water from her eyes.

Of course, the damn woman was trained.

Tempest jumped from the tub and lunged for the kitchen blade left on the table carelessly. Nyx swung her leg out and Tempest tripped, her feet slipping on the wet floor. She crashed belly first into the table and her hand curled around the blade just as the shifter woman grabbed her by the hair and yanked.

A familiar calmness settled over Tempest as she spun toward Nyx, her scalp stinging. She grabbed a handful of the woman's dress and held her in place, pressing her knife between Nyx's breasts just as the shifter's own blade touched the vulnerable skin beneath Temp's chin.

Both women stilled, and Tempest held Nyx's once warm gaze with her cool, stormy one.

"We're at an impasse," Tempest stated. "This does not need to end in bloodshed. Since you arrived, you've done nothing but care for me, and, for that, I am grateful. You can walk away now unscathed if you leave me in peace."

Tension filled the space around them as Nyx's fingers tightened in Tempest's hair. Cool air teased Tempest's skin, and water dripped down her nude body and plopped onto the floor in a constant staccato as she waited for the shifter woman's reply. She scanned Nyx's expression for any hint of her next move. If she didn't agree to a parley, then Tempest would have to take matters into her own hands.

"Even if I do go along with your plan, he won't let you go," the shifter whispered, her brown eyes serious. "You wouldn't make it to the river."

"I'm resourceful," she argued. "Let me go. You look like you've been in fight. It'll be easy to convince the men that you were attacked."

Nyx pursed her lips and dropped her blade. She stepped warily away and walked to the table. The shifter woman waved a hand at the door. "Give it a go, Lady Hound." She chuckled. "This will be the highlight of my day."

Tempest kept the woman in her vision as she tossed Pyre's tunic over her head and used the bedsheet to roughly dry her wet skin. She sliced the huge blanket in half and tied it around her throat and hair in a makeshift cloak, then cut a smaller strip to create a belt and secured it over her hips. Her wet hair dripped down her back, but she didn't bother with it. There wasn't time.

She backed toward the door, surveying Nyx, while Nyx stared back at her. It wasn't any use tying up the woman because she'd just break through the bonds. Tempest's best chance was speed.

"You're not what I expected," the shifter woman murmured softly. "Best be off with you."

"Take care of yourself, Nyx," Tempest said as her hand curled around the doorknob. "The company you keep is dangerous."

"You have no idea, little Hound."

With the parting remark, Tempest pushed through the door and sprinted into the woods, just far enough so she couldn't see the cottage anymore. Tilting her head back, she located the sun's position. To her right was west and her left east.

Pine needles poked the soles of her feet as she searched for a good climbing tree. If she could clear the top level of the forest, she would be able to tell which way was south.

Spying a tree, the perfect tree, she tucked up the blanket into her makeshift belt and began to climb, ignoring each ache and pain. Her arms trembled, and her stomach swooped as she neared the top, and the tree swayed in the wind. Only a few more paces to go.

Tempest slung her leg over a thin branch that she hoped would hold her weight and hugged the trunk, not caring that sap now clung to her arms. If anything, it would help disguise her scent. Her breath caught and awe filled her as she stared at the immense forest and the massive mountain range that kept the monsters of the wilds from Heimserya. All but the dragons. The mountains made the perfect home for the scaly, flying lizards and were located on the farther northern tip of the kingdom.

She turned her face to the south and lay her cheek against the rough bark. The shifters had carried her much farther into the woods than she'd anticipated. Blowing out a rough breath, Tempest went over her options.

She couldn't go back to the king without the Jester's heart. Her cover was blown *if* the shifters that had captured her were in association with him—which she highly suspected they were. Now, her kingdom's enemy would be expecting her.

Tempest grunted. That would make it a lot harder to kill him. *But not impossible.*

A strand of periwinkle hair blew into face. If she cut her hair and disguised herself as a boy though... that might work. But cutting it here wouldn't do. She mustn't leave any evidence. She needed to go south and find a bigger town to lose herself in. Then she could regroup and attack the Jester at a different angle.

With her chosen path in mind, Tempest climbed down as fast as she dared. She paused twenty feet from the ground and surveyed the forest around her tree. Nothing seemed amiss. Tempest waited an excruciating five minutes just to make sure a trap wasn't lying in wait. Now was not the time to make a mistake.

Her feet complained as she landed silently on the forest floor. She crouched before running south. The river should be close if the men had brought back water for her bath. Out of habit, she hid her smile. They tried to keep so much from her, but inadvertently they'd given her an escape route.

Her footfalls were silent as she ghosted through the forest, keeping to the long shadows of the trees. Her skin tingled and her eyes scanned the surrounding area constantly for threats or followers. She didn't feel like she was being hunted—yet—but that didn't mean anything. No one was infallible. Madrid had taught her that. Arrogance killed more than any assassin ever did. She mustn't get cocky.

A babble of a creek reached her ears, and she slowed as it came into view. She gritted her teeth and did what she had to do. Tempest hissed as the icy water washed over her toes when she waded into the creek. Hopefully, she didn't die of exposure. Too much time in the icy water was a death sentence.

She picked her way down the creek as fast as she dared. It was one thing to have one's feet in frigid water, another thing to be submerged in it. The sun moved across the sky and began to sink. Shivers wracked her body, and she stumbled, slamming her left foot against a sharp rock, but she didn't even feel it.

That wasn't a good sign. Time to leave the water.

Tempest slogged out of the widening stream. She wrapped her arms around her body and forced herself to pick up each foot instead of dragging them like she wanted to. A dull roar of thundering water filtered through the woods, and her shoulders sagged in relief. The river was close and that meant villages. A boy could easily disappear in a town or village.

She trekked to the edge of the creek and pulled her

filched blanket-belt she'd created. Tempest tipped her head to the right, her long hair dangling. She wrapped her left hand around the mass and lifted the blade.

A clawed hand squeezed her right hand and forced her to release the knife while another arm banded around her left arm and middle. Tempest choked on a gasp as pain radiated through her fingers and up her arm. Heat suffused her back, and a spicy scent invaded her nostrils.

"Led me on a merry little chase, didn't ya, luv?" the kitsune whispered hotly against her neck as he pinned her to his own body.

Chapter Twenty

Tempest

She hated the lot of them.

Not because they tortured, starved, or beat her. No, because they continued on like everything was just fine. Tempest had been prepared for the worst, but the kindness they doggedly showed unnerved her more than any threat. Except for Pyre.

He seemed hellbent on charming her one moment and then was icy cold the next. The whiplash put her on edge more than anything, and he knew it. The devil.

Fourteen days had passed since Briggs and Pyre had captured her and brought her back to recover in the cottage. Fourteen days of being babysat by Briggs as well as being visited by Nyx and the kitsune shifter himself. Fourteen days of listening for any slivers of information she could use to work out what was going on. Fourteen days of being frustrated that she did not find out nearly enough to satisfy her raging curiosity.

Each and every day, without fail, Briggs would come and sit in an old, worn rocking chair by the fireplace and read. It made him appear old before his time—sitting by the fire, nose twitching to keep his spectacles in place, poring over a leather-bound tome about who knows what. His spectacles had surprised her, and she'd said as much.

He'd said he was just as likely to have poor eyesight as any human. Like Nyx, he displayed no outward signs of being a shifter, but, given his size, Tempest had come to assume he was probably a bear.

A hibernating one, given how laid-back and quiet he is.

Tempest did not mind his company; rather, she had come to enjoy his easy, non-intrusive presence. But her problem was that, for the life of her, Tempest could not work out *why* he had been sent to watch over her. She couldn't possibly escape. They'd made sure not to give her anything for the pain this time as she healed. Except she wasn't injured anymore. At least, not to the extent that the shifters believed.

She'd become a regular liar.

Tempest snorted so loudly at the thought that Briggs looked up from his book, a frown creasing his brow.

"Something wrong, Temp?" he asked, using the nickname her uncles had bestowed upon her and that Pyre had so brazenly stolen for his own use.

Pyre had gleefully used her real name the first morning after her failed escape attempt. Once her hair had revealed its true color, it wasn't too difficult to figure out who she was. News of the first Lady Hound had spread over the kingdom.

She shook her head. "Just remembering something amusing one of my friends said, back in the capital." It was a lie, and a poor one, but Briggs respected Tempest's privacy enough to leave her to her own thoughts and returned to his reading—or, at least, he was pretending to.

Just as well he cannot see inside my head.

Tempest bit her thumbnail anxiously as she fake-limped over to the window. It was raining outside; fat, heavy drops of water slid down the warped pane of glass like they were racing each other. If Briggs could read her thoughts then he'd know what she was really up to and she'd really be in danger.

She rested her forehead against the warped glass and sighed. What was she thinking in taking the king's offer? As each day passed, the pressure in her chest increased. It felt as if the walls were closing in on every side. How was she supposed to find the Jester? His men had captured her, and it was unlikely that she'd ever kill him. Which meant if she escaped, disgrace and prison awaited her. Disgrace she could handle, even the dungeon she could bare. But it was the idea of being chained to the king that made her stomach knot.

What was even worse was that the shifters were slowly growing on her. None of them were what Tempest had expected them to be. Even though she was their enemy, they treated her as a guest. A small part of her believed if *she* were a shifter, she would have reacted the same way to an enemy in her territory, especially after Nyx's story.

"What is on your mind, Temp?" Briggs asked softly after an hour had passed by in hazy silence. "The rain cannot be all that riveting."

Tempest shrugged her shoulders, then sighed emphatically. "I do not know why Pyre is still keeping me here. I have nothing you need, nor am I a danger to you. We are at a standstill. What is the point in that? All he's doing is wasting food and resources on me." The other shifters from her first hazy night floated through her mind. "The other shifters won't appreciate that."

She did not need to look at Briggs to know that he was smiling at her.

"That sounds awfully like you're concerned for the clan's wellbeing, you know."

"I have to assume there are children and other innocents who live around here, right?" she fired back, turning to face Briggs as she did so. Just as she suspected, the man was smiling at her, but it wasn't in the least bit condescending. Instead, he seemed rather pleased that Tempest clearly had a heart—and a conscience. "It is difficult enough to feed oneself, let alone an enemy."

"Is that what you are—our enemy?"

Careful, Tempest. "You've broken the law by keeping me here. By all accounts we are natural enemies."

Briggs closed his book and laced his fingers together. "Natural enemies? All I see are two people here with different ways of life. Why should that make us enemies?"

"I'm not referring to our bloodlines." Time to take a risk. "I was referring to your other alliances."

"If you actually communicated with anyone maybe you'd not be so ignorant." He leaned back in his chair and closed his eyes. "You and Pyre would not be at such a standstill if you tried to trust him even a little, Temp," he murmured. "We are not the enemy."

"And who is my enemy?"

"Those who would seek to hurt innocents."

"I agree. I've sworn to protect the innocent."

"And yet you serve a man who deceives and kills his own people for his own selfish gain."

Now they were getting somewhere.

"Every ruler has selfish whims, and while King Destin rules with swift justice—"

"Justice?" Briggs said tersely, opening his eyes. "That man knows nothing of justice, only of greed and depravity. You've asked questions about the plague, but something tells me you know it's not a plague but a poison."

Finally, we were getting somewhere. "I do believe it's a poison."

"And who do think is responsible for such a crime?"

Wisely, she kept her mouth shut.

He shook his head. "You don't need to say anything. The blame is always placed before Talagan feet. The innocent judged as guilty and the guilty pretending to be innocent."

She bristled. "That is a blanket statement. Not all humans are evil, just as not all shapeshifters are evil. I don't consider you a vile degenerate because of your heritage."

"But you don't trust me," Briggs said softly. "Even now, every line of your body is stiff as if preparing for an attack. I've cared for you for weeks now and still you're wary."

"Old habits." Tempest shrugged. "Not everyone is who they say there are. Blind trust isn't something I give. Ever."

"If I was human, you wouldn't act the same way."

She snorted. "If you were a woman, I wouldn't act the same way. It has nothing to do with you and everything to do with the threat you pose to my person."

"My point exactly. You're threatened by what you don't understand. You've been conditioned to be suspicious of shapeshifters since you were a child."

"So you're telling me that the poison doesn't originate from the Jester?"

"The Jester's never been a mass murderer."

And how would you know, Briggs? She'd come back to that. "So where is it coming from?"

"I don't think you're ready to hear it."

"Don't keep me on pins and needles."

The healer leaned forward, his expression intent. "Do you honestly believe the Jester—or anyone from the clan, for that matter—is responsible for the poison that's killing people all throughout the forest?" Briggs's tone was sharper now. Tempest realized he was watching her from one half-closed eye, which she suspected missed absolutely nothing. "There are members of this clan who have lost all their family, you know," he continued. "Mothers. Fathers. Children. Best friends. And that's not to mention the entire villages who have been wiped out far closer to the Talagan mountain ranges."

"Some believe a sacrifice is justified for the greater good," she remarked. "Winning a war against the Crown would change things for all shapeshifters."

Briggs's laugh at Tempest's remark was entirely humorless. "Tell me, Tempest. Who would win in an all-out war: Heimserya or the old kingdom of Talaga? You're a smart, capable young woman. I do not believe you are so naïve as to think the answer is the latter."

Tempest said nothing. He was right. The shifters wouldn't wage an absolute war. She would not put it past the shifters to undermine the kingdom that took them over one hundred years ago by way of sneaky attacks and civilian casualties. There'd be no hope of a full-frontal attack. They'd go about it a different way.

How would she do it? The hairs along the nape of her neck rose. The surest way to change the state of the kingdoms would be to get rid of the ruler and his line. Is that why the king wanted the Jester's heart? Because the lord of the underworld was plotting to have him killed?

Briggs eased out of his chair and onto heavy feet, closing the distance between himself and Tempest in two easy strides. He pointed out of the rain-smeared window in the direction of the other cottages Tempest knew to be just out of sight.

"If the shifters—if my people—were responsible for the poison that's spreading around the forest, then answer me this, Tempest. Why are *we* the only people who are dying? Why is it *our* villages that have been affected?"

"I'd hate to think you're mixed up with someone like the Jester. I think you're a good man," Tempest whispered. "You've shown me kindness but there is a storm coming and bodies will litter the ground if we do nothing. I refuse to stand by and watch. We'll have to choose a side."

"What if the sides aren't human against shifters? What if they are corruption against innocence? Where do you think you'll find yourself, Lady Hound?"

"With the innocent." Her first thought should have been the Crown. The thought didn't sit well with her, just as Briggs's increasingly difficult questions made her stomach twist uncomfortably.

"I hope so," the healer murmured. "The innocent need someone like you."

Tempest bit her tongue and slumped back into bed, rolling onto her side so that Briggs could not see the ongoing conflict within her mind.

She had no answers. She *needed* answers. The healer had finally opened up to her, and she knew what he was hinting at. The shifters were trying to turn her against the Crown. Without trying, Tempest was infiltrating their ranks.

If they wanted a Hound for their cause, she'd give them one and then she'd destroy the Jester's vile court, stone by stone.

Chapter Twenty-One

Tempest

Tempest was becoming seriously affected by cabin fever. It wasn't surprising; almost three weeks stuck inside a cottage barely bigger than her room back in the Hound barracks was bound to make her tetchy and restless. It didn't help that Tempest was entirely healed from her wounds, which meant she had to keep pretending to be hurt.

But the last few weeks in the cottage had granted Tempest one thing: time. Time to think about King Destin's veiled threats. Time to criticize what the people of Dotae thought of the shifters who did most of the kingdom's labor. Time to contemplate that everything she had been told about the sickness decimating the villages simply did not add up. To top off Tempest's frustration and confusion, since deciding to play to Pyre's little game,

Pyre himself had deigned not to show up to see her even once in the last week.

All in all, Tempest felt rather like a trapped animal.

She'd spent most of the last five days looking out the solitary window of the cottage, tapping her fingers on the glass and holding back a scream that was longing to be let out. It had rained constantly for a full five days; now, finally, it had let up. A weak ray of sunshine filtered into the cottage through the warped windowpane, promising better weather to come.

Not that she was allowed to enjoy it.

Tempest banged her head against the glass over and over again as if she might have been able to smash it through sheer willpower alone.

That was how Pyre found her on the afternoon of Tempest's nineteenth day in his custody.

The cottage door flew open and crashed against the wall near her elbow. Tempest scowled as the kitsune swaggered in, cool forest air cutting some of the heat from the fire. She turned slightly and curled her hand around the door and slammed it closed.

"Someone's a bit testy."

So he's to bless me with his presence today. Which personality would she get, the charmer or the interrogator?

She grunted and eyed him from beneath the curtain of hair that hung over her face. The shifter couldn't help but make a spectacle everywhere he went.

"I've been told you've been highly productive with your

time, Temp."

His use of her nickname grated on her nerves. Charmer, it was—her least favorite characteristic.

He was maddeningly at ease as he strolled over to the fireplace and lounged in Briggs's favorite chair, since the man had disappeared on other business that morning. Tempest kept a constant watch on Pyre out of the corner of her eye, though she didn't move from her position at the window.

"It's hardly as if I have anything better to do," she muttered.

Pyre indicated to a pile of old, leather-bound books sitting on the kitchen table. "Surely reading would be a better pastime than trying to crack your skull open?"

"I've read them all."

"I somehow doubt that." He laughed, which only made Tempest angrier. She turned around fully to face him, crossing her arms over her chest as she did so.

"And what do you even know about me, Pyre, to believe I couldn't *possibly* have read all those books already?"

He chuckled, but his face looked altogether more serious in response to Tempest's indignation. "Well, three of them are written in Talagan, for one—"

"I don't see your point."

Pyre crossed his arms and cocked his head to one side, his fox ears twitching in interest and surprise. "You understand Talagan? I thought you hated all things shifter."

She held up a finger. "I've never said that. And even if I

did harbor a bit of hatred, I hate getting up before sunrise, but still I do that when I know I have to," Tempest countered. "Understanding Talagan is important to be able to translate texts from before the original rebellion. It's standard for Hound trainees to learn the language."

The look Pyre gave Tempest then was almost appraising. Something dark slithered through his eyes, but it was gone in a moment as his rakish façade slipped back into place once again. He arched his back lazily against the chair and stretched his arms above his head.

"Too bad the only pre-rebellion texts you've likely ever seen are ones that don't contradict the Crown's poisonous view of my country."

Tempest scowled. "And there you go again, assuming I'm a hopelessly naïve, blind follower. I know things are not always what they seem. And besides, it was actually my mother who originally taught me the language, so I could read Talagan folktales with her. Hardly the most inflammatory of texts, one way or the other." *Make of that what you will.*

"Your mum was Talagan?"

"Oh Dotae be good, no," Tempest corrected quickly. She looked out of the window, closing her eyes against the sunshine streaming through it for a moment. She realized she was holding a tense breath in her lungs. Fighting with Pyre wouldn't bring her any closer to her goal. Tempest let out a low whistle through her teeth. Now, to set the bait. "We lived close to the mountains, though. I think she'd grown up there, too. She loved Talaga. She loved

233

shifters. Too bad they didn't love her."

Pyre stood up, taking a few, careful steps toward Tempest before coming to a halt closer to her than she would have liked. Initially, she'd frozen but she worked at keeping the tension from her body. Nothing would be gained if she couldn't get over her aversion to his presence. He hadn't intentionally harmed her yet. Despite his mercurial temperament, she didn't believe him to be a complete brute without conscience.

"You told me you lived in the forest before moving to Dotae, back when we first met," he said. "I assumed you were lying, that it was part of your cover story."

"It wasn't."

"So, what do you mean, shifters didn't love your mum? What happened to her? You mentioned before that she passed away."

Tempest realized she was far too close to crying. She didn't want to share any of her life with him, but for her plan to work, she needed to gain his trust. *A little information isn't the end of the world.*

She straightened her back and stood to face Pyre properly, though, in truth, the wiry, lean-muscled shifter towered over her. She tilted her chin up to stare at his face. Gone was any trace of laughter or arrogance, but Pyre's ever-present curiosity was still there alongside something that Tempest dubiously thought might be concern.

A master of manipulation.

"What happened, Temp?" he pressed.

When Pyre reached out a hand for her shoulder,

Tempest twisted to avoid it, just barely remembering to put on a limp as she walked away from the man to stand in front of the fireplace, instead. She couldn't stomach looking at his face when it displayed such disarmingly genuine emotions.

He is playing you. That's what he does.

"Did you cause them?" Tempest whispered, more to the fire than to Pyre.

"Cause what?"

"The deaths," she said, louder this time, though she kept her eyes on the flickering, dancing flames in front of her. If she stared for long enough, Tempest could almost see her home being engulfed in them and her mum inside it. "The plague. Did you start it? Are you responsible for it?"

A tense beat of silence. Two. Three. And then—

"Why the hell would I be responsible for it?"

"I spoke with Briggs last night."

"I heard," he said, his voice slightly strained.

"I told him I don't give blind faith ever. Not to him, not to you, not to the king." The traitorous words were supposed to be a lie, but they weren't. "I need to know you're not part of the deaths—that you're not supporting the Jester."

Several seconds of silence passed between them.

"And if I was?" he whispered.

"Then I'd kill you."

Even if what Briggs had said was true about the Jester not poisoning the people, all the horror stories about him couldn't be wrong. Someone like that couldn't be allowed to spread their corruption and terror and go unpunished for their crimes.

"And here I thought we were doing so well," Pyre murmured, his voice cool and clipped. "You're nothing but the king's bitch. Rolling over to his every whim."

Here comes the icy persona.

Tempest closed her eyes for the briefest moment at the slur. It wasn't like she hadn't heard something like it growing up amongst men, but she still hated it. "Please refrain from using such language or I will lose my temper."

"You like to think you're not blinded by lies, but you can't think past the shite Destin fed you himself," Pyre growled, from right behind Tempest.

She hadn't even realized he'd closed the gap between them again. She could feel his breath tickling her neck. It was possible she'd pushed him a little too far. Tempest tried to move away, and Pyre grabbed her forearm and hauled her around to face him.

"Let go," she said sternly, looking him in eye. Her strength was nothing compared to his, but she wouldn't be cowed by his anger. "Pyre, let—"

"No, not until you *listen* to me," he cut in.

The sharp points of his canines peeked from between his lips, and her brows snapped together as she realized that *all* of his facial features were growing sharper. Glancing down, she saw that the nails of the hand he'd used to grab her were growing longer, too. She needed to tread carefully.

"All this time you've let your prejudices blind you to

what's in front of you. You aren't stupid, that much is obvious. So why do you still believe that my people are responsible for the deaths in the forest? That *I'm* responsible for them? How could you think such a thing?"

Pulling away was useless, and his rage was so palpable that it infused the air. If the kitsune wouldn't be reasonable, Tempest had to be calm and collected for the both of them.

"I'm sorry I upset you," she said softly. "That was not my intention—"

"Answer the question," he demanded darkly.

"Do you trust me?" Temp asked. His lip curled, and she fought to keep from stepping back. "Do you?"

"I haven't accused you of being a mass murderer. This isn't about me."

"Well, what would you have me believe?!" she fired back. "That everyone else in Heimserya has the wrong idea about the Jester? That it's all a lie? Propaganda spun by the Crown? That he's not as bad as he seems? That he's really the good guy?"

"Yes!"

"You haven't given me one single reason to believe that. I've only seen evidence on the contrary. Give me proof. Let me meet him."

"And you haven't given me one single reason to trust you with that information."

"Then we are at an impasse." She pointedly stared at his hand around her arm. "If you'd kindly release me, I'd be much obliged."

"All you've done so far is act as a lapdog to your king, completely blind to the truth," Pyre said, pinching the bridge of his nose and closing his eyes for long enough to steady his breathing. Tempest watched in reluctant awe as his features slowly but surely returned to the way they usually looked, and the pressure of his pointed nails on her arm lessened. "Your king—the entire Crown, really—has hurt so many people. His *own* people, not just mine. He blames others for his misdeeds. Just look at how he's using you as a puppet to act on his behalf. You think you are doing good when all you're doing is aiding an evil man who owns you. The Hounds are assassins, nothing more."

"Don't you dare speak about my family like that." A spike of anger flared in her chest that she ruthlessly stomped down. If she lost control of her emotions, it would spell disaster for them both. "You don't know me. Think before you start to cast stones."

"Wise council from a glass house," Pyre retorted.

Wicked hell. She was going to slap him. "I think it'd be best if you leave."

His brows rose almost to his hairline. "You're not the mistress here." He leaned down, his nose brushing hers, his gold-amber eyes glittering. "Don't *ever* presume to command me again."

"Understood. But if you ever touch me like that again, I will cut your heart out," she said simply and meant every word. No one touched her without her permission. If she had to use her bare hands to rip his heart from his chest, she would. "Release me."

She jerked her arm from his grasp and took a step away from the kitsune, trembling with anger, fear, and a touch of unwanted attraction. What was wrong with her?

"I didn't mean to make you feel unsafe," he growled.

"You didn't." No way would she admit such a weakness to him.

"Whatever you say, luv." He eyed her, shook his head mockingly, and touched the tip of his nose. "I'm Talagan, I can smell it all over you. A predator can always smell the fear of prey."

He. Did. Not. "Come closer again, and I'll show you a predator," she hissed, baring her teeth.

"Such a little bloodthirsty thing," Pyre crooned. "No wonder the king likes you. You may think you're in control of your destiny, but make no mistake, King Destin owns the Hounds. He owns you."

She hated that he was right.

"But he doesn't have to," Pyre added.

"And what is that supposed to mean?"

"We're going for a walk tomorrow morning."

"What?"

"You heard me," Pyre said, stalking over to the front door as he spoke. Despite the air of calm he was clearly fighting to keep in place, Tempest could see his shoulders were shaking. She had riled him up even while trying to calm him. Tempest didn't like how that made her feel, like she'd failed somehow.

"What does a walk have to do with anything we just talked about?"

Pyre smirked, but there was no humor behind it. "You'll see," he replied, infuriatingly vague, and then he thrust open the door and was gone, leaving the door wide open. No explanation. No goodbye.

"That—that no-good *fox*!" Tempest huffed, at a loss for any words that could form a more appropriate insult. She stomped to the door and slammed it closed before storming back over toward the table. In her frustration, she kicked one of the stools sitting innocuously by the kitchen table; it toppled violently and broke into several wicked-looking shards of wood. She bent down to inspect them and ran a finger along the edge of the sharpest piece. It cut her skin and she winced.

"Briggs won't be happy about this," Tempest murmured. She sucked on her finger, tasting salty blood on her tongue as she thought long and hard about what Pyre's walk was really all about. She stared at the broken chair then, slowly, pocketed the piece that had cut her finger open.

A Hound always needed a weapon. She tossed the other broken bits into the fire and stashed the sharp piece beneath the mattress. Who knew what the kitsune had planned for the walk tomorrow? He wanted her trust and yet he hadn't given her a good reason to trust him.

It was better to be safe than sorry.

She was the only one she could trust, after all.

Chapter Twenty-Two

Tempest

"I hope you're ready to have all your prejudices turned on their head, city girl."

Tempest scowled at Pyre, who had barged into her cottage, unannounced, as if he owned the place. She supposed he did.

"I could have been getting dressed," she complained.

Pyre's resultant smile spoke volumes, and the way he jokingly leered at Tempest spoke even more. Ass.

Tempest half-snarled at him. "You're disgusting."

"Only to rile you up, Lady Hound. You know I would never creep upon you while you were in a state of undress. That is most ungentlemanly behavior."

"Oh, and mentally undressing me with your eyes is so much better?"

"Having thoughts is not a crime," he pointed out,

wagging a fake disapproving finger at Tempest as he did so. His nose wrinkled. "Plus, a man does not wish to pick flowers that are venomous. There are prettier flowers in the world to decorate a man's table."

She sighed and brushed off his calloused words that pricked her. Tempest had always known she wasn't some great beauty. Suitors were few when one wore a pair of trousers and fought more fiercely than most men themselves did. Not to mention she lacked certain feminine graces that men seemed to find appealing—like simpering. She didn't simper well.

At. All.

But at least Pyre seemed to be back to his usual, easy-going self, as if the argument the two of them had engaged in during the previous afternoon had not happened at all. The man was ever-changing. She could handle his playfulness, but when he let his darkness peek out, it unnerved her. She couldn't figure him out and that's what bothered her the most. Normally, she was excellent at reading people, but it was impossible to get a read on the kitsune. His masks were flawless. Tempest could probably learn a few things from him.

She shoved the last piece of bread into her mouth and traced a swirling pattern on the table with her finger. Last night, she'd been too restless to fall asleep and had replayed their confrontation over and over. Her gaze slid to the kitsune. Had Pyre even been half as bothered by their fight as she was? Did it matter? It shouldn't have. Going by the way he'd lost his temper yesterday she'd thought yes. Perhaps she was wrong. Perhaps his anger was all a ruse to get inside her head and—

"Why do you do that?"

Tempest pulled herself from her thoughts, frowning. "Do what?"

"That," Pyre said, waving a hand toward Tempest's head. "Get lost in your thoughts mid-conversation. Am I really that uninteresting to you?"

Tempest chose her tried-and-tested route of saying absolutely nothing. Pyre was baiting her once more, trying to see if she'd play his game. Either way she answered, she'd look like a fool. Tempest rested her chin in her hands and gazed at him with a bored expression plastered across her face. He'd have to try harder than that to get a rise out of her this morning. She was too tired for games.

"Let's go, city girl."

Pyre smiled disarmingly and opened the door, waiting expectantly for her to join him. Her heart skipped a beat and an answering smile touched her own mouth as the winter sunlight poured into the cottage. She barely noticed his stunned expression as she stood and fake-limped to the door, pausing at the threshold. Her fingers twitched as the temptation to sprint from the cottage enticed her.

She took her first step outside and onto the porch, gazing at the greenery. It would be easy to stab the shifter with the wooden shard hidden in her pocket and escape. But escape would not help her find the Jester. The king's face flashed through her mind and she shivered. Her captivity in the cottage would be nothing compared to her confinement at court if she failed the king and her sovereign got his way.

"Honestly, Temp, what's the matter?"

She abandoned her escape fantasies and allowed a small smile to curl her lips as she focused on the kitsune. Pyre cocked his head to one side. *Like a fox,* Tempest had worked out rather quickly, when she wondered why he did it so often.

"I thought you'd be happy to get out of here for once."

"I am," she replied, draping a cloak Nyx had lent her over her shoulders before taking a few, slow steps toward the stairs leading from the cottage into the woods.

He thinks you're still injured. Do not slip up now.

"But?"

"But I am decidedly wary of *why* you are taking me on a walk," Tempest said, smiling slightly at Pyre's astuteness. He was, perhaps, the most observant person Tempest had ever met. She'd had to be so careful over the past three weeks not to let anything show on her face that Pyre could read. Even then, she was not sure if she had managed to do such a thing successfully. *For all I know he's worked out everything about me by now.*

"You look like you're thinking I'm taking you into the forest to murder you, Temp," Pyre said, throwing his head back to laugh as if the idea were ludicrous.

"Well, you might."

"But I won't." He shocked her by pushing a piece of her hair behind her ear.

"But you could," she insisted, putting more space between them.

"I'd wager that you could do the same to me, so we're even."

Tempest blinked in surprise, taking far too long to respond with, "If I wasn't still recovering from my injuries, perhaps."

The expression on Pyre's face was almost knowing, though Tempest was not sure if she was reading too much into it or if her brain was seeing things that simply were not there. He sidled closer and indicated outside with an outstretched arm. "Perhaps. After you, my lady."

"How many times do I have to *tell* you." Tempest scowled, "I'm not—"

"A lady. Yes, you may have told me half a hundred times. But you don't like me calling you Temp, either. And you always look like you might murder me when I call you *Lady Hound*."

Though Pyre snickered at his comments, and he'd clearly meant them in good fun, a chill ran down Tempest's spine as she took a few genuine unsteady steps to the edge of the porch. It was a gloriously warm and sunny morning, but the mere mention of *Lady Hound* kept Tempest feeling freezing. The thought of King Destin's uncomfortable advances made her shiver, but hearing the name he'd used to address her sent Tempest straight back to the night he'd ordered her up to his chambers.

Tempest followed Pyre down the rickety stairs and trailed behind him into the woods, lost in her thoughts.

That night changed everything, in more ways than one. If she escaped today without completing her assignment, the king would be waiting for her and her dreams of adventures as a Hound were over.

She examined the woods for danger when a prickly sensation ran up her neck. Tempest flicked a look in Pyre's direction and ignored how he stared at her. The kitsune shifter's ears were flat against his head, a frown of concern shadowing his brow. How long had he been studying her? Had her expression given away any of her thoughts? She needed to be more careful. He wasn't her friend even if he was beginning to pretend he was.

"What?" she barked, feeling like she needed to scrub the king's lingering attention from her skin.

"You're a strange creature, luv. I can't figure you out."

"What every girl wants to hear," she muttered, picking her steps carefully. "I hear men like mystery."

"There's some appeal, I'll admit. But I have a feeling I said something wrong."

"It's got nothing to do with you. I'm fine," she mumbled. And then, though Tempest wasn't sure why she felt the need to say it, she added, "Well, I'm not fine, but it doesn't matter. It'll all work itself out in time."

Pyre weaved a little closer and risked the lightest touch of her shoulder. "So, I haven't offended you?"

"Oh, you've offended me many times, but it's no matter. Water under the bridge."

"What put that haunted look in your eyes?"

He was studying her, and she'd let her guard down.

Damn it. Just how much had she revealed?

"I said it didn't matter," Tempest replied coolly, increasing the pace of her walking as she realized how stupid she'd been to let some of her emotions leak onto her face. Her jaw clenched as she remembered that she should not have been able to walk that fast, so she slowed down far too quickly and tripped over her own feet.

Pyre clucked his tongue. "You are not nearly so graceful as I thought you'd be, given the fight we had the day we met."

"If I was fully healed and hadn't spent three weeks on bedrest with no exercise and was wearing my own clothes, you wouldn't be making such a joke."

"Then I sincerely hope I get to see *that* Tempest again. She was far more sociable, too, as I recall," Pyre said, scratching his chin as if in deep thought. "So wide-eyed and innocent. You didn't look too bad in that skirt, either, though I must confess I rather liked it when you tore it off, to—"

"You insufferable *rake*," Tempest growled, knowing her cheeks must be red as warmth crept into her face. *What is your problem, Tempest? You've heard much worse growing up with boys.* "I'd appreciate it if you'd keep your lascivious comments to yourself."

Pyre merely laughed. "That isn't the first time I've heard such a curse, and it won't be the last. It's good to see you in higher spirits though, Temp. Being in the cottage for so long clearly didn't agree with you."

"Nobody likes to be held somewhere against their will,"

she said, very quietly, though Pyre's fox ears pricked up at her words.

"I know." His expression blanked. "I didn't want it to be this way, but as I said yesterday, you hadn't given me any reasons to trust you. I couldn't let you out."

"So why are you letting me out *now*?" What was this whole little walk about? She certainly hadn't behaved very well so it wasn't a reward. Another way to try to gain her trust?

Pyre pointed directly in front of them, down a winding path through the forest. "I've come to the conclusion that you are the type of person who needs to *see* something, rather than be told it. Which is by no means a bad thing; taking anything someone says at face-value can be incredibly stupid and dangerous."

Tempest raised an eyebrow. "So if I'd believed you from the beginning you'd have thought me stupid?"

"You and I both know that was never going to happen."

"True."

The two of them fell into an easy silence as Pyre led Tempest through the trees with a precision that meant he could probably navigate the area blindfolded. Tempest did her best to take note of every little thing around her: the soft ground beneath her from all the recent rainfall, which would make her more likely to slip if she took a wrong step; the warm south-easterly breeze, which Tempest would have to make sure she stayed upwind of to ensure Pyre could not smell her after she escaped; the dull roar of the nearby river and the sounds of thrushes, woodpigeons, and larks, which told Tempest she was not too far from the outskirts of the forest. All of these sensory inputs were vital for her to understand, if she was going to get away from a fox shifter at some point.

She cocked her head and listened hard as a faint sound caught her attention and put her on edge: the sound of someone approaching on light, nimble feet. Tempest loosened the wooden spike from the waistband of her trousers. Not for the first time, she wished she could have worn her bow and quiver of arrows. There wasn't a single member of the Hounds who could best her aim. One true-flying arrow was all Tempest would have needed to take down an enemy. But she didn't have her bow, or her arrows, so it was pointless to wish she had them. No, all Tempest had was a wooden spike and a will to fight to the end.

She got into a fighting stance before she could stop herself, her fingers clenching around her wooden spike, and then—

A small boy with the beautiful, elongated ears of a fawn and the warmest brown eyes Tempest had ever seen came bounding toward them and jumped into Pyre's arms with a glee only seen in children.

"Fox!" the boy cried, delighted, as Pyre ruffled his braided hair and tossed him up onto his shoulders as if he weighed nothing at all. "You have not played with me for days and weeks and months and—"

"It has been three weeks, young one," he laughed, startling Tempest right out of her fight-or-flight mode. It wasn't the amused-at-someone-else's-expense laugh he usually used, nor was it arrogant or humorless. No, his laugh was full of genuine, unrelenting joy and affection, the likes of which Tempest had rarely experienced for another in her life. Except for Maxim and her mum.

Her heart twanged in her chest. Winter's bite, she missed her uncle. He would know what to do with the cocky kitsune.

Tempest stared at the little fawn shifter, and, with the memory of her mother fresh in her head, she quickly tucked away her makeshift weapon. She smiled at the precious little boy as he babbled on about a new boat he'd carved. It had been a long time since she'd seen someone so carefree. Full of love. Not suspicious of everyone and everything.

Innocent, in a way Tempest had not been since her mother was killed.

What if the sides aren't human or shifter? What if they are corruption against innocent?

Briggs's question had haunted her for days. And, looking at the boy, she already knew her answer even if it meant standing against her king.

Traitor.

Chapter Twenty-Three

Tempest

Tempest followed Pyre and the boy into a clearing earmarked by two tall, carved, wooden wolves. She coolly eyed the statues and turned her attention to the pair of shifters ahead of her. The little fawn boy still sat upon Pyre's shoulders, singing a nonsensical song as he played with the kitsune's ears. Pyre did not seem to mind at all, which surprised Tempest to no end.

Was the child his? From her interactions with him, she'd have pegged him as someone who avoided the wee beasties. But then Tempest paused. What did she really know about Pyre? They were strangers playing a dangerous game. All she knew was what she had witnessed herself, which wasn't much at all.

Was this another ploy to gain her confidence? If so, she'd pretend to let it work. *Keep your wits about you. You have to have a clear head. Don't let pretending slip into real feeling.* She had to see what Pyre wished her to see and not let any previous judgments cloud her.

"Tempest?"

Pyre was watching her with serious amber eyes. Tempest ducked her head quickly to avoid showing him any of the thoughts that might have slipped onto her face. She scurried forward to catch up with him, making sure to limp as she did so.

"What's wrong with the lady? She looks pitiful," the fawn shifter asked from up high.

Pyre made a tutting noise. "Now, now, Aspen. That was a rude question. My lady was injured, you see. She's still recovering. She might not wish to talk about it."

Aspen looked horrified. His face grew ashen, and his lovely doe eyes became impossibly wide. "I—I'm sorry, my lady!" he stammered, close to tears.

Tempest shot a glare at Pyre as he wiggled his brows, amused at the mess he'd now left Tempest to clean up.

She'd wipe that grin from his face.

Tempest closed the gap between them in order to reach up and tickle Aspen beneath his chin until he giggled.

"Do not listen to the silly fox," she said with a mischievous smile. "You can ask me anything you want, little one. Do you want to know how I got injured?"

Pyre's amusement slid from his face, and something truly scary rippled across it. "Tempest," he said softly. A warning.

She ignored him when Aspen's face brightened with the

kind of excitement only children have at the idea of a gruesome story.

"Yes, please!" he exclaimed happily, pulling on Pyre's ears with such force that the man winced.

Tempest smiled sharply and leaned against the kitsune's arm to take Aspen's small hand in her own. She ignored how the fox stiffened, and she hid her amusement at his discomfort over her having so boldly entered into his personal space and deliberately kept her eyes on the fawn. The ass now knew how it felt.

She grinned at the fawn. "I fought a lion."

"A *lion*?!" the boy gasped. "Not a lion shifter or—"

"No, an honest-to-goodness lion." She kept her gaze pinned to the boy as Pyre's attention intensified on the side of her face.

"Was he scary?"

"Oh, very."

"Was he strong?"

"He almost ripped my arm off with one swipe of his paw!" Tempest swatted Pyre's arm as she spoke to emphasize her point; he watched her do so with an unreadable expression.

Aspen looked frightened, as if he were the one now facing the lion. "How did you escape?"

Tempest smiled sadly. "I killed him. I didn't want to, but I had to. I wish it could have turned out different."

"Did you hear that, Fox?!" Aspen cried, bending over to look at Pyre's face upside-down. "She killed a lion!" He looked back at Tempest. "What kind of shifter are you? You must be so strong to—"

"She's not a shifter," Pyre said, just as Tempest took a step or two back from him in response to the question. "She's not one of our people."

Her smile fell a little, but she managed to keep it in place. A little shifter could never have imagined an ordinary human could best a lion. Before she'd managed it, Tempest had never imagined it to be possible, either. But it still stung, because it reminded Tempest of what she'd been taught back in Dotae.

Talagans think they're better than us. Stronger and smarter and faster. The only thing we beat them in is numbers.

Well, they were wrong.

Tempest could not blame Aspen for his question. He was but a child, after all, and children believed what they were told by adults. But it was Pyre's abrupt reply that really got under her skin. He claimed she was the one that was brainwashed and prejudiced, but couldn't he see he was just the same?

Aspen was still staring at her in awe. "Are you a goddess?" he asked, without a hint of sarcasm. "You have hair like the skies."

Pyre's lips twitched, and Tempest held up a finger.

"Don't you dare," she warned.

The kitsune bust out in laugher, flinging his head back so abruptly that the boy slipped from his shoulders.

Tempest lurched forward to catch him just in time, the little one clinging to her with wide eyes.

"A-a goddess?" Pyre sniggered, almost inconsolable in his mirth.

Tempest clutched a bewildered Aspen to her chest protectively, as if he could somehow deflect Pyre's scathing disbelief. She stroked her hand along one of the boy's ears and smiled.

"If you think I am a goddess, maybe I am one. Your fox is a jester, after all," she needled to get a reaction out of the kitsune. "So why can't I be a goddess?"

Upon hearing the word 'jester' Pyre immediately flinched, and his laughter stopped. He plucked the fawn shifter from Tempest's arms and placed him on the grass.

"Why don't you run ahead, Aspen?" he said, patting the boy's back as he did so. "Your mother will be looking for you. I wish to show your *goddess* around the village."

Aspen looked crestfallen. "I thought I could show her around..."

"But then you couldn't ask your mum for some of that wonderful bread she bakes to give to her, could you?" Pyre reasoned. "You always help your mum bake the morning batch, don't you?"

The fawn brightened immediately. He nodded, then grinned at Tempest. "I won't be long, I swear I won't! Don't leave without the bread!" And then he was off, bounding away with the speed and grace of a deer.

An uncomfortable silence followed, and Tempest became aware that Pyre was unabashedly staring at her. They had stopped right on the cusp of the village; Tempest could smell smoke and cinnamon on the air whenever the wind carried the scents over to her.

"You like children." Pyre stated.

"That's not a question."

"I never expected an assassin to like children."

Tempest forced herself to look at Pyre. The man's sharp features seemed ever more pronounced in the morning sunlight, making him look less human than normal. It twisted her stomach in a way she could not describe and reminded her of the stark difference between them.

A fox and a Hound.

"I have always been surrounded by children," she finally replied, "being an orphan and all. When I wasn't training with the Hounds, I spent my time playing with the street urchins of Dotae."

"How long did you train with the Hounds?"

"Since my mother died."

"That's not exactly protocol."

"Neither is being a female trainee, either, yet here we are."

"Here we are." A pause. "You called me a jester. Why?"

"I didn't call you *the* Jester, just a jester. You like to play tricks and games at the expense of others. The description seemed appropriate." Tempest lifted her chin in the direction of where the fawn disappeared. "I didn't think you would like children."

Pyre shrugged, then indicated for them to continue walking through the village. "We're a very close-knit community around here. I suppose as a rebellious teenager I didn't like kids much. Things change, though, when you're put in a position to protect them. Each and every child becomes precious, then."

Tempest swallowed heavily, not sure how to respond to what Pyre had just said. It was the closest thing to a backstory he'd given her so far. *I suppose I just gave him the same information about myself, though. Perhaps he felt he owed me an answer in return.*

She glanced around at the cottages they passed as they made their way through the village. Children were running everywhere, darting behind trees and hiding in wooden buckets and making so much noise Tempest could scarcely hear herself think. But she was smiling; whether in a city or a tiny, secluded village hidden in the forest, children were children.

Then she noticed the women: they were cleaning, cooking, shopping, arguing, and corralling children back indoors. Some ways off from everyone else, two girls a little younger than Tempest were sparring each other. Something wasn't right. She scanned the village again.

Where are all the men?

"Clearly a vicious, conniving bunch, right?" Pyre remarked, sidling into Tempest's personal space just as she'd done to him earlier. When she tried to move away, he slung an easy arm over her shoulders to keep her in place. "Just relax. I didn't take you here to bait you. I took you here to show you... what 'here' is. Most of the villages along the mountain range are just like this one: women, children, the elderly and the infirm outnumber men of fighting age three to one across these parts."

So, he was trying to get her to sympathize.

Tempest kept her eyes on what was in front of her, searching for anything suspicious as they passed what looked to be a baker's shop. She wondered if that was where Aspen lived. "Why is there such an imbalance?" she asked Pyre, fighting to keep her tone as neutral as possible.

He barked out a laugh. "Why do you think, Temp? Destin's had so many of us rounded up and killed since he took the throne. His father—and his father before him—was hardly any better. Shapeshifters are a race on the brink of being destroyed altogether. What is left of us works on the farms until we die. So why do you believe we'd kill our own people as collateral damage in our vendetta against the Crown?"

"I—" Tempest began, but then Aspen came bounding out of the baker's shop and crashed into her excitedly.

"Try this, lion-killer!" he cried, holding up a small loaf of bread twisted into the shape of a tulip for Tempest to take.

She accepted it from his hands, glancing at Pyre uncertainly before ripping it in two and handing him half of it.

He quirked an eyebrow. "How gracious, Tempest."

"You *have* been feeding me for three weeks, after all."

"The entire village has been feeding you for three weeks, city girl." Pyre chuckled. "Did you honestly believe I had the time to cook you three square meals a day for that long?"

She sniggered. "You haven't done any of the cooking. It's been Nyx and Briggs." But she hadn't thought about where the food was coming from, if not Pyre himself.

The little fawn boy was watching her expectantly. "Well, is it good? Is it? Is it better than city bread? Ma says—"

"You might want to let her try it first, Aspen," a woman said patiently when she reached the boy's side. She looked to be about ten years older than Tempest, with the same ears and eyes as the fawn who was clearly her son. Her long, oak-brown hair was braided in a similar fashion to his, too. She smiled at Tempest. "You must be the lion-killer Aspen has been telling me about. I'm Rina." Her eyes lingered on Tempest's hair, her defining mark of being a Madrid. A Hound. "It's not every day we meet one of your kind."

A shifter-killing assassin was implied. "A lion killer," Tempest ventured, deliberating misunderstanding the woman's meaning.

Rina laughed softly. "Exactly right. How have you been finding the forest? Although, Briggs has been telling me you've been on constant bedrest, so I guess you haven't seen much of it."

"Is Briggs your husband?" Tempest asked, hazarding a guess at their relationship.

The woman shook her head. "He is my uncle," she explained, wrinkling her nose in amusement. "His sister—my mother—is much older than him. Usually we get mistaken for siblings. It's not often I hear someone ask if we are married!"

"Oh," was all Tempest said, feeling embarrassment flush her cheeks. "Well... I guess there's a first time for everything."

Pyre squeezed her shoulder, reminding Tempest that his arm was still around her, which only served to make her flush even harder. She shifted out from beneath his arm and ignored the curious glance Rina cast between the two of them. Tempest barely kept herself from scowling at the woman. The kitsune might be handsome, but she'd stab herself in the eye before anything happened between them.

"Temp is a little out of her depth today," Pyre said, not unkindly, though Tempest was sure that if she looked at him he'd laugh at her. "Perhaps you could help her feel at home in the village today?"

Rina beamed. "Of course, Pyre. We'll take good care of her."

Tempest managed to keep her surprise hidden and snapped her jaw shut as Pyre turned on his heel and left her. Right in the middle of a shifter village. Either he was the stupidest man ever, this was a test, or he trusted her.

Don't be an idiot. This is a test. Use your time to spy.

Rina and her son swept Tempest away from the bakery, introducing her to what felt like every person in the village. She was given apples to eat, and a smoked sausage pie, and a cinnamon pastry that reminded her of the one Juniper had given her before her trial. With every person she met Tempest was given more food than she knew what to do with. Eventually she could take no more.

"Rina, I could not possibly eat another bite!" Tempest exclaimed when they finally sat down on the rim of a rough-hewn well. "Everyone is so generous with their food. Why are you being so nice to me?" She eyed the fawn and gestured to her hair. "You know what I am."

Rina gave her the same patient smile she used with her son. "You are not like the others."

"Because I am a woman?"

"Because you have compassion and you're not blinded by prejudice. Not once today have you treated anyone you came across as inferior. That is why we are kind to you even though you're suspicious of us. We have no intention to harm anyone. Our village only wants to live in peace."

Tempest nodded. There wasn't anything so much as a pail of water out of place in the village. She had been welcomed into homes and shops and gardens, and nothing was awry. Nobody acted as if they were hiding anything or as if they wanted Tempest gone.

It was simply... a village. She wanted to trust it was true, but it felt too surreal. *Places like this don't exist in the real world.*

"Not everything is as it seems, Tempest," Rima said. "Trust only your own observations and experiences. Those in power on any side always have an agenda."

Wasn't that the truth. "I'll think about what you've said," she replied truthfully.

"Pyre believes—"

"That she's got a good heart," Pyre cut in, seemingly

appearing from out of nowhere. He sat down beside Tempest, his forest-green cloak flouncing about his shoulders as he did so. It was the same cloak he'd worn the night Tempest had fought him, though the hole her dagger had cut into it had been repaired with golden thread.

"You don't know anything about my heart, you stupid fox."

"I know that in the time you've spent with Nyx and Briggs, you've treated them with respect and dignity. That isn't for show." He touched his nose. "We've a great sense of smell. You can lie to yourself but not to me."

"Everyone deserves to be treated with kindness and respect, no matter to whom they were born."

"A rare sentiment," Rina commented softly. "For anyone."

"Except for me," Pyre retorted. "My Hound doesn't quite like me."

"No one likes you," the shifter teased and waved a hand, walking away.

Tempest squinted at his gaudy attire. "What was supposed to attract me to a scoundrel? The pompous clothes or devilish tongue?"

A wicked gleam entered his eyes. "I'd be happy to show you exactly what—"

She slapped a hand over his mouth and shook her head, laughing before she could stop herself. It sounded like something Maxim would say. Perhaps it was because she'd finally been allowed outside, or because she had spent a day with people who did not want something from her, or because she had been allowed to simply be *Tempest* instead of a Hound or a captive, but she was in a good mood. It made her want to laugh and joke and mock-insult people, just as she had done back in Dotae with her uncles and servant friends.

Pyre's golden eyes narrowed for but a moment. His long fingers wrapped around her wrist and pulled her hand away from his mouth, but not before nipping one fingertip. "So, you have a sense of humor, after all. I was beginning to wonder if you were as straight-laced as your arrows."

"You don't know me very well."

"How about letting me get to know you, then, and I'll do the same in return?"

Tempest hesitated. This was exactly the opportunity she was looking for and yet... it seemed even more dangerous now. Like the stakes were higher. "Only if you give me back my bow."

"And so begins the bartering," he groaned. "I'll let you get to know me first. And the entire group of rebels, really."

She darted her head up at the mentioned of *rebels.* "You wouldn't be so stupid." Surely, he didn't mean to introduce her to those helping with the rebellion. It couldn't be that easy.

"We have a meeting tonight that I'd like you to join."

Her mouth bobbed, and she didn't know what to say.

The skin around Pyre's eyes tightened. He was no

longer smiling. "I'm doing this to show I trust you. To show you how much I want you to know what is truly going on. Will you go to the meeting?"

This was the opportunity she had been waiting for. And, after spending a day surrounded by the kind of people the plague was killing off—the kind of people Pyre kept insisting he was protecting—Tempest needed answers to all the question she'd been asking since leaving Dotae.

There was no other answer she could give Pyre but *yes.*

Chapter Twenty-Four

Tempest

Tempest spent the entire evening after returning from the village pacing back and forth in her cottage, cursing the skirts she wore that hampered her movements.

Pyre had said the rebel meeting was that night, but not *when* during the night it would be, so she had no bloody idea when he would show up at her door. At one point, she threw a wooden cup of water into the fire, frustrated and confused beyond reckoning, but she immediately regretted it when she watched the vessel char and crack and, eventually, burn right down into ash.

It had been easy to believe the shifters were innocent when she was sitting in the sunshine surrounded by generous, welcoming strangers. But one village was not the entire shifter population, and though Tempest had no doubt in her mind that the people she'd met today were genuine and innocent, that didn't mean she trusted the rebels. Far from it. The shifters Pyre led—the ones who had protested her presence, the ones who had attacked her—were the people Tempest trusted least of all. Who, in turn, did not trust her. They had been willing to kill her without knowing anything about her, so deep was their hatred and suspicion. Pyre hadn't outright said they were from the rebellion but Nyx's reaction to Tempest's identity was a dead giveaway. She could not imagine they would like her being privy to their plans and secrets.

And yet Pyre *was* trusting her, by taking her to the rebel meeting. The question was why? Were they that desperate to have her on their side? Tempest hated having such expectations sitting heavy on her shoulders. She already had the wishes of King Destin and the Crown upon her, the weight of which was so extreme that Tempest felt like curling up in bed and pretending to be ill when Pyre came to collect her.

"I cannot do this," she sighed, shaking her head in the process, the empty cottage saying nothing in return to her mutterings.

Tempest laced up her boots—the only part of her own clothing she still wore, since the rest of her garb was either torn or dirty—and searched her bag for a comb. She dragged it through her long hair without paying much attention to what she was doing. She simply needed to keep busy and distracted until Pyre showed up, otherwise Tempest felt like she might go insane.

The kitsune shifter knocked on the cottage door a mere

ten minutes later and let himself in without waiting for Tempest to tell him he could enter. Wordlessly, he stood by the doorway, which unnerved her to no end. What was going on in his head? Were they really going to a meeting or was it an execution? That was another thought that kept popping up. He nodded toward the door, and she took the silent hint to exit the cottage. Pyre closed the door behind her and lit a lantern.

"Since you can't see as well as me in the darkness," he said. Going by the tone of his voice, Tempest realized that he didn't mean this as a jibe or insult—it was merely a fact.

She nodded her thanks, then took the lantern's handle from Pyre when he proffered it to her. "How far away is the meeting?"

"Not far." Pyre sniffed the air, scowled, and then looked at Tempest. She inched back a little.

"What is it?" she asked, more nervous than ever. Could he smell her emotions? The fear?

His scowl deepened. "Are you cold?"

"I—what? What made you ask that?"

"Normally I can smell you," Pyre explained, tapping his nose. "But I can't right now, which means you're retaining body heat. Don't you have a cloak?"

Tempest didn't know how to interpret this knowledge of Pyre's hyperawareness of her. *He is a fox, he's hyperaware of everyone.*

She focused on the lantern as she said, "My cloak was badly damaged, remember? Torn to shreds by the spikes in the bottom of that pit I fell in." A pause. "I've been stuck indoors for three weeks, and Nyx needed her cloak when she walked home tonight. It didn't even cross my mind that I'd need one tonight."

Pyre's expression was thoughtful as he considered this. "I should have Briggs knit one for you."

"*Briggs?*"

"Oh, he's an avid knitter." He grinned, back to his usual, easy-going self in an instant. It startled Tempest to see how easily Pyre could shift from one mood to the next. The grumpy old man. "Do you have a color you'd prefer?"

"Violet," she said on reflex. The half-cape of her Trial outfit had been floating through her mind upon the mere mention of a cloak. She had thought it was ridiculous at the time. A useless addition to the outfit. Now, away from the fear and nerves of the actual trial, Tempest realized she had liked it.

Pyre chuckled. "I imagine wearing the same white and brown clothes for three weeks would make anyone long for a bit of color. Unfortunately, we don't have the expensive dyes needed for something so vibrant. You may have to settle for muddy red or muddy orange or—"

"Can Briggs make one the same color as yours?" When it was time to escape, the green would help her blend in with the forest.

"I... I don't see why not," Pyre murmured, his gaze scrutinizing her.

"What? Is there a problem with that?"

"No," he said, weaving around another tree. "Right, we're here. Best behavior... or I shan't be held accountable for my actions."

"If you're asking me not to attack anyone, I won't. I'm hardly in the best position to win a fight." But if they attacked *her*, then all bets were off.

"Even though you're completely healed?" he said sarcastically.

Tempest schooled her expression. "Excuse me?"

"You can't have expected me not to notice, Temp. Your acting's good, but not *that* good. You were bound to slip up eventually."

She kept her gaze on her boots as she scuffed them against the earth, like a teenager caught past curfew. "If you knew, why say nothing?"

"I wanted to see what you would do."

"So it was a test?"

"If you want to see it that way."

Lovely. Lies upon more lies.

"Pyre. Tempest. Good of you to finally join us."

Tempest turned toward Nyx's voice. She was standing in front of a small crowd of shifters, most of whom Tempest vaguely recognized from the night Pyre had beaten some of his men.

Wait. Nyx said good of you to join us. Wasn't Pyre the leader? She frowned at the kitsune. "Why has the meeting begun without you?"

"Not everything is about me, luv." Tempest scowled at him. "Relax," he said. "No need to be so on-edge. I never told you I was the leader. Nobody did. You just assumed."

Pyre inclined his head toward Nyx, and Tempest

followed the movement with her eyes. It was like she was seeing the female shifter in a brand-new light. No wonder she liked her. She was a woman in charge.

Nyx smiled at her. "Come and stand by me, Tempest. I'm sure this meeting will be illuminating."

If there was any dissent among the rebels at the idea of Tempest witnessing their meeting, nobody spoke out about it. Clearly Nyx had things well in hand.

Cautiously, Tempest made her way to the front to stand by Nyx, closely followed by Pyre. Her hand crept to the stake tucked into her belt and some of her worry drained away as she noticed Briggs standing near the front. The giant healer nodded at her encouragingly.

"Now that we're all here," Nyx said, throwing another pointed glare at Pyre, who shrugged, "it's high time we discuss our biggest threat."

And here we go, Tempest thought, steeling herself for whatever it was that would come next. She jerked when Pyre's hand brushed against hers and gave it the slightest squeeze. What the hell? She looked at him out of the corner of her eye. What game was he playing now?

She pulled away slightly, flustered, and tried to listen to what was being said. Tonight could mean everything for her.

"Another village a few hours from here has hit breaking point," Nyx announced, pulling Tempest sharply out of her own head. "We don't know the death toll so far. I want a few of us to head out and investigate tomorrow."

There was silence following Nyx's words, though the

entire crowd nodded their acceptance of this grim piece of news. Tempest was shocked by how easily they took the news. *Just how many villages have been wiped out like this?* She'd been given no official number back in Dotae. All she'd heard from the palace soldier Rane was that it was more than the Crown was admitting to…

"Of course, mostly all of us know by now that the *plague* is, in fact, a drug problem—"

Wait, what? A drug, not poison?

"—and that the drug in question is the most addictive substance we've ever come into contact with—"

Tempest's mind scrambled with implications.

"—and that King Destin is using his Hounds to spread the drug around to encourage addiction."

No. Tempest didn't speak. Everything inside her screamed to refute the allegations, but that wasn't her purpose. All she could do was numbly listen and learn as Nyx continued on.

"It's not clear if the Crown are aware that the drug eventually causes death. I wouldn't be surprised if that had always been their intention. Either way, considering the death toll around the mountains the king now must be aware that the drug causes death, whether he knew before or not. Now, we *were* running on the assumption that the drug had originally been manufactured in one of the island kingdoms as a means to attack Heimserya. It's one of the primary reasons Destin wishes to go to war with them. However, given what the king told Tempest—that the Talagan shifter *Jester* is responsible for the drug—we are now running on the theory that King Destin himself is responsible for the drug's creation and it is being distributed by the Hounds. We believe it may well have been created in the capital."

Given what the king told Tempest?

Tempest slowly turned and glowered at Briggs and Pyre. What sort of nonsense were they spreading? She'd never said it was a drug or that the Hounds were spreading it. She felt sick to her stomach at the implications of what they suggested. Her family would never do something so heinous as to kill their own people.

She trembled but didn't deny Nyx's revelation. It would do no good. She was among the enemy and her purpose was to gather information and kill the Jester. Clearly, these people weren't on the inside of his operation. Creation of such a drug would take a master distiller, a master of apothecary...

A memory sprung to mind. Of Aleks, working with a strange herb when Tempest was small. She had asked if she could help, but he'd shouted at her to leave the room. Aleks had never shouted at her before—not even when he'd been working. He had apologized for shouting but had practically thrown her out of his clinic. *The herb smelled horrible when he added it to the pot over the fire. It had smelled...*

It had smelled like the same concoction he'd been working on in the healer's tent before Tempest's Trial. A smell so sickeningly, cloyingly sweet that Tempest had almost vomited.

A smell like death.

Tempest abruptly turned, feeling as if she'd gone so numb her legs might not support her. She had it all wrong. The shifters were messing with her head, and she was looking for connections and monsters where there were none.

"Please excuse me," she said, though it was so quiet nobody noticed.

It fit Tempest's mood; all she wanted to do was melt away. To disappear and avoid facing the possibility that the people who had welcomed her into their family with open arms could be murderers. The men who raised her could be monsters and Tempest had been well on her way to becoming one herself on their behalf.

Dima and Maxim had been right when they said she wasn't ready for an assignment.

Chapter Twenty-Five

Tempest

"Please excuse me," Tempest repeated, louder this time to ensure she was heard. A wave of quiet washed over the entire clan.

"What, the king's lapdog can't stand to hear what the mangy group of dogs has been up to?" someone in the crowd yelled at her. Tempest bristled at the viciousness in his tone.

She felt a hand on her arm: Nyx.

"Tempest?"

She stared back at the woman, then glanced at Briggs and, then, at Pyre. All three of them were watching her with concerned expressions on their faces—a far cry from the lingering suspicion she could see on everybody else's. They were genuinely worried about her. About the way she'd taken the supposed truth that her entire family were murderers.

Tempest straightened out her shirt and smoothed non-existent creases from her skirt. She tossed her long hair over her shoulder, noticing in the process that the moonlight almost turned it silver. If there was even a sliver of truth to their suspicions, she wondered if she would dye it again, so as not to be marked as a Madrid.

Traitor.

She looked over the group again. She couldn't do this right now. There was just too much confusion. "Sorry," Tempest mumbled, and then she stalked away.

It did not matter that she no longer had a lantern to guide her, nor that her eyes were full of tears obscuring her vision; her feet pounded along the path Pyre had taken her through the forest as if her subconscious had committed the journey to memory.

Nyx is misinformed. The Hounds couldn't—my uncles couldn't...

As she ran, a storm was brewing inside her, threatening to be let loose as a scream that Tempest had held back for weeks now.

But if Nyx and her rebels were correct, then everything Tempest had been led to believe was a lie. The way she'd been brought up was a lie. Her prejudice toward shifters, which began the moment one had been responsible for the murder of her mother, had made it so easy for Tempest to believe everything she'd been told. She had been so critical about almost everything else in her life—except the shifters.

It isn't true. None of it is true. It's not. It's—

"Tempest, for the love of all that's holy, slow down!" Pyre yelled from behind her. "You do not know where you are going!"

Tempest swung her head back and forth and realized Pyre was right. She did not recognize where she was at all. *So much for muscle memory.* She must look like such a fool. She had two jobs. Find the Jester and kill him. And she couldn't even keep it together at a rebel meeting. How could she call herself a Hound? Did she still want to be a Hound? Why was everything so damn confusing?

"Leave me alone, Pyre," she muttered, swinging around to face him in the process. She didn't have it in her to care that he could see her tears in the darkness with his keen eyes. Embarrassed didn't even begin to describe her feelings. Disappointment in herself weighed down on her. Each pathway she took seemed to betray someone. "I don't want to—"

"If you think I am leaving you alone in this state then you really don't know me at all, city girl." He closed the gap between them before Tempest had a chance to back away, encircling her forearm with an iron grip before weaving her through the trees on her right. "Dry your eyes. I don't want you breaking your leg on a log or something because you cannot see."

She scrubbed at her face, irritated that she'd turned into a watering pot. Tempest had never been one for tears or hysterics, but when one's world had been flipped on itself it seemed as good as any other reason to cry.

After fifteen minutes of silence traipsing through the forest and trying to pull herself together, Pyre broke through the trees to a handsome, well-built cottage that looked to be at least four times the size of the one he'd had Tempest stay in. Her footsteps slowed when he bounded up the steps and opened the front door.

She hovered below the stairs, not wanting to take another step.

"Get in here or I'll carry you," he threatened softly.

Tempest's lips pressed together at his command but she trudged up the stairs and walked in first. She stood motionless in the middle of his dark kitchen, the moonlight peeking through the windows just enough to reveal a table and stove. She rubbed at her arms to dispel the gloomy feeling. He lit several lanterns, illuminating the place and chasing away some of her melancholy.

"Sit down, Temp," Pyre said gently, indicating toward a thick, wooden table surrounded by several matching chairs.

Gingerly, she sat and blankly watched him as he hung his cloak on a hook on the wall, sighed heavily, then left the kitchen for several minutes. Tempest eyed the door and wanted to leave, but it would have been stupid. Even with a stolen lantern she wouldn't have been able to find the isolated cottage on her own.

Pyre entered the room and brushed his sooty hands together to rid himself of the ash. "I've started a fire in the guest bedroom, so it'll be warm enough for you. I'll make you something to eat."

"I'm not hungry."

"Don't give me that," he replied, before getting to work, chopping vegetables and boiling some water.

Half an hour later, he handed Tempest a bowl of soup and a loaf of tulip bread that she recognized as one of Rina's. From personal experience, she knew both would be delicious, but to Tempest, in that moment she couldn't imagine anything worse than putting food in her mouth.

She shook her head and pushed the bowl away. "I'm not—I can't. I'll be sick. I think I'm going to be sick."

Pyre sat down beside her. He pushed several errant strands of Tempest's hair out of her face with a gentle hand, and she didn't pull away. It felt nice to be comforted.

"Temp," he said, very softly, "you're in shock. You had to see with your own eyes that everything you thought to be true didn't make any sense. You had to be asking your *own* questions, before I told you what was happening. You can't be blind to what is happening."

Tempest could barely hear him. Her ears were ringing; she thought if she opened her mouth to respond then she really *would* be sick. But she didn't need to reply, because Pyre soldiered on.

"I can't promise that things will get easier for you now," he said, still stroking Tempest's hair even though it was no longer in her eyes. "In fact, it will probably get much, much harder. But at least you know the truth. You're always seeking the truth, aren't you? I could tell from the moment I met you. Lies aren't enough for you, even when they're much easier to swallow than the truth. Even when they keep you safe. So, join us, Tempest. Do you know how much good you could do, if you were on the *right side*? You could save so many lives—innocent civilians like Aspen and Rina and—"

"There's no proof." Any liar with his skill could spin a web of half-truths that sounded like truth.

"What?"

"There's no proof," Tempest repeated in a monotone. The only way she could process what was happening was to remain unfeeling—to cut off her emotions and think *logically.* If she wanted the truth, she had to put aside all feelings and truly look at the evidence.

And there was no proof.

Pyre looked at her incredulously. He pulled his hand away from her face. "Temp, you can't be serious right now. You saw—"

"I saw nothing," she cut in. "I saw a village unravaged by anything. I heard some people throw accusations around. That's it." What galled her was that she still wanted to weep bitterly. What the devil? Her forehead wrinkled, and she began to count the days since she'd left Dotae. It had been almost a month.

A month. Her moon time was near, she guessed. That would explain her fluctuating emotions.

"You—impossible woman!" Pyre roared, pushing himself away from the table so violently his chair fell to the stone floor with a clatter. Tempest straightened, feeling, for the first time since having met Pyre, that he was dangerous.

He will kill me now. I'm useless to him.

"Are you going to kill me now?" she asked, her tone wooden. It's what she would do. She was a liability.

The kitsune jerked, and he stilled. Pyre took a flowing, predatory step toward her and curled a finger beneath her chin. Tempest met his fiery gaze without flinching when he growled into her face.

"Eat your damn food and get some sleep," Pyre whispered heatedly. He released her face and stormed over to the door. He grabbed his cloak and wrenched the front door open. "I'm going out."

With a slam of the door he was gone, leaving Tempest stunned beyond belief. Of all the things she expected Pyre—her enemy—could have done, storming out in a mood was not one of them.

Chapter Twenty-Six

Pyre

Damn woman.

Pyre didn't understand Tempest Madrid.

When he'd first met her in the tavern—when she'd pretended to be an innocent, overly-curious city girl named Juniper—he'd been sure he could charm her into saying yes to just about anything. Then, after saving her life and watching as she struggled with the knowledge that everything she'd learned about shifters might not be true, Pyre had been sure he could easily convince Tempest to join his cause. She had a strong sense of justice, and both Nyx and Briggs liked her. It was a solid recommendation of Tempest's character. They didn't like just anybody, after all.

His lips curled in disgust. But still Tempest remained loyal to the Hounds and King Destin, despite everything she'd now discovered. Today was the final straw. Pyre had shown his entire hand to her: the plague, the drugs, and her precious adoptive family – well all he could show her.

And yet Tempest still would not break. She would not join Pyre's side.

"That stupid, indoctrinated, silly girl!" he snarled up at the moon, beyond frustrated. Pyre had been so enamoured with his own idea that he had never considered the possibility he could fail. Having one of the king's lapdogs working for him would have been a huge blow to the Crown, and a huge win for the Talagans. For the people of Heimserya and farther out, too. It had been so long since he'd had someone defy and challenge him like she did.

If only she would yield.

The kingdom was only moments away from an all-out war with the Fire Isles and the Hinterlands. If Destin fabricated proof that the Fire Isles had joined forces with Heimserya's enemy's then all would be lost. He could not let things get that far. The king's lust for wealth and power had to stop now.

Without someone on the inside things *would* get that far.

Pyre ripped a low-hanging branch from an oak tree as he passed by. He had already spent too much time in this village putting his plan into action with Tempest. He needed to return to his court. Whispers of mutiny had already reached his ears from a few of his commanders. That couldn't stand, but now he had to deal with the wench currently in his home. He really didn't want to kill her.

You know you can't kill her.

"Damn Hound!" Pyre bellowed, not caring who could hear him. He had largely kept himself entirely composed for the past three weeks, no matter how infuriating Tempest had been. How obstinate. He'd made sure not to appear too passionate, or insistent, or demanding, or desperate. He'd carefully conditioned her to trust his people. Pyre's plan had to work. He'd already sent in too many agents who'd ended up dead. He *needed* someone on the inside. He needed the bloody Hound.

His lip curled remembering how her hollow voice had asked him if he was going to kill her. Pyre had fed and cared for the girl, beaten one of his own men to keep her, and still it wasn't enough. Never had a female made him so crazy. It was like she enjoyed intentionally needling him.

He had tried every tactic he could think of with the young woman to crack her open: giving her space; talking non-stop; being calm and patient; being lazy and good-natured; being cryptic; being understanding; getting angry, and, finally, simply telling Tempest what exactly was going on. He had demonstrated his trust in her as a person.

It still wasn't enough.

"Bloody—"

"*Pyre, that's enough!*" His sister scolded in hushed tones, appearing in front of him as if she had literally constructed herself from the shadowy night air. *"You will wake everyone up in a three-mile radius."*

Pyre merely scowled. "What would you have me do? Tempest has refused to help."

"She outright told you she wouldn't?"

"Yes."

Nyx pursed her lips, then splayed the fingertips of her left hand across her forehead and sighed. "Pyre, you knew this was, in all likelihood, what was going to happen."

"I know," he growled.

"She works for Destin—spent most of her life with the Hounds. Don't get me wrong, I like her. She's a strong, intelligent girl. She would have been an asset, had you been successful in bringing her to our side. But it won't happen. It'll never happen. She's the king's dog; she always will be."

Pyre turned his back on his sister, not trusting the way his temple had twitched at the insinuation that Tempest could not change. Hadn't he just thought the same thing? "Then I will have to kill her." The words tasted bitter on his tongue.

"I can make it painless," Nyx said softly. "She won't feel a thing."

He ran a hand over his face. "I'm as bad as Destin. Killing innocents."

"Never," she breathed, forcing Pyre back around to face her with an iron grip on his shoulder. "You'll never be like that monster. There is blood on our hands, but we fight for justice and he fights for selfish personal gain. You're nothing like the king."

"Yet, I'm planning on killing an innocent."

"She's a Madrid. The blood of murderers runs through her veins."

"You spent time with her. She's no murderer."

"We all have the potential for it. But it comes down to numbers. One girl for an entire village."

Pyre barked out a laugh. "You've always been a mercenary, Nyx. That's why you make such a great commander." There was a firm, knowing smile on her face. Pyre hated it, because he knew what Nyx was going to say next.

"I live to serve, my lord."

"Just stop. I'm no more royalty than Briggs."

His sister's smile melted away. "Don't think I can't see through your masks. You may be the Jester, but I'm still your sister. You're not going to let Tempest go, are you?"

And it came back to his Hound. *His.*

"Tempest has learned a lot," he murmured.

His sister snorted. "About us, yes. Not everything I presume?"

He chuckled humorlessly. "She hates the Jester. Her view of shifters may have changed, but she still hates him with her entire being. I'd lose her if she knew." Pyre shook his head. "We've turned her entire life upside-down with the revelation that the people who brought her up are not who she thought them to be and we expect her to accept it, just like that?"

"Brainwashing is hard to fight. I can see with my own

eyes that she's already unlearned a lot of the lies she was taught, and she's evaluating the rest," Nyx grudgingly admitted. "We might need to give her a little more time."

"We don't *have* time, Nyx," Pyre bit out. "I need to return."

His sister said nothing for a long, drawn-out moment. Then she hung her head and sighed. "You've tried the nice way, brother." She met his gaze, her eyes like onyx chips. "We've discovered much about our Lady Hound since we discovered her identity. Formidable as she is, Tempest is inexperienced and has weaknesses. She *loves* the men who raised her. They would make perfect incentives for her to work with us."

He pinched the bridge of his nose. "It won't work. She'll dig her heels in."

"You don't know that. Why are you hesitating with her? You never have before. Hesitation spells death. You know this. Release your alter ego and secure her allegiance."

"Fear accomplishes compliance, not allegiance."

"Compliance is better than death, brother." Nyx rolled her neck. "I can bring in Brine to handle it from here. He'll secure her cooperation in a couple of hours."

"She is my responsibility. That still hasn't changed. I'll give her one more day and if that doesn't work, she'll get a taste of my hard side."

"Are you sure?" Nyx eyed him. "I can sense your protectiveness of her."

"Have I ever failed in doing what is necessary?"

"Never," she whispered. "But nobody is infallible."

His lips thinned. "One day."

"You're not alone in this. Call for me if you have a need." Nyx stepped close and kissed his cheek. "And get her out of your bloody home unless you plan to seduce her into compliance." With that parting remark, his sister disappeared into the woods like a forest sprite.

He wasn't naïve; he knew she was right. Pyre had already given Tempest far more leeway than he'd ever given anyone else. There was something about her that he couldn't walk away from. She was the answer he'd been looking for.

"Infuriating and obstinate and brainwashed, but still our best shot," Pyre repeated like a furious mantra as he stormed through the woods and reached his front door. He tried to get his emotions under control before dealing with the Hound.

He glanced through the kitchen window; he could see Tempest had eaten the food he'd made her.

That was a good sign. At least, she wasn't a brat. He'd met many women who'd have thrown a temper tantrum. On impulse, he slipped around to the back of his house and saw there was light coming through the window of the guest bedroom.

She hadn't drawn the curtains.

Heat rolled through him, and he froze where he lurked in the shadows, not able to believe what he was seeing. Tempest was undressing right in front of him.

"That naïve idiot…" Who didn't draw the bloody curtains? Surely, she knew better than to undress in front of an uncovered window? She lived with a group of men for Dotae's sake!

He watched as she shrugged one shoulder out of one of Nyx's large linen shirts, exposing a massive scar. He still couldn't believe she'd bested a lion. His spies reported it was quite the Trial. No one had ever had to defeat a lion. Tempest had done something to catch the king's attention. And not in a good way if he'd set a lion on her.

"Just who are you?" he whispered to the darkness, not taking his eyes off the woman brazenly stripping off her clothes to change into the large night shirt Pyre had laid out on the bed for her before he'd stormed out. *His* own night shirt. He glanced away to give her some privacy, feeling uncomfortable with his satisfaction that she was wearing his clothing.

She's a means to an end. Nothing more. You might still have to kill her. And she is not the first pretty girl you've seen, naked or otherwise.

Subconsciously, his gaze moved back to her lithe figure. Tempest was elegant in a way Pyre had rarely seen a woman be before. He watched in interest as the firelight in the room flickered across the muscles of her back when she pulled off her shirt. His keen eyes picked up on the scars the lion had left her with; no amount of Mimkia paste was ever going to make them fully disappear.

Tempest tugged his shirt over her head and pulled her long hair up and out of the way as she began to unbutton her skirt. The night shirt covered her interesting bits as the skirt dropped to the floor in a puddle, revealing long, creamy legs.

Legs he wanted to run his hands and mouth along. *Legs of the enemy.*

"Damn it," he growled and abandoned his perch next to the window. She wasn't a whore or his own woman to look upon. It was wrong for him to watch as long as he had. Pyre stalked around his house, keeping his footfalls soft. He was a bloody degenerate.

"Pyre?"

He turned around and scowled. Briggs was standing by his front door, clearly waiting for him.

"How did you know I wasn't inside already?" Pyre asked.

"I could smell you on the forest air." Briggs shrugged, a smile splitting his face. "With the way you're riled up, I hope you weren't doing anything indecent."

"Me, indecent? Never."

"Pyre—"

"What is it you wanted to say, Briggs?"

The healer stared at him long and hard, brow furrowed, but then he ran a hand over his face. "Nyx thinks we should leave for the village we discussed during the meeting at sunrise."

"An hour before everyone else?"

"To scope it out, clearly. Your skills haven't been used to their full potential over the past three weeks. Tempest—"

"Tempest!" An idea slammed into Pyre.

Briggs's frown returned once more as he stared at Pyre.

"What about her?"

Pyre glanced at his house as if he could see through the stone wall to where she was no doubt lying in bed. He didn't want to do this to her. It was cruel. It was heartbreaking.

But he only had one day before things got a lot more brutal.

"Take her with you to the village tomorrow, Briggs," he ordered his friend, a grim smile curling his lips as he did so. "She needs to see what her family has done."

Chapter Twenty-Seven

Tempest

"Temp. Temp, you need to wake up."

Tempest blinked groggily as she was forced to rouse from sleep. For a few moments, she had no idea where she was, then she remembered with a start that she'd stayed the night in Pyre's house. She bolted upright, searching through the dim, early morning light for who had spoken.

Briggs.

The giant of a man rested a large midnight hand on her shoulder and sighed. Going by the look in his eyes, he was not looking forward to what he had to do next. Tempest's stomach lurched.

"What is it, Briggs?" she asked, very, very quietly.

He looked away. "There's something you need to see. Some*where* you need to see. Get dressed, Temp. Wrap up warm; it's cold out this morning."

Oh no.

Tempest wasn't stupid. Considering the topic of conversation at the rebels' meeting the night before, there were very few things Briggs would take her to see with such a grave expression on his face.

Either I'm walking to my death or I'm being taken to the village Nyx was talking about.

She nodded her acknowledgement of Briggs's order before waving him out of the room so she could get dressed. With a furtive look out of the window—Tempest had kept the curtains open all night to stop her feeling like she was trapped in a box—she threw off the nightshirt Pyre had laid out for her and began pulling on her clothes from the day before.

Speaking of the devil... Where was he? She twisted in front of the window, using the reflection to help her braid her hair. Tempest hadn't heard the kitsune return to his house after storming out. But that didn't mean anything. The shifters had a knack for moving without making a sound.

Tempest worked a crack out of her shoulder then spent five minutes stretching out her limbs. She had not felt limber in weeks; she knew she'd have to train hard to get her body back into the shape it had been when she'd walked into the Trial arena to face the lion. If an attack did come, she needed to be prepared.

She glanced out of the window again, and her stomach fluttered uncomfortably, though she didn't know why. Last night, it had almost felt as if someone was watching her, but she'd searched the house and found nothing.

Though considering what she said to Pyre the night before, she wouldn't be surprised if he'd had someone observing his house as a safety precaution.

She let out a whoosh of air before exiting the bedroom. Tempest didn't regret what she'd said to Pyre the night before, but she regretted the *way* she'd said it. Regardless of the truth of the whole plague debacle, there was one thing Tempest had realized for sure: the kitsune shifter was not a bad man.

He might be on the wrong side. He might be on the right side. But, either way, he's fighting with good intentions. Like me.

"We're going to have to eat on the move, Temp," Briggs told her, tossing a hunk of bread and cheese her way when she appeared in Pyre's kitchen.

Pyre was nowhere to be seen, which meant he was clearly still out.

"Where's Pyre?" Tempest asked, deciding there was no point in wasting time by dancing around her questions.

The healer grimaced. "You'll see him in a few hours. Come on, we have a long walk ahead of us."

She was surprised to find three more rebel shifters waiting outside Pyre's house for them. They glared at her, so obviously disapproving of her inclusion in this journey that Tempest could do nothing but stare at the ground.

If they were angry at her presence, then she could assume they weren't going to kill her – surely they'd be a lot more cheerful if they were marching her to her execution. *One less thing to worry about.*

But none of the shifters said anything about her joining them so, despite the looks they gave her, the entire group set off through the forest in the opposite direction from the sound of the river. *Deeper into the forest, then.* Tempest nibbled on the bread and cheese Briggs had given her; though her stomach was roiling, she simply needed to have something to do with her restless hands. They kept twitching, wishing to hold a sword or a dagger or a bow and arrow to defend herself.

Tempest had none of those things with her, only her pathetic wooden stake.

What a sorry Hound she'd become. *Out of shape, weaponless, and sympathizing with the enemy. My uncles would be ashamed.*

But Tempest's uncles weren't here. Tempest was alone, and she had to make her own decisions and form her own opinions without their help. She'd never thought it would be so difficult to do.

As morning stretched into midday the forest grew much warmer. The sunlight on the trees brought out the smell of pine needles and sap, which Tempest found refreshing. She breathed in deeply through her nose, revelling in the memory of such scents from her childhood—from before her mother's death. Dotae always smelled of a dozen different things at once; there was something to be said for the beautiful simplicity of a forest smelling exactly like a forest, and nothing else.

Until it didn't.

At first Tempest didn't notice the new scent, though her

shifter companions clearly did. They wrinkled their noses and slowed their steps, clearly reluctant to move forward. Briggs waved them on regardless, and Tempest, confused, followed on behind them all.

Then, as the first buildings of the village came into sight, Tempest's nose wrinkled when an odor invaded her nostrils. A cloying, nightmarishly sweet smell that Tempest was sickeningly familiar with.

Please no.

It smelled exactly like the concoction Aleks had been brewing. It had to be a coincidence.

Except it was worse, Tempest realized. A hundred times worse, because it was all around her, suffocating the air out of her lungs until she could scarcely breathe. *This isn't just the smell of some drug.*

She coughed heavily and wiped tears from her eyes as she forced herself through the village. *There's another smell here. It smells like—*

"Everybody is dead," she gasped.

The words caught in her throat like a hook. All around her were corpses strewn across the ground like dolls. At the end of the cobbled street was a blackened mound that looked disturbingly like a pile of burned bodies.

Not a soul in the village was alive.

"No," Tempest whispered over and over again as she numbly checked every cottage and shop she passed by for survivors. Someone must have survived. But there were none—not even a stray dog or cat or chicken hiding in a corner. "No, no, no—"

Her stomach rebelled as she spotted a little foot poking from around the corner of a house. She retched and fell to her hands and knees, vomiting up the breakfast she'd blindly eaten on her way over.

"Let's get you out of here, Temp," Briggs said, very softly. "I'm sorry you had to see this. I'm—"

"No," she moaned. Tempest wiped her mouth with the back of her hand and staggered to her feet. Briggs wrapped an arm around her to keep her upright. "They're dead. I'm not. I got the better end of the deal."

"Temp—"

"Just need—to breathe," she said, swaying dangerously against Briggs as he led her out through the other end of the village, where the sound of running water over gravel could be heard. It was a shallow stream, but substantial enough for Tempest to stoop down and slam her face into the bracing water to clear her head. But even after she dried herself, Tempest's cheeks continued to grow wetter and wetter.

She was silently sobbing and couldn't stop.

Tempest strode back toward the village. Briggs tried to grab her arm, but she jerked away. Death surrounded her, and she dropped to her knees, gazing at the vilest crime she'd ever witnessed. Who could do such a thing? Her gaze kept straying to the small foot. Who could hurt children? She dry-heaved again, tears and snot mixing on her face.

It took her a few moments to realize that she and Briggs were not alone. A few feet in front of them stood a green-cloaked figure with flattened fox ears, hunched over another dead body. Another lurch in Tempest's stomach insisted that she look away—that she run away and never come back—for the sight that lay in front of her was one that she desperately did not want to see. But she forced herself to look and to inhale the cloying scent she knew wasn't a coincidence.

"Pyre," Briggs called over to the kitsune shifter. "Pyre, who is that? Do you know them?"

Pyre took far too long to answer. It was the kind of pause that made Tempest certain that she should cover her ears to avoid hearing what he'd say.

She didn't.

"Grandfather," Pyre said, his voice flat and devoid of all emotion as he stood. "He was my grandfather."

Chapter Twenty-Eight

Tempest

She didn't know what to say to Pyre. He stared out, desolate, at the remains of the village as if he didn't dare look at his grandfather. Perhaps he was scared of what he would see in the old man's face—or, rather, what he *wouldn't* see.

Either way, Tempest was a novice at dealing with such situations. Though she had lost her mother at a young age, Tempest had been fortunate enough to never have to deal with another death that directly affected her. Since living with the Hounds, no one she knew who had fallen victim to illness or grievous injury had ever died. Even Juniper's family was healthy.

She did not know what to say other than, "I'm so sorry for your loss," though the words felt hollow. Of course she was sorry for Pyre's loss—that was a given. But she couldn't think of any words that could make the man's entire frame stop shaking.

Perhaps there *were* none.

Pyre's visible display of grief achieved one thing, though; Tempest finally managed to stop crying and regain control of her mental faculties. She followed his stare to look at the village with less emotional eyes. The place had been all but torn apart, and several outlying cottages were smoking as if their roofs were on fire. *The final blow to this place was sudden and recent.*

Guilt weighed down on her. She somehow felt like it was her fault.

Tempest braced herself for the stench of death once more and left both Pyre and Briggs and wandered through the village again. Old, young, male and female alike hadn't escaped the plague.

The drug. Someone did this on purpose.

Her heart hurt whenever she saw the frail figure of a child lying in their bed or on the street, never to open their eyes or take a breath again. When she found a mother huddling a baby, she began crying again, and all of Tempest's hard-fought-for control was lost.

"Evil," she said, not bothering to wipe away her tears. She *wanted* to feel them—wanted proof that she was not part of the evil. If King Destin and the Hounds were truly responsible for the massacre in front of her...

Then I want no part in it.

But that wasn't enough.

She turned to look at Pyre and discovered that he was

already staring at her. She nodded her head.

I will take down whoever is responsible for this, no matter who they are.

But, though anger and vengeance were swelling in Tempest to overcome her grief, there was an undercurrent of dread beneath it. How was she supposed to discover the truth? How was she supposed to go home and confront Aleks about the herbs and the drug? Was he innocent? What if he admitted to knowledge of the crime? How was she supposed to do anything? She was only one person. A chill ran down her spine. What did she do if all of the Hounds were in on it?

And what about King Destin?

Tempest shivered despite the warmth of the afternoon sunshine filtering down from above her. The king had scared her when she'd met him, and he terrified her still, but Tempest had not thought him possible of this kind of mindless depravity. He seemed to rule well, after all. Dotae was flourishing with trade deals, and the level of poverty in the city was no worse than it had been under the rule of his father.

Dotae is but one part of a very large kingdom, Temp. You're not so naïve as to assume the state of one place reflects what life is like everywhere else.

Which meant that Tempest had to be smart about what she did next. Careful. Calculated. If King Destin had perfected his veneer as a good and just ruler, and the Hounds truly were his unrelentingly loyal lapdogs come thick or thin, then Tempest could not come blazing back to Dotae with wild accusations, screaming of murder.

I must have cards of my own. Think, Tempest. Think.

And then it hit her.

King Destin's war council. She needed to be on his council and gain his trust.

She rushed over to Pyre's side, her footsteps thumping across the cobbles. He watched her do so with a completely expressionless face, his fox ears completely downcast.

She hesitated and then squared her shoulders. "You brought me here for a purpose."

He laughed hollowly. "I did."

"Again, I'm so sorry…"

"You have already said that you're sorry for my loss," he said. "Do not feel as if you have to express such sentiments a second time. I believe your grief for me to be genuine, no need to worry that I think you are lying." His words were sharp and held an aristocratic tone of indifference.

She shook her head. "I wasn't." *Don't hesitate.* If Tempest didn't ask Pyre now, then she was fairly certain she'd lose her resolve altogether. She forced herself to lock onto Pyre's glassy, dispassionate eyes. The gold of his irises had never looked so dull.

"Do you trust me?" she asked.

Pyre barked out a humorless laugh. "After all this time, you want to know if I trust you? I've trusted you all that I can so far. That is all I can give you." He gestured to the carnage around them. "I can offer death and decay."

"Then, Pyre, can I..." Tempest trailed off, the next words of her sentence stuck in her throat as if she were choking on food.

Spit it out. Just spit it out. Even if it's outrageous. Even if he'll never say yes.

A faint spark of interest lit up Pyre's dead expression. He frowned at her. "Can you what, Temp?"

She closed her eyes. Took a deep breath. She knew she had to ask.

"Can I have your grandfather's heart?"

Chapter Twenty-Nine

Tempest

"His heart," Tempest said again, hating herself for having to push on with the request but knowing she had to. Only a kitsune shifter heart would suffice for the king, for her ruse to work. "Can I have it?"

Pyre stared at her in confusion as if Tempest had lost her mind. His eyes grew wide, golden irises flashing with anger.

She took a step toward the stunned man. "Pyre, I know it sounds insane but—"

"I'm assuming you have a particularly valid reason for asking for it?" he bit out.

"I do."

He scanned her from head to toe, his lip curling. A growl rumbled in his chest. "I can't deal with this." Pyre jerked his chin toward Briggs. "Take her home."

"I need you to listen to me," she said with quiet desperation.

"Not now. My grandfather is dead, and I can't look at you without wanting to hurt you."

She fell silent and allowed Briggs to lead her away. Her resolve grew with each step they took away from the village. She'd been thrown into a game she knew nothing about, but she'd sworn to protect the innocent and bring justice to those who found delight in hurting others. Tempest had always believed herself to be strong—she had been through so much and come out fighting at the other end, regardless—but now everything Tempest had previously associated with strength felt hollow.

What use is being a Hound if the entire group is corrupt? What use is physical strength when there is nobody to protect? What use is intellect and logic in the face of senseless massacres and illegal wars?

Tempest glanced over her shoulder as Pyre bent low by his grandfather's side, stroking the man's sparse, graying hair away from his forehead with a tenderness Tempest herself had experienced first-hand the night before. She turned abruptly away, feeling as if she was watching an intimate moment that shouldn't have spectators.

"I stand on the side of the innocent," she said with conviction, tipping her head up to stare at Briggs. No one should lose their loved ones to such senseless violence.

The healer nodded gravely. "Good. They need all the protectors they can get."

Tempest sat on a wooden stool before the fire, drumming her fingers on her knee. The day had faded into night and Pyre still hadn't come home. Her ears pricked with every sound, but each time it was nothing.

She'd spent the rest of the day going over what she knew to be absolutely true. The king wanted the Jester dead to stop the rebellion. He also had a desire for more power. Tempest had smelled the drug before in Aleks's infirmary. It was villages along the mountains that had been targeted—isolated enough that people wouldn't go poking around, but well-known enough for stories to travel. From what she'd learned, the Jester wasn't the cause of the mass murders. But why would the Crown kill its own people? That didn't make sense. Even if the king hated the shifters, he wouldn't kill his own for the fun of it, would he?

The front door silently swung open, and Pyre stepped inside. She blinked at his ensemble: the gaudy, stripped coat and silky top hat from their first meeting sat at an angle atop his head. Tempest had only seen him in leather trousers and linen shirts for weeks. It was disconcerting to see him looking so much like a... a courtier.

His empty, amber eyes ran over her, and he turned his back, closing the door and hanging his hat on a hook. "What are you doing here?"

"I know it's a terrible time, but I need to speak with you. If only to apologize."

He slowly unclasped his cloak and hung it on the wall. "Apologize for what? Your bloody heritage, your murdering king, or wanting to desecrate my grandfather's body?"

"For my insensitivity this morning. I shouldn't have asked you like that. I'm sorry."

Pyre turned and rested a shoulder against the wall, regarding her. "You're forgiven. Now get out."

"That's not all I have to say."

"I'm poor company tonight. We can speak in the morning."

Tempest steeled her nerves and ignored his dismissal. "I'm sorry, but it can't wait."

"I don't know how I can make this much clearer," he enunciated. "I don't want you in my home. I still have the stinking reek of that drug singeing my nose and looking at you makes me want to hurt something. I'd prefer it not to be you."

"I know you, Pyre. You won't hurt me," she said softly.

"You don't know anything about me, little girl."

"No, you don't know anything about me," she said calmly as the kitsune moved to the kitchen and poured himself a drink. "Or why I am here."

"You're poking around into the plague," he sneered.

She unfolded herself from the stool and crossed her arms. Once she revealed her true purpose, there was no going back. "I'm here on behalf of the king."

"Oh?" Pyre murmured, swirling the spirits in his glass. "Do tell."

Tempest ignored his attitude. Grief affected everyone differently. "The king took an interest in me, and I found myself in a precarious situation." Just thinking about that night in his room made her sick.

"Did he harm you?" Pyre whispered, his voice so dark it sent shivers across her skin.

"No, but he made me a deal." She swallowed. "My mother was killed by a shifter. I wanted time to hunt that shifter down, and I'd heard of the sickness. The king promised me the assignment, with an added task." Time to lay all her cards on the table. "He tasked me with killing the Jester."

Her heart pounded in her chest as she waited for Pyre to react. She knew he had some connection to the crime lord. The kitsune took a slow sip from his glass and stared at her over the rim.

"And what do you get out of this?" he murmured.

"A chance to exact vengeance for my mum's death, and he promised me a place on his war council if I succeeded."

"And if you failed?" he whispered, sauntering up to her.

Tempest swallowed hard and backed toward the hearth, the flames heating the back of her calves. "I am to become his," she gritted out.

"You foolish, foolish girl," Pyre crooned. He reached a hand over her shoulder and set his drink on the shelf above the fireplace. "You're playing games with a man who never loses."

"He didn't give me a choice. I did the best I could with what I was given. One doesn't turn down a king when he calls for you."

The kitsune ran a finger down her cheek. "Did you give

it up to him, Lady Hound?"

Her face flamed, but she held her ground and slapped his hand away. "No."

He flashed a smile. "Of course not. Tempest would never sully herself with such base emotions."

"We're getting off track." She ducked under his arm. "I can't go back without the heart of the Jester. Which brings me back to my insensitive question this morning. The king knows the Jester is a fox. I promised him a heart. Was your grandfather a kitsune?"

Pyre picked up his glass and tossed back the remaining contents. "He was." He faced her and laced his arms across his wide chest. "Why does it matter?"

Tempest exhaled heavily. She had no idea if one could tell what kind of shifter someone was by their heart, but she wasn't going to take any chances. For all Tempest knew, Aleks had some kind of chemical test that could work it out. "I don't have time to track down the Jester, and, even if I did kill him, another would rise up in his place. But if I were to approach the king with a kitsune's heart... well, then I would be appointed a place on his council."

"The king sent you to assassinate the Jester?" Pyre repeated. "An inexperienced woman with the acting skills of a potato?"

Tempest jerked and blinked at his hostile tone. "Did you not hear what I said? If I had a position on the council, you'd have a direct line of information from the Crown." She closed the distance between them and placed her right hand on his arm. "What transpired today can't occur again. I'm not completely sure what's happening, but I'm going to find out."

The kitsune smiled softly at her and uncrossed his arms. He touched the tip of her nose. "The king sure knows how to pick them. He knew exactly what he was doing, like a lamb to the slaughter."

She stiffened when his right arm slipped around her waist and pulled her flush with his body. "Pyre?"

He bent his neck and sniffed at her throat, a husky groan reverberating in his chest. "Oh, luv, what a web you've been caught in."

"Excuse me?" she squeaked.

"If you want the Jester so badly," he whispered in her ear. "Strike true and my heart is yours, city girl."

Chapter Thirty

Tempest

Tempest stopped struggling against Pyre and blankly stared at his jacket, his heart steadily thumping beneath her right palm. "W-what?" she stuttered, trying to make sense of his words.

"You heard me, Hound. If you want your precious Jester so badly, I'm standing right here."

A dull ringing started in her left ear, and her breathing sped up. It couldn't be true. He was too young. "You can't possibly be," she reasoned. "You're not old enough."

"That's the lovely thing about being the Jester: the name passes from one person to the next, continuing on the legacy. No one can really kill the lord of the underworld."

Bloody hell. Even if that was true, the horror stories she'd heard in the past five years were enough to give her nightmares. Fear pooled in her belly, and panic began to creep up her throat.

Remember your training. Panic is the enemy, not fear.

Tempest slipped her left hand into the pocket of her skirt, her fingers curling around an abandoned kitchen blade she'd stolen from the baker a day earlier, so thankful for her foresight. The Jester's arm tightened around her, and she wheezed. She needed to get out of his arms this instant. Close-quarter brawling would end in her death.

"You think you're so clever," she said, maintaining his cold amber gaze. "But you're nothing but a crook with stolen top hat." Tempest stomped her foot on his instep and jerked her knee into his groin.

The kitsune's grip loosened as he dodged her blow. "And you're just a little girl playing at being a warrior." He caught her arm in a brutal grip, his fingers locking on her right wrist.

She jerked against his grip, but it was immovable. The firelight lit his face, highlighting his sharp, fae-like features and the slash of his cheekbones. His amber eyes seemed to glow, and he looked like the devil himself. His hard lips formed a cruel smile.

"You think it would be that easy to escape me? To kill the Jester?" His voice was a soft, seductive murmur, the voice of someone who expected his word to be obeyed and was never defied.

"No," she agreed, tightening her fingers around her hidden blade. Tempest slid the thin, six-inch blade from her pocket, keeping her weapon hidden. "But I've been a quick study."

Tempest stabbed hard, stepping forward with her body to strengthen the thrust. Pyre caught her wrist, jerking it to the side so that the blade skittered across his ribs, not between them. He shoved away from her and held up his fingers, blood covering them.

She danced back out of his reach and eyed the doorway. It was so close and yet so far. Her gaze darted back to the kitsune as he looked up through a fringe of wine-colored hair, his eyes burning with intensity and the promise of revenge. The blood in Tempest's veins turned cold at the sight, and she held her bloody blade tighter. It was like looking at a completely different person.

The Jester sucked in a sharp breath and brushed the wrinkles from his shirt, like he was getting ready to have tea with a lord. "That wasn't wise, luv."

She eased a foot behind her and shifted, swiping her blade at the fox as he came at her, his form moving so quickly she could hardly track him. A hand caught hers, and his thumb dug into the nerve that ran to her thumb.

"Damn it," she cursed as the knife dropped from her useless hand.

The kitsune yanked her arm behind her and he spun, shoving her face-first against the cottage wall. She hissed as the rough wood scraped her cheek, but it was the least of her worries. Tempest had been taught hundreds of ways to kill a man, but none of them would apply if she couldn't get a little space between their bodies.

Pyre leaned against her, towering over her with his great height. He shoved her between the shoulder blades and yanked her arm farther behind her back. Black dots danced across her vision, but she managed not to cry out. The fox expected her to fight and that would make it worse. Tempest relaxed against him, the pain softening a touch. She'd suffered many injuries before, so pain was like an old friend. A physical ache was something she could fight—death was not.

The Jester's firm body pressed against her, one knee driving into the back of hers. There was nowhere to go, she was well and truly pinned. But she had one more trick up her sleeve. The damn shiv from the stool hidden in her corset.

She wiggled her right hand that was pinned beneath her breasts. With some maneuvering, she'd be able to reach it. The shifter ran his hand along her left arm.

"No more blades? I'm almost a little disappointed." He laughed, a short barking cough of amusement. "Nothing to say?"

Tempest kept her mouth shut and schooled her expression, blankly staring at the fireplace to her left. Silence hung between them. Only a couple of inches, and she'd have her weapon. Winter's bite, did she ever wish she had her blades.

"Cat got your tongue, city girl?"

She needed to keep him distracted. "You and I could come to an understanding." There were always ways to manipulate a man. Even the Jester had to want something, desire it.

"You're trying to bribe the wrong man," he hissed.

"From the stories I've heard, you're exactly the type of man who enjoys a good bribe." *And arson, larceny, prostitution, and assassinations.* "You've been at me for weeks to join your side. So what do you want from me? To be your own personal assassin? Information? Access to the king?"

Tempest wiggled her right hand to the top of her corset and paused when his grip slacked and his left hand slid around her waist, his thumb splayed over her ribs, just beneath her breast. A touch below her stake.

"What about something a little more personal? I love thwarting the king, so maybe I'll take you as my mistress."

Her stomach twisted. She would play along for now, but she'd never be anyone's mistress. *Ever.*

He released her arm, and she quickly plucked the shiv from the top of her corset. Grabbing a handful of her skirt, he spun her around, one hand wrapping around her throat. The Jester stared down at her, haughty contempt written all over his face. His other hand curved around the back of her skull, and he grabbed a fistful of her hair.

She inhaled slowly, even as her pulse raced when he dragged her head back, exposing her throat. His nose brushed along the edge of her jaw and then down to the smooth skin just behind her ear. "Are you going to tear my throat out?" she asked, her tone serene despite the storm brewing in her chest. "Like an animal?"

"You'd like that, wouldn't you? If anyone is an animal here, it is you. You who kill without conscience or question." His cool breath fanned over her skin. He lifted his head, his hand still cradling her skull. Tempest met his gaze evenly. "Even now, you show no emotion. Did they train all humanity out of you? Even animals don't kill like the slaughter we saw today in the village. I'm no animal, but you are."

She peered up at the seething kitsune and studied him. Anguish and rage were clearly riding him hard. Tempest wrapped her leg around Pyre's and slid her foot up the back of his calf. A flicker of surprise touched his face, and he softened. *What a stupid male.* It was just the opening she needed.

She launched herself off the wall and toppled Pyre. They collapsed onto the floor. Tempest scrambled up his body and pinned his shoulders with her knees. Her scalp stung, and his hand still tangled in her locks as she placed the wooden shiv beneath his jaw. "Don't move."

He blinked slowly, and she snarled when his hands curled around her ankles. "It seems we are at an impasse, luv."

Tempest pressed the makeshift weapon hard against his neck, a small drop of blood leaking down his throat. "You'll bleed out before you could make a move."

"Now that you have me where you want me, you're going to kill me?"

Pursing her lips, she glared down at the kitsune. He'd turned her world upside-down. By all accounts, she *should* kill him and take his heart back to the king. But Tempest couldn't ignore the evidence. Even *the Jester* couldn't concoct such an elaborate scheme. Seeing the village had changed everything. She couldn't blindly look the other way when innocents were suffering.

Her eyes narrowed on the man laying beneath her. Even if she did kill the Jester another would spring up in his place. The devil she knew was better than the demon she didn't. Whether all the stories were true or not didn't matter. He was a means to an end.

"Thank your stars tonight. I should kill you," she whispered. "But we're embroiled in something much bigger than ourselves. Only your grief and the love Aspen has for you have stayed my hand. No one can fake emotion like that. The slaughter of that village affected you just as much as it did me."

"How magnanimous of you, Lady Hound." He quirked a wry smile at her. "So where do we go from here?" His fingers crept up her legs.

Tempest pressed harder against his throat. "We come to a truce. My first condition: get your bloody hands off me."

His fingers lingered for second longer than necessary on the backs of her calves and then extricated themselves from her skirts. "Agreed, and I won't tear your head from your shoulders when you release me."

She laughed at his chilling words. "You and I both know you wouldn't kill me." Tempest leaned close and sniffed at his throat like he'd done to her. "I don't have your sense, but desperation clings to you like a foul odor. You didn't nurse me back to health out of the goodness of your black heart. I'm your only shot at the king."

FROST KAY

"So impertinent. Where have you been hiding this side of yourself, Temp?"

"Probably the same place you hid your Jester identity," she retorted hotly.

Pyre clasped his hands behind his head and arched a brow. "As much as I love being nestled between your sweet thighs, you think you could get up?"

Heat scorched her cheeks at his crude words, but she didn't move, her gaze boring into the Jester. "Don't make me regret trusting you."

"Don't trust me. I wouldn't trust me."

Her lips twitched at his humor, but she managed to keep a straight face. Tempest slid back and started to stand, but his hands landed on her hips, pinning her in place. She lodged her shiv against his sternum as Pyre levered up and looked into her eyes. His eyes scanned her face, and he brushed his nose against hers.

"In my culture, we seal our deals with a kiss."

Her stomach flipped, and a thrill of dread and excitement ran through her. Tempest scowled and squashed the feeling. It would be pure stupidity to allow such an emotion to take root in her heart. The Jester was dangerous.

She kept her weapon in place and lifted her left hand, sliding her fingers through the deep red strands of his silky hair. The amusement fled from his expression and something hotter replaced it. The blackness of his pupils expanded in his eyes, and his fingers clenched in her skirts. He might not like what she was, but he was

317

attracted all the same. Tempest had him.

His warm breath fanned against her sensitive lips when she leaned closer. Tempest brushed her nose against his once and then placed a gentle kiss on his left cheek. His heavy breaths heated the side of her throat. A shudder swept through his massive frame when she pulled back and stroked his clenched jaw.

"Afraid to kiss the Jester, luv?" he taunted.

She cocked her head and made a decision that could change everything. He'd lost his grandfather that today and a whole village of his people. Pain and grief like that needed comfort, even the lord of the dark courts. They were enemies, to be sure, but when she was in a sorry state, he'd protected her—even if it had been for an ulterior motive. Tempest pulled her weapon back and wrapped her arms around his neck, hugging him.

Pyre stiffened, but she didn't let go. A minute passed, and he slowly relaxed, enfolding her in his own massive arms. He held her tightly against his chest and tucked his face into the crook of her neck. The fire crackled in the hearth, and minutes drifted by, but she didn't move until she felt some of the tension in his body melt away.

She carefully pulled back. "Make no mistake, we are still enemies, but in this matter, I will help you. What happened today must never take place again."

"So, we're allies."

"So it seems."

She squeaked when the kitsune rolled to his feet and set her down. Her lips thinned as she stepped out of his arms. The bastard could have dislodged her at any point. Damn Talagan strength.

He turned his back to her and poured another drink. "A toast to our new partnership?"

"No, thank you."

"Afraid I'll poison you?"

"It seems prudent to keep my wits about me in the current company."

He chuckled. "There's the old pragmatic Tempest I know." Pyre turned and rested a hip against the kitchen table. "What happens next? You feed us information about what's going on, straight from the horse's mouth?" A vicious grin spread upon his face. "Although comparing Destin to a horse is an insult to the horse. I always considered him more of an—"

"I won't promise that," Tempest said sternly.

Pyre quirked an eyebrow. "Oh? Even after everything you've seen today, you still won't join our side?"

"That isn't what I said," she said. "I'm not on anyone's side. Not yours, not the king's, not until I truly know what is happening."

"Very wise, but I certainly hope you'll be on mine. Your prickly nature has grown on me some."

She ignored his comment as Briggs's question once again returned to her mind. "I stand on the side of the innocent." Tempest lifted her chin and stood taller. "You certainly aren't innocent."

"My delicate sensibilities are so offended," he cried.

"I'm sure," she muttered dryly. "I need to collect more

evidence."

"You want me to let you go."

"To corroborate your theories, yes. If you're correct, I'll feed you the information you need."

Pyre swirled his spirits. "And if you can't?"

"I'll stay silent." *For now.*

"You want me to trust you?"

"You don't have a choice," Tempest murmured.

"I could toss you back into a pit."

She flinched at the memory of falling into the dark pit. "True, but you'd be back to square one. Spyless."

"I have plenty of spies."

"Not ones on the king's war council."

The Jester appraised her. "You're a bold one. No wonder he likes you."

Her lip curled just the tiniest bit. There was no doubt who the *he* was that Pyre was speaking about.

"You truly aren't the king's tart." The kitsune's smile widened, and he pointed at her face. "You better get that facial spasm under control, or it'll make you even more desirable. He relishes conquering things."

"I'm not discussing that with you. Let's focus on what really matters," she bit out. "*If* I find out that the king and the Hounds are responsible for all of this, I will stay undercover on the council for as long as I can to feed you more information. If I discover nothing, this will be the last conversation we ever have before I find you and throw you into a windowless prison for your prior crimes."

Pyre contemplated this for a long time in silence. "The enemy of my enemy is my friend."

"I'm not your friend, but I am your ally." For a moment back then, she might have thought they could be, but not now. A gulf of depravity and sin lay between them. She pressed her lips together, hating what she needed to say next. "I need to return, and I can't return home empty-handed," Tempest said very quietly.

"You need a heart."

"I do… and my weapons."

He gazed impassively through her. "It'll be done. Give me an hour."

Tempest ran her fingertips over the grain of the heavy wooden table in Pyre's kitchen as she thought out her next steps. She looked at the front door.

She could leave now. Without the heart. Without saying goodbye. Without any responsibility being thrust upon her shoulders. She could simply…run away. She'd always wanted to see the giants of Kopal. It wouldn't be easy crossing the mountains, but she'd be able to do it.

She shook her head at her fantasies. Of course, she would not leave. She was in too deep, and she had a job to do. It was her responsibility to help if she saw a need. And someone needed to stop the poisonings. She wanted to prevent another village from being wiped off the map before it was too late.

Pyre returned stone-faced and grim, his mouth set in a determined line. Her traitorous heart skipped a beat. He looked like a dark, avenging angel: dangerous and alluring.

He held out her leather satchel. Knowing what must be inside, her hands trembled as she took it. She ignored how the Jester's fingers brushed her own as she reverently opened the bag and examined her weapons. It was like she had a little piece of herself back.

"It's needless to say, but what you're doing is extremely dangerous."

"Isn't that why you need me to do it?" she asked, closing the satchel.

"I suppose so." His hand wrapped around her wrist, and she lifted her eyes to meet his gaze. "I may be the monster who lives under your bed, but you have a choice. I won't force you to do anything."

"No one makes me do anything I don't want to do." She slung the bag over her shoulder, feeling the sharp edge of a box within it against her hip. She looked down at it, then back at Pyre. "I understand the risks."

"Be sure you do," he murmured, a familiar smirk curling the corner of his mouth. "Lion-Killer. Goddess of Little Fawns. Lady Hound. You have much to lose."

The two of them stared at each other in silence. Pyre scratched one of his fox ears and shifted his amber gaze to the door. "Come in, Briggs."

The door swung open, and the healer's massive frame filled the doorway.

"Time to go," Briggs said, breaking the increasingly awkward silence at the best—or perhaps, the worst—

moment. Tempest wasn't sure which it was. Briggs handed Tempest all of her previous gear, which she attached to her person with a joy she had not felt in weeks. She no longer felt so exposed, not now she had her sword and daggers and, most importantly, her mother's bow and quiver again.

She stroked the intricate pattern engraved into the bow with her thumb, before slinging it onto her back. "What now, then?"

Pyre pulled his forest-green cloak from the wall and threw it over Tempest's shoulders. She gawked and then snapped her mouth shut when the kitsune pulled the hood low over her face. She held out a hand to stop him on instinct, and he caught it in his own with ease.

"We can't have you knowing how to get back here, if you end up deciding not to help us," he explained. "Briggs will return you to where my clan first picked up your scent."

"And if I need to contact you?" Tempest asked, flinging back the hood in order to look at Pyre for what could well be the last time. "How will I find you?"

He flashed an achingly familiar grin at her. "Why, we'll find *you*, of course."

Chapter Thirty-One

Tempest

Briggs and Tempest did not speak to each other as they passed into a stretch of trees—trees that had been impressed into Tempest's mind for a long time.

The woods where I started my journey.

She glanced at the huge man walking beside her as he hummed a soft tune. He really did remind her of Maxim, though Briggs was quiet and thoughtful whereas Maxim was boisterous and impulsive. Maybe it was because both men looked after her in the same practical way.

Her lip curled when the pair of them splashed through the shallow banks of a babbling stream, and some water slogged over the top of her right boot. Her bad luck hadn't run out, it seemed. Tempest paused at the edge of the stream and plopped down on a large, sun warmed rock.

"I need a moment," she told Briggs, before dropping her

bag, bow, and quiver to the ground in order to yank her shoe off. Her whole body ached as she dumped the water from her boot. She grinned when she imagined a small fish pouring from her boot.

Unprompted, Briggs stepped closer and began massaging her sore shoulder. "It's healing well," he commented. "How's the pain?"

"Nothing I can't handle." *But can you handle what's to come?*

A strange mix of relief and dread filled her soul—Tempest was pleased she was free but... the truth seemed deadlier and more terrifying than she ever could have imagined. Could her family really have been part of the deadliest set-ups in history? She brushed the idea away—Maxim and Dima couldn't have been part of it. As for Aleks... She just couldn't get the sickly-sweet scent from his healing tent out of her head. *Does that really make him a murderer?*

"Tempest?" Briggs questioned, a frown of concern furrowing his brows. "Something wrong?"

She shook her head. "Just thinking." She wiggled her boot one more time and tugged the damp shoe back on. "There is much that will be decided once I return to Dotae. I don't relish lying to my sovereign," she said bitterly. It was only a matter of time until he discovered her betrayal. *So why are you doing this? Are you really going to believe the Jester's word?*

The Jester.

She glared at her distorted reflection in the stream. The

name tasted like ash in her mouth; Tempest wished she could wash it away as easily as she had done the black dye in her hair. The Jester had trapped her so nicely. And, now with her reunion with King Destin, she felt like a helpless fly caught in a spider's web. Her stomach lurched sickeningly.

She placed her hand over her belly and steeled her nerves. Tempest had to stay strong, not just for herself but for all the innocent people who'd died so senselessly. Doing what was right never meant it was easy.

Briggs placed a heavy hand on her shoulder. "You carry a heavy burden." He sighed. "But if I have learned anything about you over the past few weeks it's that you're resilient and headstrong. And you have a good sense of right and wrong and a desire for justice just as powerful as Pyre's." She barely kept her skepticism from her face. The Jester was no saint. Briggs continued. "You will not fail us… or yourself. I trust you."

Tempest gulped back a lump in her throat. When had anyone placed that much trust in her? She'd never been one for crying in public and didn't want to start now. She squeezed Briggs's hand for a moment, then gently removed it from her shoulder as she got back to her feet, reattached her bow and quiver and slung her bag on her back once more. Feelings needed to be irrelevant in what was to come.

"Thank you, Briggs," she said, very quietly. "Thank you for looking out for me. For supporting me. For not judging me the way I initially judged you and your people. I won't promise anything, but I will say that I hope to see you again someday."

He nodded, stoic as always. Tempest turned from him and began walking through the forest in the direction of the royal city.

"I pray it will be sooner than someday, my lady. Stay safe," he called out after her.

A stubborn, lone tear dripped down her cheek, followed by a few more silent comrades.

"I cannot be emotional right now," she mumbled a few minutes later, wiping away any evidence of her tears. Tempest glanced down at the metal box attached to her belt, innocuous and innocent to look upon if one did not know what it held.

Unbidden, the expression on the Jester's face when he discovered his grandfather's body seared itself into her mind. Pyre had looked like part of himself had died. Tempest clenched her jaw and picked up her pace. She couldn't afford to think like that. Dead was dead. She needn't feel guilty over a heart that wouldn't do anyone any good buried in the ground. If anything, she imagined his grandfather would be proud to help such a noble cause.

It was time she completed her task to perfection.

After all, that was what she'd trained her entire life to do.

The black velvet of night had descended and gem-like stars had begun to wink into existence when Tempest finally approached the immense metal gates to Dotae. The chill of a frosty night nipped at her exposed skin, so she tied her cloak a little tighter across her chest and pulled up its voluminous hood to protect her ears, Pyre's spicy scent enveloping her. Her lips turned down. Why did he smell so good?

She shook her head and refocused. Tempest studied the warriors guarding the entrance, their body language stiff and intimidating. They were on edge. A month ago, they hadn't been. What had changed in the city to make them act so?

A hulking guard stepped toward her and held up a hand, his other settling over the hilt of his sword. She eyed him. The man was spoiling for a fight.

"State your business," he grunted.

"I seek my bed. It's well past time that I get home."

Another warrior to her right crept closer, his eyes narrowed in suspicion. "And what is a girl like you doing out so late? You should know it's not safe to travel alone." His squinty gaze roamed over her body in a lecherous appraisal.

Tempest's nose wrinkled. Even though her whole frame was covered by her cloak, it still felt like he could somehow see through the heavy cloth.

"Answer me," he bit out.

The warriors were testy and lecherous. She'd have to speak to Dima about that. The guards were supposed to protect their people, not frighten them.

She slowly reached for her hood, careful not to startle

the two men and lowered it to reveal her infamous hair. Its long strands fluttered in the freezing night breeze, leaving no doubt about which family line she belonged to. The guard to her left visibly paled and bowed.

"My lady," he murmured, much more respectful.

She fiddled with her leather glove. "I see you've heard of me. I am Tempest Madrid, and I've not got time to dally," she said, making sure to keep her voice level and commanding. "If you'd be so kind as to let me pass, I'll be sure to pass along to King Destin how diligent his men are at the gate."

Both guards backed away from her as if she'd burned them. They lowered their heads immediately. "Of course, my lady. Our deepest apologies. We were only doing our job."

Tempest said nothing, choosing instead to stroll right past them. She paused and glanced over her shoulder at the men. "I would consider it a favor to me if you kept my appearance a secret."

The lecherous guard bobbed his head comically. "Consider it done."

She nodded and lifted her hood once again to avoid drawing attention as she wound through the streets, straight to the barracks. King Destin would know of her return within the hour, now that she'd announced herself, which gave Tempest very little time to prepare for her impending meeting with him. The men wouldn't be able to keep silent. They might keep her presence quiet for an hour but that would be all the reprieve she'd get. Winter's bite, she didn't want to face him yet. But she was sure she'd receive the summons shortly.

All she wanted was to sleep and pretend that everything that had happened over the past month was but one long, horrible nightmare.

Just for one day.

But those slaving for the kingdom didn't have the benefit of procrastination. She had a job to do and she had to do it now. Even if the next part of it was unpleasant and dangerous. It wasn't anything she hadn't been trained for. Except for the way the king looked at her. Gods, she didn't know how she was going to deal with that.

One thing at a time, Temp.

Some of her confusion, fear, and anxiety faded as she caught sight of the achingly familiar Hounds' barracks in which she was raised. There was a large fire burning in a pit in the center of the training rings. Hounds and trainees were sitting around it enjoying a drink, food, and easy conversation. She hid her smile and ghosted into the group. She held her hands out to the fire and waited.

Tempest closed her eyes when Maxim released a deep belly laugh from across the fire. It was so good to be home. For the first time in weeks, she felt like she was wearing her own skin again. Her uncle dropped his head and glanced across the flame. It was pure accident that his gaze snagged hers.

"Lass?" he called over and then stood up immediately. "Tempest, is that you?"

She once more lowered her hood, smiling for the large,

boisterous man who bounded over to smother her in a bone-crushing hug before she had a chance to reply. She wheezed but didn't ask him to let go. She had sorely missed Maxim over the past month. She had missed all of her uncles—even Aleks. *Don't judge until you have the complete truth.*

"You were gone so long Dima was considering sending out a search party for you," Maxim rumbled in her ear. He pulled back and ruffled Tempest's hair, before clasping her cool cheeks between his enormous hands.

"I'm okay," she said softly.

"I was not planning to do that," Dima said from behind him, inclining his head politely toward Tempest as he did so. "How did your trip go, Temp?"

She kept her smile in place, barely, which completely belied the shocking revelations that had turned her entire world upside-down. "I came back in one piece, did I not? That implies it went well enough." They could take that as they pleased.

Maxim laughed. "That's my girl. Come, join us by the fire and have a drink. You deserve it."

"I have a feeling King Destin will want to see her before she can relax, Maxim."

Tempest turned her head. Aleks appeared from the crowd of Hounds, his hair sticking up in all directions. His strong arms wrapped around her, and she hugged him without thinking the gesture through. A little body flashed through her mind, and her stomach twisted.

"It is good to see you, Tempest," he murmured into her

hair. His voice was low and serious, and it sent a chill running down her spine that she hated.

How did he know about the king? Suspicion wormed its way through her. Did he suspect that she knew about the true origin of the sickness decimating the mountain villages? She squeezed her uncle a little too tightly as if the action would somehow make everything she now suspected of the man to be completely untrue. But Tempest could not shake her fear away. If Aleks was involved with all the deaths in Heimserya—and in pinning it all on the shifters—then she wouldn't know what to do.

No, that was wrong. Tempest knew what she *had* to do. She simply didn't want to face off against the man she oftentimes still believed to be her father. How did the world get so messed up?

She glanced up at Aleks as they broke away, searching for some kind of answer in his eyes. But his expression was carefully composed; Tempest would find no answers there. So, instead, she asked, "Where is Madrid?"

It was Dima who replied. "He is at the palace with the king, I believe. Do you need to speak to him urgently?"

Maybe he could help her, or he could be part of it... "If that's at all possible. I—"

"Lady Tempest?"

Tempest and her uncles turned at the sound of an unfamiliar voice. She frowned when she spotted the source. It belonged to the servant girl who had shown her to King Destin's chambers. It was a feat to hide her distain, not for the girl, but the uncaring way the king sent his female servant out into the night into a barracks full of randy warriors.

She fought the violent urge of desire to strangle the king. Tempest nodded gently as worry and rage waged war in her chest.

"Your Grace requests your presence at the palace immediately," the servant said, in a tone that told Tempest there was no way she could find a way to delay the meeting.

She glanced at her uncles. "I must go."

"Did you not wish to speak to Madrid first?" Maxim asked, concerned. Clearly, Tempest's face betrayed more of her unease than she was capable of hiding.

"I can speak to him later," she said, knowing that she probably wouldn't. What was she supposed to ask Madrid, anyway? If the Hounds were completely corrupt? If Madrid had a hand in it all? If King Destin was an evil, manipulative man? If she asked any of those questions, and the answer was yes, she'd be dead before morning.

Tempest followed the servant out of the courtyard without another word. Levka swaggered around the side of the barracks opposite of the fire and paused, eyes wide with surprise. But before she could utter a greeting, he averted his gaze and rushed off toward the Hounds.

She frowned. He usually had no problem showing his distaste of her. Tempest peeked over her shoulder at his quickly disappearing figure. He was acting odd. What was wrong with him?

There wasn't any more time to mull over it. She needed

to get her thoughts straight. Before Tempest knew it, she found herself in front of the heavy, mahogany doors to King Destin's chambers. An eerie sense of déjà-vu crept up Tempest's spine when the servant lightly squeezed her hand. She blinked at the servant and realized she didn't know the girl's name who offered her comfort in exchange for nothing. When the gut-wrenching meeting was done, she'd make sure to find out what her name was. The young woman was a good person.

"Lady Tempest is here to see you, Your Grace," the servant said, opening the one of the double doors in the process.

The dreaded voice of King Destin answered, deceptively soft, "Let her in."

Tempest closed her eyes and took a deep breath before entering the king's chambers, preparing herself for the worst. Several potential but terrible outcomes came to mind. She could be outed as a traitor and killed, or she could betray the Jester and his people and doom them to die instead. Or Tempest might successfully lie, and then...

She'd be subject to the attentions of the king.

To her relief, King Destin was fully clothed when she laid eyes on him, though he was lounging in his throne-like chair just as lazily as he had done the last time they'd spoken.

He grinned. "My Lady Hound. How I have missed you. You have good news, I hope?" he crooned.

Everything she'd rehearsed in her mind to say disappeared like smoke. For half a second, her mouth bobbed, and then she decided to jump straight into the deep end. If she were to die tonight, might as well not stand around waiting for it.

She removed the metal box from her belt, closed the distance between herself and King Destin, her muddy boots sinking into the soft rug. With care, Tempest held out the box, opened the lid, and bowed.

"The heart of the shifter responsible for the sickness around the mountains," she announced, bowing even more deeply.

Her pulse pounded in her ears, and she focused on her boots, hyperaware of the king. Destin said nothing, though he took the box from Tempest's outstretched hands almost immediately. She tried hard not to shift on the spot as the silence between them grew longer and longer. Sweat dampened her temples and the nape of her neck. Eventually, after several very long, painful minutes, the king set down the box on the table to the side of his throne.

"Rise," he commanded. "How did you come to take him down?"

Tempest straightened her back to look the man in the eye. *Here goes nothing.* "I fell into a pit his shifter group had dug in the forest. Foolish, I know, but when they discovered that they'd accidentally entrapped an innocent girl they allowed me to stay with them while I recovered from my injuries. Throughout my time with them I learned about where they planned to attack next and visited one such village which they had ravaged. Considering everything I saw and heard, I decided it was too dangerous to leave the current shifter in command—he was too proficient in his planning and attacks to keep alive—so I took him down."

King Destin considered everything Tempest said with a somewhat surprised look on his face. *Do not insist that what you say is true. He will know you are lying if you do so.* She had to bite back the urge to speak.

The king stood up to face her, a smile playing on his lips and a predatory glint in his amber eyes. "You have done well, my Lady Hound," he said. "And you did the right thing in taking the fox leader out. You can debrief the war council on everything you saw and heard at their next meeting when you take your seat with them."

It was Tempest's turn to feel surprised. In truth, she had not expected King Destin to honor his promise to her. Her eyes darted to the floor and then back to the king's eyes. "That is... thank you, Your Grace." *That was too easy, wasn't it?*

"Well," he replied, moving closer to Tempest in the process. Much too close. "We did have a deal, after all. And if I'm upholding my end..."

Destin wrapped an arm around Tempest's waist, pulled her face to his, and brushed his lips against her cheek. She inhaled sharply, heart throbbing and head spinning at the uncomfortable proximity of the man. He moved way too quickly. She may be a Hound, but he was a lion.

You bested a lion once before.

"Forgive me," she bit out, "but I have traveled far today in order to give you this information as soon as possible. I am weary and would like Aleks to check on the wounds I sustained from my fall in the pit. Could we... continue this another time when I have had a few days to recover?"

King Destin paused, lips horrifyingly close to Tempest's, before sighing good-naturedly and pulling away. "What kind of gentleman would I be if I refused you? Be off with you, Tempest, and sleep well. You will have a busy day tomorrow—we must have a celebration in your honor!"

She smiled for the man, hoping it looked genuine. "You flatter me, my lord."

"It is not flattery if you have earned it. Sleep well."

Tempest did not need to hear more than that to be off, making sure not to run away as she had done the last time. She took slow, purposeful strides out of the king's chambers, and did not once look back until she was well out of the palace.

She couldn't push him off like that again. She needed a plan. A proper plan. What she really needed was the truth. Toeing the line between her king and the Jester would not be easy. The sooner she uncovered evidence either way, the better.

How in the hell was she supposed to find out what was going on? Tempest readjusted her bag and moved purposefully through the darkness in the direction of the barracks. As it was, her body ached and her mind was foggy. Any planning would have to wait until dawn.

All she wanted to do was fall into unconscious oblivion and dream of nothing at all. Maybe things would make more sense in the morning. She huffed at her own whimsy, her breath turning to a puff of white fog.

She'd always been a realist. Without a doubt, tomorrow would be worse than today.

Chapter Thirty-Two

Tempest

Once more, Tempest found herself at a celebration held in her honor, and, once more, she found herself feeling decidedly out of place.

At least she didn't have to wear an obscene dress this time.

She picked at one of the raven-black feathers on her bodice and shifted the half-cape onto her back. Aleks had dutifully replaced the purple fabric that the lion had torn to shreds in her Trial. A phantom pain ran up her arm at the reminder of the wounds she'd suffered. Tempest rubbed at her bicep and studied the court peacocks prancing around the room. A smirk played about her mouth. Even though she'd shown up in her overly dramatic Trial outfit, nobody had noticed or they'd been too afraid to mention the fact that she wasn't dressed appropriately for such a celebration. No one seemed to know what to make of her as the first of her kind.

She was a Hound first and foremost, and a woman second. *Is that really true?*

At the moment, she didn't feel much like a Hound. It was as if she was a completely different person since her Trials. Tempest took a half-hearted sip of her ale. So much had changed in such a short time.

Her gaze flicked to the king. Tonight, he celebrated merrily, but what would he be like at the war council meeting tomorrow? The man seemed to swap personalities like a man changed hats. She scanned the group of men and women fawning over their sovereign, noting several other advisers that would be on his council. How would they take her appearance? Would she even be heard, or was her place more decorative?

Her nose wrinkled, and she took another sip of her ale. She'd never be decorative. They'd experience how outspoken she could be on the morrow—and how well she could lie. A ripple of unease roiled in her gut. Hopefully, she was doing the right thing. If not, she'd be betraying a group of people sworn to protect the kingdom—one she had equally sworn to protect.

Dima's saying popped into mind, *"Cautious as a serpent, innocent as a dove."* The advisers could equally be innocent or guilty. Whichever it was, she needed to be careful. If she poked the bear too much and it was an inside job, Tempest could find herself hanging from the gallows.

She swallowed down the rest of her ale in one go. The idea that King Destin and his inner circle were inciting a war was too much for her to cope with right now. The bitter ale soured her tongue. And all the while they danced, drank, and engaged in general revelry.

"You are alone."

Tempest flinched at the words. She set her cup on the table near her right hip as she gathered her thoughts. His voice was one Tempest was used to hearing waspish indifference from. She turned to face him, crossing her arms across her chest on instinct. Levka towered above her, like his father did, watching her with tan-colored eyes that, for once, were not shadowed beneath a frown. What did he want with her? When they were alone, they usually ended up fighting.

"Indeed, I am," she said wearily. "I don't know what you have up your sleeve tonight, but I don't have the time to hear you spout insults, so if you'll excuse—"

"I wasn't—I wasn't going to say that," Levka cut in quickly. He put his hands on Tempest's shoulders and pushed her into the shadows of a nearby corridor, taking her enough by surprise that she blindly allowed him to do so.

Alarm pricked her. "Levka, what is it?" she demanded, keeping her voice low simply because it seemed as if the situation warranted it. He stared at her. Her throat tightened. "Is it Maxim? Is he okay? Levka—"

"My father is okay," he said tightly. "I do not hate you."

Her brows snapped together in confusion at the subject

change. "That's good to know," she said slowly.

His fingers tightened on Tempest's shoulders. He closed his eyes, took a breath, and then opened them once more. "I've never hated you." His words rushed out in one stream. "I always thought—I don't know… that when I got older, things would be easier, you know." Frustration tinged his voice. "But it has only become bloody harder. When you passed your Trial, I thought I finally had my chance to make things better between us. But then you left."

A thread of hope unfurled in her chest. She'd always wanted Levka to see her as an equal, to treat her like a sister.

"You left," he continued, "and the month you were gone felt like the longest four weeks of my life. It wasn't the same without you in the barracks, eating with my dad and me, sparring in the morning, drinking in the evening…"

"What are you trying to say, Levka?"

"Isn't it obvious?" he huffed, clearly a little louder than he'd intended to speak. He waited for a couple of drunk soldiers to pass their way, then said, "It must be obvious, even to you. Tempest, I… I really like you."

She almost laughed. Her absence had brought about something good. "I like you too."

He cocked his head and scanned her face. "I don't think you understand." Levka brushed his thumb up the column of her neck. "I like you."

Her attention narrowed to the familiar, *intimate* way he touched her. She gurgled and caught the incredulous laughter from breaking free. Levka liked her? Tempest studied his expression and glanced around his shoulder. Not one of his friends were lurking nearby. He didn't lose some sort of bet, did he? But then she thought back to something Juniper had said the morning of her Trial. She had hinted that he liked her and she'd totally disregarded it.

Levka looked wildly uncomfortable. His gaze shifted to the wall behind Tempest's head then back to her eyes. "Why aren't you saying anything?"

"I don't know what to say," she admitted. "I never... I honestly thought you hated me."

He laughed softly. "Trust me, I don't. Though I wanted to, all the time. But how could I *hate* you, Tempest, when you're practically part of my family? When I've known you most of my life?"

"Well you certainly did a good job of pretending you did..." Tempest muttered, though not unkindly. It was bizarre and oddly nice to be talking to Levka without them at each other's throats—or speaking about something that wasn't do-or-die, bloody, traitorous, or revolting. It was reassuring to know that her world hadn't *entirely* collapsed over the past month.

His lips quirked into the slightest of smiles and his thumb moved a little higher to the skin just behind her ear. "You haven't rejected me."

"That's because I have no idea what to think," Tempest replied, blunt as ever. What was she supposed to think? She'd always thought of him as a brother.

She had a moment's warning that Levka was about to kiss her—the hint of him gulping back his nerves and tilting his head—and then his lips were on hers. It was distinctly different from when King Destin kissed her cheek. It was... comfortable. She knew Levka—he was the cranky, sullen boy she'd lived with her entire life.

Tempest parted her lips before she had the time to really think it through, leaning back against the wall behind her when Levka pushed her against it. He ran a hand through her hair, deepening the kiss with an intensity Tempest had only ever seen from him in sparring practice. His tongue ran along her teeth, and she clenched her fingers into the front of his finely-woven shirt in response, determined to pull back, when he let out a growl of longing that vibrated against her chest.

Another face and embrace imposed itself over Levka— that of Pyre.

She gasped when Levka pulled away with a dazed and happy expression on his face. Shame flamed her cheeks red. Had she really just thought about the Jester? There was something seriously wrong with her because there was a handsome warrior that liked her who was wholly acceptable, and yet, she felt nothing. The kiss had been good—great, even—and it hadn't been unwelcome. But that was all it had been. No sparks. No excitement. No longing for more. It hadn't been the way Juniper had once explained kisses should be at all.

"I—I should go," she told Levka, face flushing as she slid away from his grasp. She eyed the corridor for prying eyes. If this little escapade got back to the king, it wouldn't mean good things for Levka.

He walked a step or two after her. "Tempest...?"

"I'm really tired," she called back, giving him an apologetic wave. "I'll see you tomorrow in the ring."

Tempest slipped unnoticed from the party and crawled into her bunk in the empty barracks. She mulled over Levka's confession for a long time in bed, wondering how she would let him down. He was practically family, and she didn't want to make it hard for either of them.

Just before unconsciousness took over, a disturbing thought flitted through her mind, clearly indicating that Tempest did not entirely believe Levka's excuses for not being kinder to her over the past few years.

Why had he waited until she was a Hound, and on the king's war council, to confess his feelings?

"...Tempest? Tempest?"

Tempest blinked. Sitting at her first war council wasn't what she expected it to be. Exhaustion had plagued her for the past two days—it most certainly had to do with her fitful attempts to sleep and the nightmares that had chased her as soon as unconsciousness claimed her. *You only had two nightmares while you were gone.* The unwelcomed thought caused her to stiffen even as she nodded at Madrid.

"Yes, it was the southern village on the edge of the mountains that had been destroyed. I saw it with my own eyes. Everyone was dead," she said woodenly.

Madrid's face was grave, as were the rest of the men's expressions. They all seemed genuinely perturbed by her findings, which suggested that they were not privy to any kind of insider attack on the villages. Tempest wondered if she could risk telling them the truth of what she had discovered—that the shifters were not responsible for the sickness killing hundreds of common folk. That someone else was to blame.

But she couldn't.

It would be idiotic and suicidal. The men around her had been in power for a long time. They could all be very good actors.

Tempest inhaled shallowly, and she could have sworn the scent of death and the sickly-sweet poison wafted through the air. The scent that had come from her uncle's tent. She couldn't trust anyone. There wasn't any other choice but to stick to her lie she'd concocted with the Jester.

Her gaze darted to the king's seat, which was blessedly empty. Who knew what he had up his sleeve and how she could rebuff any more of his future advances? She needed to invent more excuses. It was also a relief that he wasn't watching her every move at the meeting. Destin was just as ruthless and observant as his forefathers. The longer he stayed away, the safer she was.

"What did you do, after seeing the village?" one of the men asked in a snide tone as if her presence offended his delicate sensibilities. Tempest did not, in all sincerity, know who he was. Nobody save Madrid seemed to appreciate her being at the war council meeting in the first place, which she expected, but it didn't make the palpable animosity any easier.

"I took out their leader, cut out his heart, and returned it to King Destin," she said, enunciating each word of her lie as if it was a vicious truth she was rightfully proud of. "I made sure to find out as much information about future attacks before I did so, of course," she added, as if in afterthought, in response to the shocked looks on the council's faces at her bloodthirsty confession.

All except Madrid.

He was watching her with an unreadable expression that she'd come to know over the years. It still unsettled Tempest greatly, though Madrid was normally an impossible person to read in the first place. But the blankness of his face against the other men in the room made him look almost sad.

No, not sad. It was almost as if he was disappointed in her, like she'd failed some sort of test. What did that mean? Was she reading him entirely wrong?

But the non-expression was enough for Tempest to open her mouth and almost confess that she'd been lying; that in truth she hadn't assassinated the Jester. That she was yet to kill a single human being in cold blood, and part of her clung to the wish that she would remain that way. Death was a part of life, but murder? That was something completely different.

You're an assassin. Death is your shadow.

Tempest kept her mouth shut.

When the meeting finished, she was fast to leave the room, her heart beating too quickly. Her lies felt thick and wrong in her mouth. She'd barely turned onto the narrow staircase a servant had shown her up earlier, when a hushed conversation in the stairwell stopped her in her tracks. She frowned and leaned against the wall, straining to make out whom the voices belonged to.

The hair at the nape of her neck rose.

King Destin.

"...that she took out their leader means we'll have to plan the next poisoning as if it was an emotionally charged retaliation," he murmured.

"Did you tell her to take the Jester out?" a second voice asked. Tempest thought it sounded like one of the men from the war council —but that wasn't possible. She'd beaten everyone in leaving the room so it definitely wasn't Madrid.

"I asked for her to bring me his heart. The bastard has been trouble from the beginning, and I knew exactly what type to send his way." He laughed, the sound sinister and sexy all at once. "I knew he wouldn't be able to resist her appeal."

Tempest jerked, sickened. He'd sent her not because of her skills but because he thought to use her as a tart. *Bastard.*

"This way the Talagans will have a far less organized front to defend against our attack once we strike."

The second voice chuckled. "I suppose that's correct, Your Grace. We should aim for a village closer to Dotae if we're going for a vengeful attack. Where was it that Lady Tempest was found as a child? We could orchestrate it to look like the shifters have gone after her personally. The people would rally behind her after such a thing. They already favor her."

All the blood drained from Tempest's face. Wicked Hell. What kind of monsters were they? She sagged against the stone wall and strained to listen to the rest of their conversation.

"That idea has merit. It will work for us twofold: she'll stay on our side *and* be completely devoted to her duty. She'll be so busy chasing ghosts, the poor little thing will be too exhausted to see the obvious," Destin murmured. "She is a sharp one, after all, so we must stay vigilant. Speaking of, where did my Lady Hound go? I was rather hoping—"

Tempest did not hang around to hear the rest of the king's sentence. She crept back up the stairs and glanced both ways. Not a soul.

Destin's voice grew louder and in blind horror and fear, she sprinted for the other parallel staircase. Temp hurled herself down the stairs determined to escape without being seen and missed a step. She stifled a shriek and curled into a ball like Dima had taught her, tumbling down the final half dozen, curving steps. Cursing silently, she got to her feet and shook out her arms and legs to ensure they had not been broken in the fall.

She thanked whatever deity that looked after her that no one spotted her fall.

Then she ran.

Tempest snuck out of the castle, filched a cloak that she swore to return, and fled the city of Dotae, not daring to stop by the barracks to pack a bag or say her goodbyes. She wound through the streets with eyes barely able to see and a brain barely able to comprehend the swirling, tumultuous thoughts inside it. When she reached the edge of the sprawling forest that marked the long journey toward the mountains she did not stop.

Tempest ran as fast as she could through the trees, though, in truth, she knew nobody was currently after her. But they would be, once they realized she was missing, and that knowledge was enough to spur her on faster and harder until her lungs felt like iron and her stomach begged for her to stop, lest she be sick as she ran.

But Tempest *couldn't* stop. She couldn't—not until she found the man she was looking for. The man who needed to know everything she'd heard as soon as physically possible.

He's the enemy. And yet, the enemy of her enemy was a friend. Her conscience would have to make peace with it.

Her brain scrambled and question after question ran through her mind. How long would it take for the king to discover her disappearance? How could the king condone such senseless murder? The corpse of the child floated through her memory.

Tempest's body forced her to halt out of sheer exhaustion. She dropped to her knees, retching and gasping for air as beads of sweat dropped from her forehead to the cool forest floor beneath her/ A thorn cut into the palm of Tempest's left hand and tears tracked down her cheeks. Children. *Bloody children.*

The telltale snapping of a twig beneath a boot cracked to her left, and she stilled. She lifted her head and scanned the flitting shadows between the trees.

Her heart thumped loudly. She'd been found. How did the king already know? Tempest curled her abused palm around a sharp rock and stood, sinking into a defensive position. The monster wouldn't take her alive and she'd slaughter as many of his minions as possible.

She smiled grimly. They'd trained her to be an assassin. Death was in her blood.

The shadows melted into humanoid shapes but not the ones she expected. A huge black wolf loped into view and growled deeply.

She held her ground and bared her teeth at Brine. "I don't know if you can understand me, but I need to see him. Now."

Brine lowered his head and the hackles rose along his spine.

"Don't you snarl at me," she growled. "I've had a bloody horrible day. I know you're not here just for anyone." Tempest's smile sharpened. "Take me to see the Jester."

A hulking shape stepped around a massive tree trunk. She held her hands up in surrender and her expression softened when Briggs gave her an encouraging smile. Tempest threw one last glare at the wolf and focused on the healer. If he was here, things wouldn't get bloody.

Well, she wouldn't draw first blood, but if the nasty beastie didn't control himself, she'd let him get very acquainted with her rock.

She took a deep breath. "The Jester," she said again. "I have information he needs."

"Oh, is that so?" a playfully, sinful voice purred.

Tempest thought her heart would jump out of her chest at the sound of the low, melodic voice that belonged to one man and one man only. She spun around and eyed the kitsune who stepped out from the shadows of a hazel tree, looking altogether like a mythical forest king in a moss-colored cloak that perfectly set off the russet of his skin. He looked at her with gold irises—true, pure gold, not the amber of King Destin's—glimmering with mischief.

Damn sneaky fox.

He sighed. "Is the rock really necessary?"

"You'd be surprised at what I can do with a rock."

"I don't doubt that." He chuckled and held out a hand. "Are you ready to stand at my side?"

"Not *your* side," she began, "but on the side of justice."

Pyre smiled a grin full of sharp, delighted canines.

"Then it's a good thing those two are one and the same."

Continue The Twisted Kingdoms with book two:
The Rook

About the Author

Thank you for reading THE HUNT. I hope you enjoyed it!

If you'd like to know more about me, my books, or to connect with me online, you can visit my webpage https:// www.frostkay.net/ or join my facebook group FROST FIENDS!

From bookworm to bookworm: reviews are important. Reviews can help readers find books, and I am grateful for all honest reviews. Thank you for taking the time to let others know what you've read, and what you thought. Just remember, they don't have to be long or epic, just honest.